The ROCKETEER

A NOVEL BY
PETER DAVID

BASED ON THE MOTION PICTURE FROM
WALT DISNEY PICTURES

EXECUTIVE PRODUCER LARRY FRANCO

BASED UPON THE COMIC BOOK SERIES
"THE ROCKETEER"
CREATED BY DAVE STEVENS

BASED ON THE SCREENPLAY BY
DANNY BILSON & PAUL DE MEO

FROM A STORY BY DANNY BILSON &
PAUL DE MEO & WILLIAM DEAR

PRODUCED BY LAWRENCE GORDON,
CHARLES GORDON, AND LLOYD LEVIN

DIRECTED BY JOE JOHNSTON

FALCON ™

BANTAM BOOKS

NEW YORK • TORONTO • LONDON • SYDNEY • AUCKLAND

THE ROCKETEER

A Bantam Falcon Book / July 1991

FALCON *and the portrayal of a boxed "f" are trademarks of Bantam Books, a
division of Bantam Doubleday Dell Publishing Group, Inc.*

Illustration on page 246 by Dave Stevens.
Designed and project supervised by M 'N O Production Services, Inc.

ISBN 0-553-29322-2

Published simultaneously in the United States and Canada

---

*Bantam Books are published by Bantam Books, a division of Bantam Doubleday
Dell Publishing Group, Inc. Its trademark, consisting of the words "Bantam Books"
and the portrayal of a rooster, is Registered in U.S. Patent and Trademark Office
and in other countries. Marca Registrada. Bantam Books, 666 Fifth Avenue,
New York, New York 10103.*

PRINTED IN THE UNITED STATES OF AMERICA

RAD   0 9 8 7 6 5 4 3 2 1

TO DAVE STEVENS,
who can fly rings around the rest of us

1 The sun was just coming up, the rays creeping over the large white letters that read HOLLYWOODLAND far in the distance as the small but sturdy caravan worked its way slowly up the steep canyon road. There was a very slight chill to the air, and the only sound around was the noise of the powerful engines of the three vehicles. They roared in protest, as if annoyed that they were being subjected to such effort so early in the morning.

In the lead was a Los Angeles County police car, two cops carefully watching the road ahead of them. Bringing up the rear was a green Plymouth sedan, also occupied by two men.

The one at the wheel of the sedan was thick-necked and square-jawed. He looked like the kind of guy who could crack walnuts with his chin, a little stunt that he had in fact performed at the occasional holiday party. The lanky man seated next to him was scanning the horizon with an intensity that suggested at any moment that they might be subjected to air attack. Then he turned and surveyed the road in front of them as if expecting, at any moment, that someone might burrow out in front of them. In short, he was clearly expecting something to happen, and almost seemed disappointed when all appeared quiet.

In the middle of the odd caravan was a heavily armored truck. It was the slowest vehicle in the assemblage, of course, and the other two were matching its speed perfectly. The black and white Los Angeles police car led by half a car length and the Plymouth followed by a like distance. On the side of the armored car was the seal of the government of the United States.

Satisfied that for the moment all was quiet, the man in the passenger side of the Plymouth picked up the newspaper that the square-jawed driver had stuck into the seat next to him. He scanned the headlines and shook his head slowly. "Guy gives me the creeps," he said after a moment.

The driver didn't turn his gaze from the road as he said, "What guy?"

"Uncle Adolf."

The driver made an impatient clucking noise. "Aw, Fitch, I tell ya and tell ya not to read that stuff. Gives ya gas."

"Gives me more than that. Gives me a swift pain is what it does, which is what I'd like to give this bird right here." He tapped a photo on the front page. "Does just looking at him get you angry, Wooly?"

"How angry am I supposed to get, Fitch?" said the one called Wooly skeptically. "I mean, look at 'im! The monkey looks like Charlie Chaplin! Now, am I supposed to get worried about Charlie Chaplin?"

"If Chaplin had just come marching into Austria with a bunch of Nazi saps backing him up, I'd be plenty worried. Hitler's bad news all around, I'm telling you. I know his type. I seen it before, lotsa times. Hitler isn't going to be satisfied until he steamrolls all over Europe."

"Ah, you're squirrely." Wooly waved him off.

"They can settle with him. He keeps sayin' he wants peace. The Brits keep sayin' they can handle him."

"Wrong," Fitch shot back, stabbing a finger at his partner. "You see, that's where your never bothering to read anything besides the funnies is causing you not to realize the big picture."

"Oh, and you got the big picture."

"Yeah, I got the big picture," said Fitch. "Not all the Brits think they can handle him. The Limey prime minister, that Chamberlain duck, he thinks Hitler's someone he can talk to. Trusts him to deal in good faith. But Anthony Eden resigned a little while back. Eden's the foreign minister and he's got more brains in his little finger than Chamberlain does in his whole head."

"Wow. Just think," Wooly said, smiling. "If they could take Eden's whole hand and stick it on top of Chamberlain's neck, they'd be okay."

"Aw, you're a riot, Wooly."

"You wanna see something that can cause a riot? Take a gander behind us."

Fitch did so. There was a tan Ford roadster behind them, and driving was a striking young woman with blond hair hanging over one shoulder. She saw Fitch glancing in her direction and waved to him, and then she honked once to indicate she wasn't thrilled about the slow speeds. She had a playfully petulant look on her face, and Fitch shrugged in a wide, what-am-I-supposed-to-do-about-it manner.

Ahead of them, for a few hundred feet, the road straightened out, and the tan roadster suddenly roared forward, sweeping past the Plymouth, the armored car, and the police car. The woman at the wheel was laughing, and she waved gaily, not caring that she was in the oncoming lane. She whipped in front of the police car and shot away.

"Now, that's a tomato with more guts than brains," said Fitch. "Pulling stunts like that right in front of a police car."

"She weren't no dope," said Wooly. "She figured the cop car was with us, and wasn't gonna go buzzin' off after her."

"Yeah, well, if they got her plate number, she might get a little surprise," said Fitch.

Wooly laughed deep in his throat. "I wouldn't mind givin' her a little surprise."

"Knowing you, it would be pretty darned little."

Wooly roared loudly in amusement. "Aw, thanks, buddy."

"Think nothing of it. That's what you're best at. Thinking nothing," said Fitch in annoyance. "Don't you see we gotta get this Hitler guy before he gets us?"

"It's none of our beeswax what he does," said Wooly. "The Limeys, the Frogs, they got their problems and we got ours. I mean, England and France don't like the guy, let England and France hash it out. It's not like this country's in any great shape, brother. Or don't the word *Depression* ring any bells?"

"Things are a lot better than they were. FDR's doing just fine. But he keeps talking about world peace and scaling back on the arms race. That ain't going to happen. Not while Hitler's running around. I'm telling you—"

" 'Hitler's bad news.' " Wooly sighed as he quoted Fitch. "Fitch, I got broken records that are more entertaining than you. He ain't done nothin' to us, and we should be just minding our own business, and whatever you say ain't gonna change—"

"*Hold it!*" shouted Fitch. "*Look out!*"

But Wooly had already been alerted by the sudden screeching of tires up ahead. The police car had slammed to a halt and the doors of the cruiser were already flying open. The armored car almost rear-ended the police car, and Wooly cut his wheel hard to the left, slamming on the brake. The Plymouth slowed and Fitch had leapt out of the car, gun drawn, before Wooly had it completely stopped. Then Wooly was out, too, the driver's side door open, and he was crouching behind it for protection. Fitch was poised on the far side of the hood.

Just ahead of them was the tan Ford that had passed them a short time before. It was crossways on the lane in front of them, effectively blocking progress.

The woman was out of the car, and clearly not willingly. Standing behind her, his back against the car and his arm around her neck in a fierce choke hold, was a thick-necked man with gnarled features and brilliantined hair. He was holding a tommy gun to the head of the young woman, and his face was twisted in a savage snarl.

Positioned on the far side of the car, holding a revolver aimed at the cops, was another man, not quite as fierce looking but nonetheless clearly meaning business. He had a face that looked kind of like a ferret, and a tweed cap perched on his head.

The woman was sobbing hysterically, and instantly Fitch worked it out. The men had been standing in the road, their weapons at the ready, when the woman had come around the curve. A guy with a tommy gun aimed at you would make you slam on the brakes pretty fast, especially if you were a dame and weren't thinking that you could just run him down. Dames didn't think like that. You could threaten them and they'd just fold up like a card table.

Maybe they had their own car stashed away nearby. Maybe they were planning to steal the roadster. Whatever it was, the terrified woman's inarticulate pleadings had definitely increased the danger of the situation.

"All right!" the tommy gunman was shouting. "All right! Everybody out of the armored car! Open up the back! Do it now, or so help me, the girl's death is gonna be on your hands and her brains are gonna be on your nice suits!"

"Oh, God, no, oh, no oh no . . ." the woman was screaming.

"You know 'em?" Wooly whispered to his partner.

Fitch shook his head. "Must be local talent. Small change with big ideas." Then he raised his voice and called out, in his most authoritative tone, "All right, you clowns! We're FBI! I'm Agent Francis Fitch, and this is Agent Jake Wolinski! You want to muck with us, you want to go up the river for the rest of your life, you just go right on with what you're doing!"

"And you want to see her die, *Franc*is!" called back the tommy gunman. He shoved the muzzle even harder against the side of her head. It looked like he might push it right through her skull. "That's gonna look real good on your report, *Franc*is. Mr. Hoover'll be just tickled pink, won't he."

"He's not bluffing!" shouted the other thug. "He's nuts! Ask anybody he's killed."

"The driver and guard get out of the armored truck,

and you open up the back now!" His finger was starting to tighten on the trigger.

"Don't let him hurt me!" screamed the woman, trembling violently.

"You got to the count of five, *Fran*cis! One! Two! Four! Fi—"

"Hold it!" It wasn't Fitch who had called out. It was the driver of the armored car, a young man with red hair. The uniform he wore looked almost too big on him. "We'll do what you want! Just don't hurt her!" The other guard was getting out the other side.

"Get back in the truck!" shouted Fitch.

The guard turned angrily and said, "Hey! I'm not gonna sit there and watch some girl die just for some piece of government hardware! It ain't worth it! Nothin's worth it!"

Wooly tended to agree, but nevertheless he had to agree with Fitch. "You know the drill!"

"She's the one gonna get drilled, brother," said the guard, "and not if I can do anything about it."

He went around to the back of the armored vehicle and moments later had the rear doors opened up. Fitch looked at Wooly helplessly. What were they supposed to do now? Fire on the guard? Run and grab him? But if they did, they'd be exposing themselves as targets to the gunmen. No matter which way it played, they were in a fix.

Seconds later the guard was slowly walking toward the tommy gunman, and he was carrying a large case. It was an odd suitcase, custom designed to hold some special instrument. The case was made from hand-tooled leather, the spines and fittings of brass. He set it down in front of the two thugs and then stood.

"Open it," said the one who was holding the young woman. She whimpered softly in protest against the fierceness of his grip, but otherwise was too frightened to say anything.

The guard reached down and did what he was told. He flipped some latches and lifted back the lid.

The contents gleamed silver in the light of the morning sun. The sky overhead was brilliant blue, and the clouds almost seemed to beckon to what was in the case.

"That's it all right. Close it up." As the guard did so, the tommy gunman said, "Wilmer, grab it."

The one addressed as Wilmer now came from around the car. He reached down and lifted the case. "Heavier than I would have thought," he muttered. "I can carry it though."

"Great. Glad you like it," said the tommy gunman. "Now get in the car and—"

All of a sudden the red-haired guard's gun was in his hand.

Fitch gasped in surprise. It was the fastest draw he'd ever seen. The guard's gun had cleared its holster before the tommy gunman had even blinked, and it was leveled right at Wilmer. Wooly nodded, impressed. Obviously the kid wasn't a total washout at that.

"Let the woman go," said the young guard with icy calm. "Let her go or I shoot your partner."

"My leg," the woman was moaning. "He hurt my leg. . . ."

"I'll kill her!" the tommy gunman shouted. "I swear I will!"

"And I'll kill him," said the guard. "Either way, you're not going anywhere."

And now Wilmer, frozen and afraid to try to aim his own gun at the guard for fear that he would fall victim to the guard's remarkable swiftness, said nervously, "Lenny, better do as he says."

"Shut up, Wilmer!"

"Do it, Lenny! Let her go!" snapped Wilmer.

"My leg," moaned the woman, and she started to sag.

"All right!" said Lenny furiously. "All right!" And he pushed the woman toward the guard.

The guard hadn't taken his eyes off of the man called Lenny. So he didn't notice when the woman, clutching at her thigh, reached under her dress and pulled out a small derringer.

She brought it up and fired at almost point-blank range. The guard staggered back, a red stain appearing just above his heart.

"*Let's go!*" shouted the woman. She scooped up the torpedo-shaped case and leapt toward the car before the guard had even fallen to the road.

"We've been had!" howled Fitch in fury. "Fire!"

"Watch the case!" bellowed Wooly. "Don't hit the case!"

The woman clutched the case to her as she ran toward the car, and Lenny opened fire with the tommy gun even as he leapt to follow. Wooly and Fitch ducked for cover. Fortunately, the armored car was blocking the direct line of fire, and bullets struck and ricocheted off the huge vehicle.

One of the ricochets struck the woman.

She screamed and staggered forward, dropping the case. Lenny deftly caught it before it struck the ground, and hurled himself into the car, firing blindly.

Wilmer was already at the wheel, but when he saw the woman on the ground he called out, "Sheila! Lenny, Sheila's been hit!"

Lenny cast one quick glance and saw the blood pooling under her. "Forget her! Let's go!"

The woman lay sprawled across the road, unmoving, as the roadster peeled out with Lenny leaving a covering fire behind him. Wooly, Fitch, and the two cops opened fire, but before they could draw a bead on it, the car was gone around the hill.

Fitch ran forward as Wooly jumped into the driver's seat of the Plymouth and backed up. Running up to the woman, Fitch saw immediately that she was dead. The other armored-car guard, meantime, was trying to staunch the blood that was flowing from the hit the young guard had taken. Fitch hoped the guard made it. He had guts. It would be a shame if those guts wound up all over some canyon road.

Then Wooly had pulled up beside him. The cop car was already in motion, and Fitch, presuming that the cops were radioing for an ambulance, ran around and leapt into the passenger seat.

The cop car roared forward, siren blazing, and the car carrying the G-men fell in right behind it.

Fitch shook his head. "The blonde was in on it. Can you believe it?"

"Maybe you're right about what you were saying before," said Wooly. "I mean, if you can't trust gorgeous blondes, how can anyone trust Hitler?"

Wilmer held the wheel tightly, watching the road while at the same time glancing fast and furious into the rearview mirror.

"Just keep your eyes front!" snapped Lenny. "Let me worry about the cops and feds, okay?"

"Sheila, Lenny . . . poor Sheila. I'm so sorry," said Wilmer. "I mean, your girlfriend, Lenny. She was your girlfriend. . . ."

Lenny shrugged and slammed a fresh drum of ammo into his weapon. "I got lots of girlfriends. She was a better shot than most, but otherwise she's a kiss-off. Now, eyes front, I said! I don't want anything, and I mean anything, screwing this up!"

2

There was an ominous rumble that echoed through the otherwise silent Chaplin airfield. It was the sound of a hangar door opening, and light flooded through into the darkened building. It was an eerie feeling. One almost expected bats to come pouring out.

The two men who had pushed open the hangar door did not chatter or waste time with idle movements. They were grim-faced, energized, excited, and trying not to show it. Part of it was professionalism, part superstition. They were mutually concerned that if they displayed too much enthusiasm, there might be some sort of arcane evil eye watching the proceedings that would feel constrained to cause that morning's activities to end in tragedy.

The two men scurried back into the comforting darkness of the hangar and then, moments later, were helping two other men wheel out what appeared to be an airplane. "Appeared to be" was a particularly effective term, for actually it was little more than a flying death trap. Many pilots had stormed their last barn attempting to master the intricacies of this particular model. This rather depressing statistic was not going to deter yet another pilot, this beautiful morning, from trying his hand at braving the skies in a plane nicknamed the Blind Bulldog.

It was, in fact, a racing plane called a GeeBee, painted black and yellow, sunlight gleaming off its propeller and fresh paint as it was rolled out onto the tarmac. It bore the number four on its tail. The stubby GeeBee was little more than a gigantic radial engine with wings and a cockpit; a hunched, aggressive animal ready to pounce.

Nearby, about a dozen fliers and mechanics had turned out to watch the plane's flight. Every single one of them was pulling for the pilot to accomplish his goal, although some wouldn't have minded this morning's pilot being taken down a peg. He was the best pilot around; he knew it, and they knew it, and they hated knowing it. It would be a nice kick in the old ego for the plane's pilot if he had a rough time of it.

However, not a man on the field for even a moment wanted anything fatal or even near-fatal to happen. Annoyingly self-satisfied and cocky the pilot may be, but he was still a pilot. They were a fraternity, a brotherhood, and one did not wish ill on someone with whom such a bond was shared. A good scare, maybe, but not ill.

The four men who were pushing the GeeBee were dressed in greasy overalls and looked like they'd been up all night, which of course, they had. Pushing on the left-hand side was lanky Goose Taylor, and grease monkey Eugene Turner was huffing and puffing on the right. Skeets Moran, who still proudly went by the name of the Loop King, was guiding the tail. And in the front, not really pushing, actually, so much as making a fairly big production of calling out, "Over here! This way! Watch it! Watch it now!" was pudgy, red-faced Malcolm Willis.

Of the four men there, Malcolm was the most envious. Then again, of all the pilots there on the Chaplin field tarmac, his career as a flier was over. His best years were behind him, and Malcolm had an unfortunate tendency to look fixatedly back at those times. And while he was looking back, he had nasty habits of tripping over things in front of him, such as the bottles of booze that he'd developed a nasty habit of crawling into.

But in the back of his mind, Malcolm knew that even in his prime, he would have thought long and hard about going up in a widowmaker like this one.

Not Cliff though. Old Cliffie, he probably hadn't given it so much as a second thought. Old Cliffie, he was that good. Or that stupid. Or maybe a little of both, thought Malcolm.

He remembered the time when Bigelow, the overstuffed, obnoxious businessman who ran the Bigelow Air Circus, where they all worked, reamed Malcolm out for some offense that Malcolm had not committed. He docked Malcolm a day's pay for it, and old Cliffie had gotten so hopped up about it that he'd snuck into Bigelow's office that night and removed all the screws from Bigelow's chair. The resulting crash the next morning and shouted profanities could be heard all over the airfield. From that moment on, Malcolm felt eternally indebted to Cliff. Most people wouldn't care about some washed-up old rummy, but not Cliff. He cared about everybody.

That's the way Cliff was. A guy who was willing to carry the weight of the world on his back.

As Malcolm guided and the others huffed and puffed, pushing the racer, two figures converged on it from the far side of the airfield. Malcolm glanced up and smiled. It was them all right. Cliff and Peevy, together as always. Practically joined at the hip.

Cliff Secord was a handsome young flier, the way that Malcolm wished that he'd looked in his prime. He sported his customary brown leather flight jacket with the silver buttons that lined the flap across the top and down the sides. His white jodhpurs were crisp and clean—he was always excessively fastidious the night before he made an important flight, although he was a perfectly decent slob the rest of the time—and his brown boots were slickly polished. Secord moved with the easy stride of a natural athlete.

Beside him strode Ambrose Peabody, who was called that by his mother and maybe his priest. Everyone else called the bespectacled, weather-beaten, and quick-tempered man Peevy. Peevy had been a part of the aviation scene for as long as anyone could remember. Now in his late fifties, he was more than a mechanic, more than an engineer. He was Cliff's friend, father confessor, conscience, all of it rolled into one.

Matching Cliff's stride, Peevy was talking quickly and with controlled excitement. Cliff, for his part, was calmly chomping away on a piece of chewing gum. It might have appeared to the uninitiated that Cliff Secord was not paying the least bit of attention, and Cliff might have even claimed that he wasn't. He was, in fact, taking in every single word. He'd just be damned if he gave Peevy the satisfaction of knowing it.

". . . and keep her straight and level," Peevy was saying. "Don't let me catch you gettin' fancy first time up."

"Who, me?" said Cliff, the picture of innocence. He was busily pulling on black leather gloves, and he worked the gum faster.

Peevy ignored the pure-at-heart act and continued. "Remember, she stalls at around a hundred. Keep your air speed up or she'll wallow all over the sky. If those ailerons start to shimmy on ya . . ."

"Peevy, I have flown a plane or two, you know," Cliff said with a laugh.

The mechanic was starting to get annoyed. It was hard to tell with Cliff if what you were saying penetrated that hard head of his. "Not like this one, dammit! She's a handful! You gotta concentrate on her every second! Sneeze once and you'll be tail up in the bean field!"

They had reached the plane, and Cliff exchanged terse greetings with the four men. He seemed faintly distracted, as if his mind were already in the clouds, just waiting for his body to follow. Absently, he removed his chewing gum and stuck it on the rudder, and then moved toward the cockpit. Peevy stopped, staring in appalled amazement at the wet wad that was now affixed to the plane's tail. "That's fresh paint, dammit!" he said.

Cliff glanced at him, looking slightly hurt. "You want me to crash?"

"You and your lamebrained superstitions," said Peevy, shaking his head. "Chewin' gum ain't gonna keep your ass in the air." He didn't bother to add that he himself was wearing his lucky socks and that they would be more than enough to keep Cliff airborne. Gum. Honestly. Kids nowadays.

Cliff slung his leg over into the cockpit and hoisted himself up. He settled easily into the tight pilot's seat and smiled. A perfect fit. It was like the plane had been measured specifically for him. Of course, he grimly reminded himself, you could say the same about a coffin.

Goose prepared to lower the canopy over Cliff

when Peevy stopped him and looked Cliff straight in the eye. All of the required posturing and role-playing was put aside for a moment as Peevy said with utter sincerity, "Cliff . . . treat her right and she'll fly us all the way to the Nationals," referring to the National Air Races, the premier event for fliers.

At first Cliff nodded solemnly, but he couldn't hold it. His roguish smile spread across his face. "Let's make some history," he said.

Peevy couldn't help but smile back, and he dropped down off the wing, shaking his head. Kids. In the final analysis, it was amazing that anyone lived past thirty.

Peevy stepped back a few paces and flashed a thumbs-up to Cliff, who confidently returned the gesture. Then Cliff lowered his goggles and spoke the two words they were all anticipating and even dreading a little bit. His voice was slightly muffled, but clear enough as he called out, "Switch on!"

"Crank 'er up, Skeets!" shouted Peevy.

A ripple of excitement went through everyone on the airfield as Skeets stepped up, spit into his palms, took hold of the propeller blade on the front, and pulled down hard. For a moment Peevy held his breath. Two or three failed attempts to get a plane started never bode well on a maiden flight. Please, he thought, give us a good omen, give us a—

The engine caught on the first turn of the propeller and roared to life. The thundering power of four hundred fifty horses turned the surrounding area into an instant hurricane.

The others backed away quickly, shielding their eyes as Cliff revved up the throttle. The only one still nearby was Peevy, who, satisfied that Cliff wasn't watching, snatched the gum off the tail and flicked it away. No stupid piece of mouth candy was going to ruin his paint job. He rubbed his thumb over the paint to clean the spot, and then backed away along with the others.

The GeeBee turned and slowly began to taxi down the runway, throbbing with barely contained, pulsing power, like a prime race dog pulling against the leash and quivering in anticipation of the release. Peevy and the ground crew quickly crossed the runway to watch from the bleachers, where the other air jockeys had gathered. There were quick handshakes and nods and words of approval. Thumbs-up all around. Peevy and the others accepted the accolades, although Peevy felt uncomfortable doing so. Never a good idea to count chickens, etc., etc.

From the cockpit Cliff tossed a quick glance to make sure everyone was clear. Then he scanned his instrument panel, checking all the dials and nodding in brisk approval at what he was seeing. Finally his gaze lit on his real talisman. The gum was what kept him in the air, but what he was looking at now was what put him up there in the first place.

It was a postcard-size picture of a stunning young woman. She had a mouth that looked beautiful when it was smiling or when it was pouting. Right now it was smiling, generating more power than all the GeeBees in the world put together. Her eyes sparkled in a "come-hither" look, and her beautifully angled face was surrounded by a cascading array of black hair. She was draped in a satin gown that she'd worn when she was an extra in a party scene during *My Man Godfrey* two years earlier, in 1936. It was her very first job in a movie and she'd been thrilled that day, more so than Cliff could ever remember. She'd chattered on for hours that day about William Powell—she referred to him as Bill—and Carole Lombard, whom she'd said was beautiful beyond all belief. Cliff merely watched her chatter on about Lombard and thought to himself that no one could possibly be more beautiful than the excited little actress right across the table from him. One day she'd managed to sneak her costume off the set and Cliff photographed her in it.

He was glad he had. It was the only chance anyone had to see her in it, because her part had wound up on the cutting room floor, although she swore if you looked real hard you could see her for a second passing behind Alice Brady.

That was the photo he was staring at now. And it had been signed, "With love from your Lady Luck, Jenny." As always, Jenny had drawn a heart with an arrow through it around her name. It was an affectation she'd developed to make her autographs more memorable. She dreamed of the day someone would ask her for one.

Cliff's gloved fingers brushed across the photo, and then he opened the throttle up. Jenny seemed to wink approvingly.

The indicator needles jumped. The plane began to pick up speed and then surged forward. Cliff gasped slightly as the sudden thrust of power shoved him back into his seat. It was nothing he wasn't prepared for, but nevertheless he felt a brief trill of surprise at the power of it. He felt like he was sitting on top of a powder keg with wings.

On the bleachers, the pilots and technicians held their collective breath as the GeeBee hurtled forward. The fixed landing gear skittered over the asphalt. It was incredibly loud, filling the entire airfield with a sound like thunder. Peevy crossed his fingers, flexed his toes inside his lucky socks, and suddenly wished for some bizarre reason that he'd left the damned gum on the rudder.

The GeeBee picked up speed. At first it had displayed the grace of a sick tortoise, but then it began to move faster and faster until it was barreling across the tarmac. The landing gear bounced once, twice, and then the GeeBee lifted and angled its way skyward.

A triumphant war whoop went up from the spectators and, for the first time, Peevy allowed himself a self-satisfied smile as several rough hands clapped him on the back.

In the cockpit of the GeeBee, Cliff watched with satisfaction as the air speed gauge passed two hundred miles per hour. His grin widened and he glanced down at the airfield that he was circling, already dwindling, the occupants receding from the status of coworkers to the lowly position of ants. "Watch this, Peev!" Cliff declared, and moved the stick with long-practiced skill.

The GeeBee angled downward, back toward the spectators, and came barreling down on the deck in a run across the field. The bleacher bums put their arms in front of their faces to shield themselves and the GeeBee rocketed directly overhead with a thunderous roar. Their heads whipped around as they watched the powerful little plane climb upward, ever upward, slowing only for the briefest of moments to tip its wings in a victory salute. Then, under the steady hand of Cliff Secord, the GeeBee angled upward, leveled off, and sailed in the general direction of the surrounding foothills.

On the ground, even the pilots who had been conservative and cautious in their initial enthusiasm now cut loose, cheering and yelling. Peevy was bounced around like a rubber ball, but he still managed to stay calm, allowing only a smile at a job well done. All around him was jubilation and cheering and—

As the GeeBee climbed up into a glorious cloudscape and accelerated away, almost disappearing from view, Peevy suddenly looked down to discover a sticky tangle of chewing gum on the sole of his shoe.

3 The tan Ford roadster whipped down the narrow cliffside road, and Lenny crouched in the rumble seat as the sounds of sirens alerted him to the proximity of their pursuers. He whipped around his tommy gun and opened fire. Wilmer, gripping the wheel for all he was worth, was made nervous by the fact that his gaze barely cleared the dashboard. The blasting of the tommy gun drowned out the sirens, and for that he was appreciative. He also floored it, trying not to think about the fact that one curve taken too quickly would mean the end of this little adventure, his freedom, and quite possibly his life.

He glanced only once at the case that sat on the passenger seat next to him. Cripes, enough was enough. After this little escapade, he was going to turn in his resignation. He'd put in enough good years with Eddie Valentine that he figured (hoped, prayed) that he'd be entitled to some sort of decent compensation. Eddie was a mug and all, but he dealt square. And Wilmer was simply getting the sudden feeling, deep in his gut, that maybe he'd been pushing his luck a little hard lately and now might be the time to get out while the getting was good.

Of course, all he had to do now was get away from the feds and cops who were breathing down his neck. That's all. Just get away from them, and then he'd never pull another job again. That's all. Just this one more time.

Lenny, in the meantime, was undisturbed by such considerations as alternative career paths. For him, nothing beat the feeling of what he was doing right now: firing on the representatives of the law with everything he had. Cops and feds and judges and everyone in the system, they always acted so high and mighty. They always came across as if they were so much better just because they drew paychecks while he drew blood. Well, bullets were the great equalizers, and Lenny felt very much in the need of some serious equality right about then. The tommy gun spit out bullets in rapid succession and he chortled, the image of the girl on the road completely gone from his mind.

Wolinski gripped the wheel of the Plymouth ferociously and cast an annoyed glance at Fitch, who was hanging out the window and trying to take careful aim. "Hey, Fitch!" snapped Wooly. "You trying to save on ammo?"

"I can't get a clean shot!" Fitch shouted back in frustration. "I wish that black-and-white would get out of our way!"

At that moment a volley of tommy gunfire shredded the cop car's front tires. The car spun out, careening off the road like a top, the sounds of the policemen screaming drowned out by the screeching of the rear tires and the constant barrage of machine gunfire. Fitch and Wooly ducked as bullets ribboned across their windshield, blowing it out in a shower of glass.

Fitch brushed shards of glass off the front of his jacket as Wooly said dryly, "Careful what you wish for." Fitch shot him an annoyed glance, then aimed his revolver out the window and started blasting. Wooly, eyes on the road, wondered why the hell the bad guys always had automatic weapons that could wipe out a platoon and the good guys got stuck with revolvers. Hardly seemed fair.

In the roadster, meantime, Wilmer was the first to feel the effects of Fitch with an unobstructed view. A slug tore off Wilmer's tweed cap. He touched his scalp with one hand while gripping the wheel. No blood. Then he checked the rearview mirror for a graze, and yelped in alarm when another slug shattered the mirror and his reflection.

He saw a back road and turned the car hard. The roadster angled off as Lenny reared up, tommy gun blazing. He stitched a pattern of bullets across the Plymouth's grille, blasting it into fragments. Steam belched up from the ruptured radiator. In the Plymouth, Wooly slammed an impatient fist against the dashboard and squinted, trying his best to see through the huge gust of vapor that was now billowing into his face. But he had to slow down to compensate for it. Fitch yelled obscenities and Wooly did the best that he could, but he began to worry that the roadster was really going to get away. And if they did, the first thing he was going to do was requisition a tommy gun.

In the roadster, Wilmer glanced triumphantly over his shoulder as he accelerated up a hill. He chuckled low in his throat as he watched the Plymouth fall back, then turned his gaze back to the road and screamed in alarm.

Chugging right toward them from the other direction was a Model-T truck. The damned thing was so wide, it was taking up the entire road. At the wheel was a farmer who was frantically waving them off.

Clearly he hadn't expected to encounter anyone on this road. Who would come down this stretch of nowhere anyway?

Wilmer cursed his luck. Even when he caught a break he couldn't catch a break. This bleak thought went through his head as he angled hard to the right, leaving the road altogether. The abrupt change of direction and bumps sent Lenny tumbling to the floor of the car, and he yelped loudly when the roadster bounced over a ditch and sailed into a bean field.

Behind them, the Plymouth carrying the two FBI men bore down on the truck. But Fitch had seen where the Ford had gone and he pointed furiously to the right. Wooly whipped the steering wheel around and the Plymouth sideswiped the truck as it pursued the roadster into the field.

The steam was subsiding now, which was good news and bad news. The bad news was that it meant they were in serious danger of overheating. The good news was that now Wooly could see. Even this, though, was promptly aggravated when the roadster churned up a cloud of dust behind them. Wooly and Fitch coughed violently and Fitch almost lost his grip on his gun.

Lenny, in the meantime, was laughing loudly as he slammed a drum of fresh ammo into his gun. This was all going great. It had been so simple. Sheila drives by with Lenny and Wilmer hiding in the back, waves to the feds, makes nice, and then a minute or two later becomes the damsel in distress. They had to fall for it. And they did. Shame about Sheila, but that's the way the cookie crumbled.

Then he heard something from overhead and whipped the tommy gun skyward.

There was a plane coming up over the hill, heading in their direction. It was black and yellow and shaped like nothing Lenny had ever seen, but it was moving like a son of a gun.

It might be nothing, Lenny reasoned, but on the other hand, it might very well be something. Just like the feds to have a backup plan. Well, backup plans were just fine and dandy. Lenny didn't subscribe to that notion though. He went through life with one plan—if it moved, shoot it. And if this was just some innocent plane jockey out for a spin, well, that was just his tough luck now, wasn't it?

Lenny opened fire on the oncoming GeeBee.

Cliff didn't know what was happening at first. He heard something like a series of explosions, and then the plane was shuddering as if someone had lit a bunch of firecrackers on the underside of the fuselage. For one wild moment he prayed that that was all it was: someone's stupid, brainless idea of a joke. He didn't see the bullet holes ripping through the underside and through the engine, but he became suddenly aware that there was more than just a lot of noise and jostling when a ricochet cracked his windscreen.

He barely had time to adjust to his mishap when the engine sputtered and began to emit grayish smoke. *Ahhhhh, why me? It was going so great!* thought Cliff in exasperation as he watched his instruments go haywire. That he might die was secondary to the concept that he was going to be embarrassed after all his boasting that he could master the GeeBee with one wing tied behind his back. Well, with his instruments doing

the trots, it was the equivalent of both wings and his
rudder tied behind his back. He fought the controls,
but it was a losing battle.

Lenny looked up with satisfaction, watching the
stubby plane spin around in the sky, clearly out of
control. Gray smoke was billowing from the front and
he patted his tommy gun affectionately. And then he
stumbled back, landing hard in the rumble seat as the
car fishtailed out of the bean field and back onto a
winding road. Then he caught a glimpse of a sign that
read CHAPLIN AIRFIELD, 1 MILE.

"Wilmer!" he shouted, and when Wilmer glanced
back he continued, pointing frantically. "Head for the
airstrip! I can fly a plane!"

The feds' car had now jumped out onto the road
behind them, skidding around before coming under
control. It didn't matter though. Unless that Plymouth
could sprout wings, Lenny and Wilmer were going to
be in the clear within the next few minutes.

Cliff struggled with the stick, feeling as if he were
trying to keep the plane in the air through sheer muscle power and force of will. Through clenched teeth
he muttered to the crippled engine, "That's it . . .
don't die on me now." He barely managed to keep
the GeeBee from plowing into a hillside as he continued hurried words of encouragement, both to the
plane and to himself. "Eaaasssssy does it . . . no more
surprises, okay?"

Someone up there in the heavens that Cliff was always reaching for decided to show just how seriously they were taking Cliff's heartfelt plea of "no more surprises." A rod blew through the cowling, and Cliff's canopy was instantly coated with a thick stream of brackish motor oil. Whacked controls, a stubborn stick, a failing engine, and now—just to make it interesting—he was flying blind. Great. Just great.

He pounded frantically on the windscreen, trying to punch his way through the bullet-riddled glass. He shouted everything he could think of in frustration and then, to his amazement, the glass gave way. Air blew into Cliff's face, a bracing, stinging sensation—

—*and another plane was coming right at him*.

Cliff screamed and jerked back on the stick, uttering a quick prayer. Not that they had been doing any good until then.

This one did, though, as the GeeBee jumped upward, clearing the oncoming obstruction with inches to spare.

Cliff glanced back to see who the hell he'd almost hit, and then his eyes widened in disbelief. It was a highway billboard advertising some movie called *Wings of Honor*. Smack in the center of the billboard was a painted image of a warplane and an actual propeller mounted on it to give it a realistic three-dimensional effect. It spun wildly in the GeeBee's wake, and had been just a bit too realistic for Cliff's personal taste.

Through a eucalyptus grove hurtled the roadster, with the Plymouth right after them. They hadn't put

enough distance between themselves and the feds for
Wilmer's taste, and he was doing everything he could
in a last-ditch effort to do so before they reached the
airfield.

The feds were getting closer and, damn! They were
now running a parallel track with the Ford roadster.
Wilmer ducked down as Lenny opened fire once more,
exchanging a furious hail of bullets with the Plymouth. Bullets were ricocheting everywhere, perforat-
ing the trees and leaves.

Wilmer spotted two eucalyptus trees to his right
and angled quickly toward them. They were side by
side, but there was enough of a gap in between them—
he thought. He held his breath, certain that they
would be able to get through, uttered one more quick
prayer that this was the last job, honest to God, and
then the Ford shot through the two trees. Paint
scraped off either side of the roadster—it was that
close a squeeze. But it was enough and the Ford made
it through. Up ahead he could make out the outlines
of airplane hangers.

Wooly whipped the Plymouth around, right on the
track of the Ford. The side-by-side trees loomed
ahead, and he saw the Ford disappearing into them.
He slammed down on the gas as Fitch, bracing himself
against the dashboard, warned, "She ain't gonna
make it. . . ."

"Yes, she will!" shouted Wooly. Wooly was determined. Wooly was positive. Wooly was unstoppable.

Wooly was wrong.

The car slammed to a jarring halt, caught between
the two trees, tires spinning helplessly.

"Like I said," continued Fitch calmly.

Wooly gave his partner an annoyed glance and then

threw the car in reverse, grinding gears. The car moaned and so did Wooly as the two front fenders ripped clean off.

Fitch quickly surveyed the damage. In addition to the absent fenders, smoke and steam were still billowing out, and the sides and front were more holey than a football field of nuns.

Their heads were going to be on the block as it was. If the crooks got away with the stolen case, Fitch and Wooly might as well just make a hard left and keep on going until they drove into the Pacific.

"Move it!" shouted Fitch. Wooly did so, going around the trees this time, in steadfast pursuit of the fleeing roadster.

The roadster tore out across open ground behind the hangars. Wilmer was looking around furiously and then saw one with an open door. He drove into it and screeched to a halt, allowing himself a small sigh of relief. They weren't remotely in the clear, but there was something vaguely comforting about being in an enclosed area. He grabbed the patent leather case and turned toward the rear of the car. "Let's go, Lenny!" he started. "We can't get caught with the—"

His eyes opened wide. Lenny would never be caught now, because he'd caught something—a bullet. He was slumped to one side, staring at Wilmer with glazed, dead eyes. Wherever Sheila was, Lenny was now with her.

Wilmer felt a tremble go through him. It just as easily could have been him. He felt the same guilty

sort of relief that any soldier feels when the trooper
next to him in line has taken the bullet.

"Lousy feds," he muttered.

In the distance he heard the screech of tires and the
sputtering of an engine that could only be one that
had sustained the sort of punishment Lenny had in-
flicted on the Plymouth. Backfiring, chugging, but determined. The feds would be there in minutes, checking through the hangars.

He was going to get caught. After all this, on the
edge of a clean getaway and a new life, he was going
to get caught. He couldn't fly a plane. Maybe the roadster could still outrace the feds. Sure. There was a
better than even chance. But what if he couldn't? And
he got nailed holding the contents of the case?

His mind was racing as fast as the GeeBee that was
wobbling into view in the distance, but he paid it no
heed. For his frantic gaze had fallen upon a vacuum
cleaner that had been designed in that obnoxious art
deco style. Wilmer couldn't stand that look, but suddenly it was starting to grow on him, especially when
he saw the duffel bag next to the vacuum cleaner.

He grinned.

The spectators in the bleachers heard the GeeBee approaching before they saw it because it was dropping
down straight from the sun like a meteor. But the
sound told as much as the view, for Peevy's trained
ear detected the telltale, labored sputter of a plane
engine in trouble. "Something ain't right . . ." he murmured, and then more loudly, to alert the others, he
shouted, "Something ain't right!"

Then the GeeBee came into view, wobbling toward the runway, a plume of smoke boiling from the cowling. The group looked up in horror and Peevy glanced once more at the bottom of his shoe, which still had traces of sticky gum. Man, if Cliff lived through this, he'd probably kill Peevy.

"Come on!" shouted Peevy. "Move yer butts! Get the fire extinguishers! Get the water trucks! Get going! Move! Move!" The occupants of the bleachers cleared out, dashing toward the hangars to get whatever crash assistance gear they could.

As Cliff hurtled downward, he frantically tried to wipe the spewing oil from his goggles. Smoke billowed up in front of him and he held his breath. The last thing he needed to do was inhale a few lungfuls of smoke and choke to death. No. Then he would miss his chance to die on the runway.

The runway, which was now only seconds away, seemed to reach up toward him and tilt crazily.

But it wasn't too fast for Cliff. It wasn't anything he couldn't handle. He told himself that over and over again. He wasn't going to let the GeeBee beat him despite all the things that had gone wrong. Cliff hadn't gotten to where he was by listening to naysayers who predicted a fiery end for him. Then Cliff realized just exactly where he had gotten to—namely, inside a falling box of metal that was going to crash and burn inside of thirty seconds, and wondered if maybe he should have taken those naysayers a bit more seriously.

No. He banished those thoughts from his head

as he concentrated on the job before him. Doesn't
have to be pretty or elegant. Just get down on the
ground. Just make it down and walk away from the
landing, and that would be enough to make it a good
landing. And he was going to be able to make it.
The ground wasn't spiraling as crazily now, and he'd
managed to wipe away enough oil to get just enough
vision.

And that's when he saw the car coming directly
toward him.

Moments earlier Wilmer had slammed the roadster
forward and shot out of the hangar like a cannonball.
He blew past the Plymouth, which skidded around
the rear corner of the building and screeched to a halt.

The Plymouth engine choked out and died, having
given everything it could and more. Desperate, determined, Fitch leapt out of the car, crouched into a
marksman's pose, and fired on the fleeing roadster.

Barreling down the runway, Wilmer's back suddenly arched in pain as a bullet hit him square in the
shoulder. *It's not fair! This was the last time!* he cried
out in his mind, his eyes slamming shut in pain.

Then he heard a roaring in his head and, through
the pain, his eyes opened, and he saw a smoking airplane descending toward him on an inevitable collision course.

Wilmer threw open the car door and leapt out. He
thudded hard onto the runway and rolled, the asphalt
tearing up his clothes and skin.

In the GeeBee, Cliff saw, through smeared goggles, the driver of the car leap clear, which wasn't going to do him a hell of a lot of good. He cried out and yanked on the stick in what he knew was an exercise in futility.

The GeeBee's landing gear bashed into the roadster's windscreen. The impact tore the wheels loose from the plane with an ear-splitting screech of metal, and then the crippled plane bellylanded in a shower of sparks.

Cliff cursed his misfortune inwardly. Any other pilot would have done a nose dive. Not Cliff. Noooo, not Cliff Secord. He manages to land right side down, but just to make it more challenging, it's without landing gear. He just couldn't catch a break.

The roadster, in the meantime, sped forward completely out of control—understandable, since no one was at the wheel to control it. Wilmer rolled to a stop and, every part of his body aching, managed to raise his head in time to see, a couple of hundred yards away, the roadster slam into a fuel truck that was parked at the runway's edge. With an explosion as if hell itself had just blossomed up from down under, the Ford erupted into a churning ball of flame and smoke.

Goose, Skeets, Malcolm, and Peevy were the first to reach the battered, unmoving hulk of the GeeBee. The former two were carrying fire extinguishers and, in the distance, a water truck and fire engine were roaring down the runway.

Peevy moved quickly, seeing the smoke rising from

the smoldering GeeBee. The last thing he was going to allow to happen was for Cliff, having survived the landing, to go up in a roar of fire afterward. "Goose!" he shouted as he clambered up on the wing. "Give me a hand!"

Goose passed the extinguisher over to red-faced Malcolm, who was huffing and puffing heavily from the run and was remembering the days when he could dash the length of a runway on foot and not be the least out of breath. As Peevy and Goose worked on wrenching open the jammed cockpit, Skeets urgently waved Malcolm over. "Get the flames out," he shouted, "before they hit the fuel tank!"

Malcolm nodded, and he and Skeets turned their extinguishers on the smoking fuselage, fighting the cowling fire with everything they had.

Peevy and Goose grunted and pulled one more time, and this time the battered canopy came loose. Cliff, miraculously, was conscious, and so it was only a matter of moments to pull him most of the way out of the cockpit. He stopped for a moment to snatch Jenny's photo off the instrument panel, and then followed Peevy and Skeets down the side of the GeeBee to safety. They ran a safe distance and then turned and stopped. Cliff looked on helplessly as Skeets and Goose put out the fire on the wounded plane.

"I knew it!" he suddenly shouted, and pointed. "Look! The gum fell off!"

Peevy looked where Cliff was pointing, then took a deep sigh, looked up at his protégé, and shrugged. "Bad break, kid. These things happen."

Wilmer's head sagged to the ground and he stared into the blackness of the asphalt. Then he heard the sound of a trigger being cocked a few feet away and heard an authoritative voice announcing, "FBI! Don't move!"

He laughed and it hurt, which probably meant that something was broken in his chest. His shoulder throbbed with pain. Nevertheless, in his best Edward G. Robinson voice, he growled, "You'll never take me alive, copper," and then he passed out.

4

"Now, let me get this straight. You chase some two-bit thugs onto our runway, they crash into my plane, and it's *my* fault?"

Cliff was dogging the heels of two guys who'd been identified to him as G-men named Wolinski and Fitch. Cliff had always had tremendous respect for the feds in their various incarnations, both in works of fiction and in the real world. But these guys were nothing like the screen portrayals he'd seen of the super-efficient, brave, and conscientious agents that he'd read about in the newspapers. These two guys seemed totally self-absorbed, as if Cliff's complaints and clear consternation were irrelevant. He was a taxpayer, for crying out loud. He paid their salaries!

The FBI men shouldered their way through the confusing mass of ambulances, fire trucks, cops, and others who had shown up in the hour following the crash, turning a usually busy airfield into a complete madhouse. Cliff and Peevy stayed right behind them, not giving a hoot about the G-men's claims that they were too busy.

Fitch and Wooly, for their part, just wished that these guys would go off and do something else to anybody else. Write their congressmen. Call a lawyer. Anything except ride their backs. "Look, kid . . . no offense," said Wooly, "but we've got more important things to do than get all sweaty over whose fault it was."

"We put three years and every dime we had into that racer!" said Peevy, bristling.

Fitch had even less patience than Wooly. Throughout the last twenty years, hotshot aviators had been tearing around the country providing barnstorming "entertainment" that more often than not ended in accidents and fiery death. Fitch laid his life on the line every day for the good and security of the country. Flyboys did the same thing to provide cheap thrills and kicks for the yokels. It showed a callous disregard for life and safety that Fitch could not abide at all. "So file your gripe with Uncle Sam," snapped Fitch. "Maybe you'll get lucky."

"And wait six months? A year?" Cliff brushed a hank of his sandy brown and slightly scorched hair out of his face. "We make our living with that plane!"

Fitch stopped and turned to face him, hands on his hips. "Guess it's time to get a *real* job," he said.

Fitch loved moments like this—letting smart-mouth punks like this Secord clown know exactly where they stood. Because Secord would undoubtedly love to take a poke at Fitch for that crack, and Fitch knew damned well that even a cloudhead like Secord wouldn't risk going to the slammer for punching a federal agent. So Secord would stand there, burning, firmly put in his place by his helplessness to respond.

The only problem with this approach was that Cliff hauled off and slugged Fitch in the jaw, his fist moving so fast, it was a blur. Fitch went down flat on his butt.

Peevy's eyes widened in astonishment, but Cliff was too burned to notice. What he did see, though, was an infuriated Fitch clambering to his feet with a snarled, "Why, you lousy . . ." and charging right at him.

Fitch was off balance, and when his punch landed, it did little more than shove Cliff back. What it did, though, was send Cliff staggering into the arms of Peevy and the ground crew, who grabbed Cliff and held him back to prevent him from adding even more years to his prison sentence. Wooly, for his part, held Fitch back with a hand against his chest. "Relax, Joe Louis!" he said.

Fitch didn't feel like Joe Louis. He felt like Max Schmeling, who'd been KO'd by Louis a few weeks before in just over two minutes. Nevertheless, he saw the angry faces of the fliers surrounding them. He could arrest them. Maybe even shoot them. And there were other feds just within shouting distance. Maybe . . .

Aw, the hell with it. The kid had moxie. Still, the last thing Fitch was going to do was admit admiration, and so in his gruffest voice he snarled, "That one's free, kid. Keep it up and you'll be eatin' dinner through a straw."

Peevy couldn't believe Cliff's good fortune. And he believed it even less when Cliff started forward again. The smaller, older man nevertheless put a hammerlock on the hotheaded pilot and whispered harshly in his ear, "He's a G-man, for Pete's sake! You lookin' for time in the slammer?" He pulled on Cliff. "Come on . . ."

He dragged Cliff off, and the other fliers, seeing the moment had passed, drifted away. Fitch for his part rubbed his jaw and then glanced in annoyance at his partner. "Son of a bitch hangs one on my kisser and you let him waltz."

Wooly smiled raggedly. "Maybe you had it coming."

Disdaining to discuss it further, Fitch stalked toward an ambulance with Wooly right behind him. They got there just as Wilmer, on a gurney, bandaged and splintered from head to toe, was being loaded on. Fitch motioned for them to wait, and they stepped back. He leaned down over Wilmer.

"Your pal in the rumble seat's playing his harp. If you make it to County General, your next stop's Alcatraz. So spill. Where's the package?"

Wilmer chuckled and mumbled through blood-spattered lips, "Blown to hell. Go look for it."

Fitch stepped back and waved impatiently. "Get him out of here."

The annoying, mocking laughter of Wilmer continued as the ambulance drivers loaded him into the ambulance. Fitch tried to choke down his frustration, and then suddenly Wooly tapped him on the shoulder. "Look. Over there. Looks like they found something."

The "over there" he was pointing to was the smoldering wreck of what had once been the roadster. Several firemen were grouped around it, along with a G-man named Stevens. Stevens signaled to Fitch and Wooly as they headed over and pointed to what the fireman was extricating from the wreck, carefully using a pair of tongs. "Hey, Fitch!" called Stevens. "Take a look at this!"

Fitch and Wooly approached the remains of the roadster. The fireman raised a charred and twisted lump of metal up in front of them, presenting it for their inspection. Its shape vaguely suggested something that once could have been a streamlined, finned object.

Fitch was afraid to say it, but Wooly had no such concerns. Indeed, he was relieved that at least they knew, one way or the other. "That's the gizmo all right," said Wooly.

Fitch was digging a nickel out of his pocket, and he flipped it to Wooly, the buffalo head flickering momentarily in the sun before Wooly caught it. "Call him, Wooly," said Fitch.

Wooly grimaced. "Why me?"

"He likes you," replied Fitch.

Wooly sighed. Fitch was right, actually. For some reason, The Man had taken something of a liking to Wooly, appreciating his open and honest air. At the very least, he didn't insult Wooly the way he did Fitch.

Wooly went off to make the call.

The balcony of the wide, plush office opened onto the Santa Monica hills, and beyond that was the ocean lapping at the shore.

Most people, when standing on such a balcony, would gaze longingly and in fascination at the Pacific. Not the man whose office this was, though. His attention was always focused on the sky. It was his second home. In some ways, it was his first.

At this point, however, his attention was not on the sky, or, for that matter, on the ocean. Instead, it was on the telephone receiver that he had pressed against his ear.

He was quite slim, and his face was narrow, even

foxlike. He had a high forehead and his hair was combed back, and his entire body and being radiated quiet intensity. He sported a pencil mustache that he had left after shaving the rest of a beard, acquired during a recent marathon flight. Just behind him on a shelf was his latest acquisition, the Harmon International Trophy for record flight achievement. Like an oversized paperweight, the trophy was sitting on top of a note that read simply: "I wish I could have been with you," and was signed by Franklin D. Roosevelt. At this moment, even that didn't matter to him. All that did matter was the news that he was getting over the phone.

"There's no mistake about that, Wooly?" he said.

"No mistake, sir," came Wooly's voice.

"I see."

"I know it was a little sloppy—"

"It was damn sloppy," the man shot back.

"Hey," said Wooly, feeling slightly annoyed. "At least it didn't wind up in the wrong people's hands."

"Well, yes," he conceded, "it could have been worse."

"That's our attitude. Now, if—"

"Right," said the man, and hung up before Wooly could continue.

He looked across his desk at two War Department liaisons, Foster and Wolfman. His lips thinning even more than they were before, he said, "That was Wolinski. They chased it to an airstrip in the Valley. There was a wreck on the runway . . . the Cirrus X-3 was destroyed."

Wolfman and Foster exchanged looks of disappointment . . . and, at the same time, relief. Echoing

Wooly's words, Foster said, "Better lost than in the wrong hands."

"How soon can you rebuild it?" asked Wolfman.

"Rebuild it?" said the mustached man. He seemed amused. "Not a chance."

This time the two liaisons gave each other glances of somewhat greater significance. Clearing his throat, Wolfman said, "My people in Washington will have something to say about that."

The mustached man gave an unpleasant laugh. "Your people in Washington want to turn anything that flies into a weapon. Apparently, someone else had the same idea." He then picked up a thick portfolio and riffled through it, gazing at a sheath of diagrams with an almost wistful regret.

Foster said, a bit more loudly, "Sir, I'm afraid we must insist. . . ."

The man at the desk sounded almost bored. He didn't look up at them as he said, "I'll remind you boys that I don't work for the government. I *cooperate,* at my discretion."

He stood and strode over to the fireplace, where a crackling fire was burning brightly. "Two of my best pilots were killed in the test phase," he continued. "God knows how many more men would've died if it had flown. I'm sorry I ever dreamed the damned thing up."

And before Foster and Wolfman could react, the tall, brooding, mustached man dropped the portfolio into the fireplace. The flames immediately began to consume the blueprints, documents, notes—all of it.

Wolfman and Foster were on their feet immediately. "You can't do that!" said Wolfman.

"What'll we tell the President?" protested Foster.

One of the objects being reduced to ash in the fire-place was a watercolor rendering of a proposed Hughes Aircraft pavilion at the upcoming 1939 World's Fair. In the sky above the structure was a flying man soaring toward golden clouds.

"Tell him the dream is over. Tell him Howard Hughes said so," said Howard Hughes, running a finger over his mustache. He looked up over his desk at a scaled-down model of another pet project of his—the biggest seaplane in history, which he called the *Spruce Goose*. The model alone, which he kept mounted on an overhead track so he could watch it cruise around his office, was as wide as a man's out-stretched arms. He sighed. There would always be more dreams.

He turned and gazed back into the flames, watching the portfolio and papers he'd dropped there being consumed.

The sky in the watercolor blackened, and the flying man in the picture burst into flame.

"Three hundred gallons?!" Peevy stared in shock at the slip of paper in his hand. "We don't burn that much in *two years!*"

Inside the airfield hangar, a heavyset man stood in front of Peevy with meaty thumbs looped into frayed suspenders. He chomped down on a cigar that he habitually switched from one side of his mouth to the other. It was Bigelow, owner and operator of the Bigelow Air Circus, and at the moment he was being shouted at by a pipsqueak named Peevy and didn't particularly appreciate it. "You burned it in two seconds when my fuel truck went up."

Perched on a chair nearby, Cliff protested, "I didn't blow up your truck, the guy in the car did!"

Bigelow, as always, had all the answers. "Yeah, after bouncing off *you!*" He waved his cigar in Cliff's direction, leaving a trail of smoke in the hangar air. "Pilots are responsible for a safe landing. You know that."

Cliff was about to protest when Peevy cut him off. The mechanic tried to sound reasonable. "Where we gonna get this kind of dough, Bigelow? The GeeBee's scrapped."

Now they were getting into the territory that Bigelow wanted. Trying to look sympathetic, he said, "Look, fellas, I hate to kick you when you're down,

45

but business is business. I'm out-of-pocket here. 'Course . . ." He paused, savoring the moment. "I could always use the old clown act."

Peevy's eyes narrowed. So that's what this was all about. Bigelow had never liked Cliff's style, his confidence, or anything else about him except his ability as a pilot and his entertainment value. But if he could keep that entertainment value and add in the pleasure of humiliating Cliff by making him dress in that stupid clown costume to do aerial acrobatics in a flying death trap called *Miss Mabel* . . .

"We don't do that anymore," said Peevy.

Before he could get another word out, Cliff immediately said, "Sure we do." He ignored Peevy's glare and said, "Fifteen bucks a show, right?"

Bigelow was loving it. Secretly he was still sure that Cliff had removed the screws from his chair that time. He still had back troubles because of it. "Ten," said Bigelow, rolling his cigar back. "Five goes against your bill."

Peevy fired a glance at Cliff, who shrugged. What choice did they have?

However, Bigelow acted as if it were entirely up to them, as if he hadn't boxed them in. "It's up to you, boys," he said expansively. "See it my way or see me in court." He turned, started to leave, and then as an afterthought added, "Clown suit's in the storeroom. First show's at nine tomorrow. Don't be late." And he walked out.

"Lousy nickel nurser," muttered Cliff.

Peevy went to Cliff and took him by the shoulders. "Cliff, are you off your nut? Doin' the clown act means goin' up in *Mabel*. She's a flyin' coffin. You said so yourself."

And Cliff hadn't been exaggerating. Barnstorming had really gotten its start after the Great War, when surplus war planes were put on the market at dirt-cheap prices. Pilots bought them and went around the country putting on shows or taking thrilled passengers for flights, usually operating out of barns—hence the term.

Miss Mabel had been one of the first purchased and, the way things were going, was working on being the last retired. It was a positively ancient biplane called a Standard, painted garish yellow. It had been dubbed *Miss Mabel* by Peevy, who, along with all the other air veterans on the field, not to mention every man, woman, and child in America, was madly in love with Mabel Cody, the daring air circus acrobat who cavorted on the wings of Standards and Jenny biplanes as if she were a monkey leaping around branches. He'd seen her in action a number of times and was utterly captivated by her verve, her skill, and her pure and obvious lust for life as she capered about, high in the air, wearing a skin-tight white jump suit that inspired pilots everywhere to rise to new heights.

So Peevy had named the plane for her, knowing that it would probably be the closest he'd ever come to climbing inside of Mabel Cody.

Miss Mabel sported the number 19 on the side, which Cliff had claimed was the number of pilots killed flying her. Each time, he said, the plane had been rebuilt by the money-conscious Bigelow, although attempts at rebuilding the pilots had met with somewhat less success.

Still, Cliff forced a smile. "I'll go real easy on her. She never let us down before."

He pulled the photo of Jenny out of his pocket,

grinned, and stuck it into the Standard's instrument panel. Behind him, Peevy went on. "The number five piston's shot! There's more spit and bailing wire here than airplane—"

"I can fly a shoebox if it's got wings," said Cliff airily.

He climbed up into the cockpit, trying not to think about the image of himself wearing that awful clown outfit. But when he tried to sit down, he jumped up moments later with a pained "Owww!"

Peevy looked up in surprise. "What?"

Cliff stepped out onto the wing and leaned back into the cockpit, the upper half of his body disappearing from sight as he rooted around in it. Finally he managed to dislodge something wrapped in a gray duffel bag from under the seat.

"What've you got there?" asked Peevy curiously.

"I don't know, but it's heavy," replied Cliff.

He carried the bag to a work table and set it down with a thud. Now Peevy said with surprise, "That's my duffel bag!"

Cliff pushed the fabric down and his mouth dropped in amazement. Peevy squeezed in behind Cliff's shoulder and gasped.

It sat upright on the work table, a device that consisted of two cylinders seamlessly joined, between two and three feet in height. It was gray steel and chrome, sleek and somehow ominous, as if suggesting potential for great good and, at the same time, great danger. There were straps on it, folded tight and buckled in place.

Peevy stared at it. "Odd-looking contraption . . ."

"What do you suppose it is?" asked Cliff. Peevy shrugged.

Cliff uncoiled a wound-up cable and held it up. It was about the length of his arm. At the end of the cable was a weird metal T, like a flat bracelet. And in the center of that T was a red button.

There was something about the presence of a button, particularly a large red one, that made people want to press it.

Cliff pressed it.

With an enormous blast of flame, the device roared and leapt off the table on a rush of superheated air. Peevy was knocked to the floor and Cliff fell back with a yelp of surprise.

The cylinder shot toward the roof. It smashed through a thick rafter, bounced off the ceiling, and zoomed back at the floor. In a screaming shower of sparks, the blazing cylinder ricocheted off a steel tool cabinet, its trajectory carrying it straight through the outer wall of the hangar's small office.

There were the continued sounds of chaos from within the office, and Cliff and Peevy looked at each other with pure terror. Peevy took a step in the opposite direction, as if contemplating simply leaving the hangar and pretending that he'd never even seen the damned thing before. But Cliff went to the hole that the cylinder had drilled through the wall and, after a moment's reconsideration, Peevy joined him. Together they peered tentatively through the hole in the office.

The cylinder, still spitting fire and vibrating furiously as its powerful engine continued to operate, was half embedded in an easy chair. It looked as if, given a few more minutes, the thing would manage to get the chair airborne.

Cliff entered the room, shying away from the intense heat of the flame. He reached out and grabbed a mop that was propped against a wall nearby and, shielding his face, punched the red button with the handle. Even as he did so he wondered, for one horrible moment, whether pushing the button a second time would, for example, push the flaming cylinder into high gear or something. He was fortunate, though, for the small jet engine promptly shut off. The only noise left in the office was the ragged breathing of Cliff and Peevy.

Automatically Cliff started to reach for the rocket to pull it from its entrapment, and Peevy shouted, "Careful!" Wondering what he could have been thinking, reaching out with his bare skin to touch something that had been a flying inferno, Cliff immediately pulled his hands back. But then, very slowly, very gingerly, he brought his hands closer and closer to the housing, trying to sense for heat. There was none. He touched the metal lightly and then more firmly.

His eyes widened. "The shell's still cool!"

Cautiously approaching the rocket, they each grabbed a side and, within moments, had pried it loose and gotten it back onto the work table. They set it down gingerly, as if afraid that they were handling a keg of dynamite that might blow up at the slightest wrong move.

There was a long moment of silence as they circled the table, trying to get some sense of the object's purpose.

"Never seen nothin' like this," said Peevy. He leaned in closer, sniffing, and scented something familiar. "It burns alcohol!" He paused, shaking his head in wonderment. "What's the damned thing for?"

And slowly it began to dawn on Cliff. It was just a hunch . . . the size of the rocket pack itself, the arm's length of the control cables . . . but maybe . . .

Wordlessly he stepped up to the table and slipped his left arm through the first strap. Then his right arm through the second. He straightened up and the rocket pack now rested comfortably on his back. He slipped his hands through the curved, T-shaped metal bracelets, taking great care not to touch the red buttons on either side. The last thing he did was snap the buckle over his chest, securing the harness.

Peevy and Cliff stared at each other for a moment, and then Cliff pointed wordlessly skyward.

The sun was setting on what had been an extremely busy and hectic day. And watching the sun go down was Lucky Lindy.

Not Charles Lindbergh himself, per se. Instead, it was a life-size wooden statue of Colonel Lindbergh, posed in his heroic best style, looking upward as if the statue expected to soar into the heavens at any given moment. It was the prime landmark that stood outside the Chaplin Field Flight School, which was called, naturally, "Lucky Lindy's Flight School."

Lindbergh himself knew nothing of the school's existence. The proprietor had not approached him on it for fear that he would say no. So they'd just gone on ahead and named it that. One of the first students had been, in real life, a sculptor, and in lieu of payment he had offered his services in creating a statue that would symbolize the bravery and nobility of the school's theoretical sponsor. This offer had been eagerly accepted, which was how the statue of Lindbergh—a quite nice likeness, really—had come to sit on the front lawn of the Lucky Lindy Flight School.

The proprietor lived in perpetual nervousness that sooner or later Lindbergh would learn of the school's existence. He wasn't sure just what the famed aviator's response would be. With any luck—and considering that Lindbergh resided on Illiec, a French island off the coast of Brittany, and so probably wouldn't be passing through Chaplin Field anytime soon—he would never know.

It was reasonable to assume, however, that Lindbergh would definitely not have approved of what was being done to his likeness. Namely, it was shaking from side to side, accompanied by the steady sound of sawing. And, after long moments of sawing, the wooden statue tumbled over with a resounding crack.

The perpetrators froze in place, the noise having been far louder than they anticipated. But no one appeared to have heard; this was a fairly deserted section of the field, after all. So, after ascertaining once more that they were unobserved, Cliff and Peevy gathered up the statue and scurried off into the approaching darkness.

6

While Howard Hughes contemplated a dream that had died aborning, and about the same time that Cliff and Peevy drafted an unwilling statue of Charles Lindbergh for a historic flight, a man in a Hollywood Hills house examined the point of a sharp, gleaming fencing sword and contemplated his next move.

The house was done up in an elaborate Mayanesque style that would have delighted your typical Spanish explorer. Parked in the flagstone courtyard in front of the house were a pair of black Cadillac sedans, glittering like beetles.

There were two grim-faced, broad-shouldered men waiting by them, alert to the possibility of trouble both from inside and outside of the house. The likelihood of the former seemed greater, though, because they could hear angry words floating down from a second-story window. They glanced up and frowned, not liking the tone of things, and unconsciously let their hands stray near the guns that sat snugly in their shoulder holsters. They looked at each other in grim-faced assessment of the situation, and decided that they didn't like it one bit.

From within the house, meantime, the man who had spoken last—the man with the sword—leaned casually against the open balcony door at the edge of his elaborately decorated library. He deliberately selected the pose for its dramatic and stylish visual look, since that was of preeminent importance to him. He was painfully aware of just how the setting sun gleamed off his silk shirt, which was casually undone, or the way the orange rays reflected through the glass of champagne that was held suavely in one hand. In the other hand was the sword, which seemed to be with him at all times, to the degree that it appeared to be a permanent extension of his right hand.

He was tall and elegant, with thick black hair and snapping eyes that reflected both intelligence and, somehow, a deep mercilessness. When the swordsman spoke, it was with a crisp British accent as he said quietly, "So what went wrong?"

The man he was addressing was named Eddie Valentine. Compact and stocky in a pinstripe suit with a bright red rose in his lapel, Eddie rocked back and forth quietly on the balls of his feet, considering his answer.

Eddie was something of a legend in the circles in which he moved. Growing up in a tough neighborhood where his father ran a grocery store, Eddie Valencia, as he was born, had come to love the country of his birth, the country that had been good to his parents when they'd immigrated years before, seeking a new and better life. So dedicated was he that when the Great War had broken out, he had lied about his age so he could serve in the army and help defend his country.

When he'd gotten home after the war, though, he found his father had gone out of business, driven out by gangsters and thugs who wanted to take over every enterprise they could so as to build a power base. They didn't care about his father per se; he was just someone to be stepped on as they went on about their business. When his father died a year later, a broken man, it hardened the heart of young Eddie Valencia and he vowed that if that was the type of man you had to become to succeed, then that's what he would do. He was not going to be stepped on as his father had been.

Eddie Valencia, for all intents and purposes, vanished, although Eddie Valentine continued to make sure that his mother, still stubbornly residing on the Lower East Side of New York City, was always well cared for and wanted for nothing. Eddie Valentine headed for California, where he became a major player, with all sorts of "legitimate interests" to cover his shadier dealings. And now one of those shadier dealings was starting to become a major sticking point.

Standing on either side of Eddie were two of his men, the lean and deadly-looking Spanish Johnny, and the broad-shouldered and thuggish-looking Rusty. Both men were leaning against a wall, a study in nonchalance, but taking in everything that was being said.

"The FBI's what went wrong. They showed up like flies at a picnic," said Eddie. "Now Lenny's dead and Wilmer's in County General wrapped up like a stinkin' mummy." Not knowing about the girlfriend, since that riff had been Lenny's idea, he didn't mention her. "You didn't level with me, mister. This was suppose to be a simple snatch-and-grab."

The swordsman paused a moment and said, "I'm sorry about your boys, Eddie. Truly. But I didn't say it would be simple, and snatch-and-grab is what they're supposed to be good at."

"They are! When they know what they're grabbin'.

What's so important about this package that the feds are nosin' in?"

"Relax, Eddie—"

"Relax!" Valentine exploded. "I'm not your delivery boy! I want to know why the merchandise I'm moving is so hot!"

With incredible calm, as if discussing the weather, the swordsman said, "I don't think that's anything for you to worry about right now."

The swordsman and Eddie Valentine stared at each other for long, tense seconds. And then Valentine made an abrupt gesture to his men. "Let's go, boys."

The principal philosophy of making a deal—any kind of a deal—is being prepared to turn and walk away from it no matter how much you stand to benefit. This was a lesson that Eddie's father had drilled into him. It had served him well throughout his life, and it served him well now, for he and his men got only a few feet before the swordsman said quietly, "It's a rocket."

Eddie turned back and stared at him incredulously. "A rocket—!" and then louder, "*A rocket*?!"

"Yeah," said the swordsman in a fair imitation of Valentine's voice. And then in his more polished tone, he added, "Like in the comic books. Now, what happened to it?"

Unsure of whether he believed the swordsman or not, Eddie said slowly, "Only one who knows is Wilmer. But the hospital's so thick with cops, we can't get near him. Maybe in a couple days when the heat dies down—"

"I don't have a couple of days!" For the briefest of moments he sounded nervous, and then he was com-

paper tape, it read simply, RENDEZVOUS CANNOT BE CHANGED.

Trying to put across the seriousness of the situation, Sinclair snapped into the radio, "I need more time!"

The next response was no less encouraging, and far more final: UNACCEPTABLE. AWAIT FURTHER TRANSMISSION. END.

Angrily Sinclair slapped the code book shut. Then, after only a moment's pause, he picked up a telephone and dialed a number.

The phone rang on the other end and he paused, tapping his foot with minor impatience. Then there was the sound of the phone being answered and a thick voice, low and deadly, responded. "Yes?" In the background the swordsman could hear *Amos 'N' Andy* playing on the radio, and then it was shut off so that he could be heard.

"That job we discussed," said Sinclair. "I'd like you to visit a friend in the hospital . . . a condolence call . . . Room 502, County General."

At the other end there was simply a grunt of acknowledgment, and Sinclair smiled. That was the pleasure of dealing with someone like Lothar. There wasn't a lot of nattering about. You gave him the job, he did it, and that was all. No excuses. No failures. And no one alive to talk about it afterward. Just the way Sinclair liked doing business.

Far away, out of sight of the Hollywood Hills, the headlights of a truck—Peevy's truck—were illuminating a metal stake that Cliff was driving into the ground near a large bean field. Despite his long and arduous day, he was throwing himself into his task with undisguised enthusiasm, swinging the mallet and sending it thudding onto the stake over and over, to make sure it was in good and solid.

The stake was attached to a chain, and the other end of the length of links had been nailed to the wooden chest of the statue of Lindbergh. The rocket pack was resting on Lindy's back as securely as it had been on Cliff's earlier that day. As Cliff hammered, Peevy unspooled a large roll of wire attached to the ignition switch.

Cliff prodded the stake with his foot and nodded in satisfaction to Peevy. Then they both scurried to a nearby ditch, ducked down behind it, and exchanged a significant look. Cliff gave Peevy a quick thumbs-up as Peevy connected the two ends of wires.

The rocket roared as the circuit was completed, and Peevy and Cliff reflexively ducked. Lindy, this time without benefit of plane or life, went immediately air-borne. The chain snapped taut and there, twenty-five feet in the air, the statue was flying in great wide circles at the end of the chain, like a great dog leashed in its backyard. The roar was deafening, but Cliff and Peevy didn't seem to mind. Instead, they stared up in amaze-ment as Peevy shouted, "If I weren't seeing it, I wouldn't believe it. . . ."

And then Cliff managed to take his eyes off Lindy and check the grounding. Immediately he shouted in alarm, "Peevy! The stake!"

And sure enough, the stake was loosening in the ground. The pull of the rocket was simply far stronger than they could have anticipated.

Cliff started to leap out of the ditch, but Peevy immediately yanked him back, pointing to the chain that was whirling around at high speed like the world's longest and deadliest yo-yo string. "That chain will cut you in half!"

But to Cliff, nothing was more important than the hardware. "We're going to lose it!"

And sure enough the stake uprooted. Lindy rocketed skyward, hurtling upward into the night sky faster and faster. The rocket's flame dwindled and finally faded into the blackness.

That was it.

It was over.

Cliff couldn't believe that, after all that—the preparation, the theorizing, the planning—it was gone as if it had never been there.

And then they got a souvenir. They were warned just in time by a strange metallic moaning, and then twenty-five feet of chain slammed into the dusty earth between them.

"Holy hell!" said Peevy in awe.

Cliff's frustration bubbled over. "We lost it! We shoulda anchored it to your truck!"

"My truck would be halfway to Cincinnati by now, you chowderhead!" retorted Peevy, no happier than Cliff.

They started to argue and then they heard something else—a whistling, like a bomb dropping. They threw themselves to the ground as Lindy had his revenge for being sawed down from his perch. He dive-bombed them from behind, skimming right over them at what seemed to be somewhere in the neighborhood of two hundred miles per hour. It missed them by inches and slammed into the ground, plowing a furrow in the bean field before coming to a stop.

They raced over to it and shut the rocket down. It gave a few last sputters of protest and then fell silent, as did the two men for a long moment.

"Peevy," said Cliff slowly, thoughtfully, "you'd pay to see a man fly, wouldn't you?"

Peevy had been dreading this moment. He knew it would be coming the second he saw the way Cliff had first looked at the thing. "I know what you're thinkin', Clifford," he said dangerously. "Forget it."

As if that closed the subject, he grabbed Lindy's feet and tugged him out of the furrow. Cliff grabbed the other end to help lug him to the truck, but he didn't stop yammering.

"But I'm talking about making some *real* money here—not just ten bucks a show, but enough to get us back on our feet and into the Nationals."

"Cliff, are your eyes painted on? That thing's like strapping nitro to your back. Besides, the feds are mixed up in this."

"Yeah," Cliff reminded him sourly, "and thanks to them we're flying the clown act and scraping for nickels. They *owe* us."

"Well, maybe they don't see it that way." Peevy shrugged, trying not to grunt under the strain of the statue's weight. "Look, we're just a couple of sky bums. I don't want to get tangled up with the FBI."

"I don't want to keep it. Just borrow it for a while."

"You do, eh? Well, if you borrow something and don't tell anybody, they call it stealing." He didn't add that borrowing something like this could also be termed "suicide."

Cliff was undeterred. "Just a week or two! Soon as we can afford a new plane, we'll give it back. I swear."

Peevy shook his head, unconvinced. "Did you see what this thing just did? You want to turn your head into a plow? The thing don't work!"

"You're always telling me what a genius you are. Fix it!" said Cliff, hurling down a challenge.

Somehow he always knew just what to say to get Peevy's goat. The annoying thing was that Peevy had already started coming up with ideas to fix the thing. He couldn't help it. The ideas just started coming and he felt the itch to try them, just to see if they would work. But that didn't mean everything was jake about the idea of turning Cliff into a flying guinea pig.

But was it that very different, really, from sending him up in things like the GeeBee? Someone had to be first with any new aviation advancement, and if anyone could handle it—

He shook his head, amazed at the direction his thoughts were taking. "We're gonna need a hell of a lawyer," he said ruefully.

Cliff grinned to himself. He had gotten Peevy thinking of possibilities—and he hadn't even needed to mention the other thing on his mind, namely, that he was trying to get together enough scratch to treat his girlfriend, Jenny, right. There were so many rich hotshots who could show her a great time, and she was always talking in significantly wistful tones about the places she wished she could go and do and see, places that needed guys with serious money to make it happen. Cliff wasn't one of those guys, and he was becoming preoccupied with the notion that if he stayed a poor pilot without two nickels to rub together much longer, Jenny was going to go waltzing off into the sunset with one of her big-bucks Hollywood pals. Hell, strapping a rocket to his back was preferable to watching Jenny slip through his fingers any day of the week.

They tossed the statue into the truck, and Cliff studied poor Lindy's head. It had been completely splintered and Cliff realized that his skull, rock-hard as it was often called, would probably not fare much better.

"*I* think we need a helmet," he said.

7

The radio in the small bedroom was cheerfully playing a big band rendition of "Smoke Gets in Your Eyes," and Jenny hummed along with it as she leaned forward into the mirror, applying her lipstick.

The black-and-white photograph that Cliff carried with him would do her justice only on the day the entire world went color blind. Up until that time, Jenny Blake remained a gorgeous creature who could be appreciated only in full living color. Her skin was soft and white, her just-decorated lips a startling and yet stunning red, and her long black hair lay meticulously about her shoulders. She wore a tight red skirt that ended provocatively just above the knee, and a low-cut striped wool shirt with a deep scooped back. She finished clipping the stocking to the garter and smoothed the red skirt, smiling at herself once more into the mirror approvingly.

Twenty-four years old and dressed to kill.

There was the sound of a car honking outside and she turned toward her friend and roommate, Irma. "Whose is it?" she asked.

Irma glanced out the window. "Yours. The flyboy. You know, I can't figure out what the attraction is."

"Oh," she laughed, "he likes me only because there's a model of plane called a Jenny."

"No," said Irma. "I mean I can't understand what you see in him."

Jenny smiled once more. "He makes me laugh."

Cliff hopped out of the truck and crossed the street toward Jenny's place. Technically speaking, it wasn't just Jenny's place. It was the place of a lot of young women, all of them actresses. The boardinghouse catered to them, and Cliff sometimes jokingly referred to it as the "Home for Wayward Girls," which usually earned him an amused slap on the arm from Jenny.

Other young men were picking up their dates, all under the stone-faced supervision of the matron, Mrs. Pye. The other men barely spoke to her beyond the formal, " 'Evening, ma'am," but Cliff was just outgoing enough—or stupid enough—to try to do more. "Good evening, Mrs. Pye," he said gregariously. "I've come to pick up Jenny."

He started forward and, pretty much as he expected, Mrs. Pye placed an immovable palm on his chest.

"You know my rules," she said stiffly. "No gentlemen after six P.M."

He winked. "I'm not a gentleman."

"You can say that again," she said. "This time don't forget the curfew. I lock up at eleven sharp."

He remembered the last time, when they'd gotten in at 11:05 and the front door had been bolted. Cliff had wound up breaking a window to get Jenny in, which resulted in police cars showing up and a mad dash through backyards and . . .

"Okay, warden," said Cliff, having no desire to repeat the experience.

Jenny swept out and chastely kissed Cliff on the cheek. She draped an arm around his neck and called out, "'Night, Mrs. Pye!"

"Have a good time, dear. If he tries anything, deck him." As she retreated into the boardinghouse, Cliff had a sneaking suspicion that that philosophy explained what must have happened to Mr. Pye.

As soon as the door slammed, Jenny threw both arms around Cliff's neck and kissed him long and hard on the mouth. The length and passion of the kiss drew good-natured hoots and catcalls from the other girls who were walking past or hanging out windows. Cliff broke off the embrace and, grinning, he and Jenny set off strolling down the street.

"Cliff!" she said in that marvelously bubbly way she had. "Guess what! I think I got the part!"

"That's great!"

"I won't know for sure till I get to the set tomorrow, but the director liked my reading best."

"You mean you have lines this time?" said Cliff, surprised.

"Just one," she admitted, and then brightened, "but it's to Neville Sinclair."

"Lemme hear it."

She stopped, threw her head back, and exclaimed, "Oh! My prince! Would that you drink of my lips as deeply!"

Suddenly Cliff felt a slight buzz of annoyance. "And then he kisses you, right?" he said.

"Naw, he's too busy killing someone."

Her response had been an offhanded one, but then the tone of Cliff's question sank in on her and she realized, barely suppressing a smile, that he was jealous.

And since she was in far too good a mood to want a fight, she said briskly, "Now you tell me."

He looked at her, confused. "What?"

"What do you think! The GeeBee, the maiden voyage! How'd it go?"

"Okay, I guess," he said evasively.

She couldn't quite hide her annoyance. "That's it? 'Okay, I guess'?" She had been sure that Cliff would be very enthusiastic about it, and it irked her that he didn't deem it all that important. "How'd she fly?"

"She *flew* great," said Cliff. "Landing had a few bumps. Got some bugs to work out." He shrugged as if it were all meaningless and then said, "We gotta hurry if we're gonna catch a movie. I hear a new Cagney picture opened."

"So did a new Neville Sinclair picture."

"Aw, Jenny, Cagney's better," protested Cliff. And he really was a big Cagney fan—had been ever since 1935, when Cagney appeared in both *Ceiling Zero* and *Devil Dogs of the Air,* two fairly sharp films about airmen, even if they were made by Hollywood types. Of course, Cliff didn't bother to add that he didn't feel like shelling out dough to go see some guy that Jenny might be talking about kissing tomorrow. He thought about Sinclair and all those pansy movies he'd made with his hoi polloi accent and snooty airs that made women swoon and men guffaw. "You won't catch Cagney lounging around a penthouse in his underwear or walking poodles in the park or—"

"Or getting shot down behind enemy lines?"

He paused in surprise. "What?"

"The movie?" she prompted. "*Wings of Honor?* Neville Sinclair?"

He realized that this was leading toward the inevita-

ble giving-in to Jenny, and he might as well do it grace-
fully. Besides, it might be worth a few laughs to see the
fancy dan trying to pretend that he's in the same class
with Jimmy Cagney or Ralph Bellamy, or even Cary
Grant, who had some of the same airs but at least
seemed like he was taking himself a bit less seriously.

"This I gotta see," he said with as much enthusiasm
as he could muster.

The show had already started as Cliff and Jenny made
their way down the darkened aisle. Cliff was loaded
down with popcorn and sodas, muttering, "Excuse me,
pardon me," as people who were already seated reluctantly moved their legs to accommodate him and Jenny
squeezing past.

As they moved toward two empty seats, the announcer of the newsreel that was unspooling on the screen
intoned, "But as rumors of war haunt the Continent,
Herr Hitler claims to be working for world peace ...
and the sovereignty of nations."

Cliff glanced up and saw the Nazis giving Chancellor
Hitler that annoying, stiff-armed salute. It bugged the
hell out of him. He'd had a lengthy argument with Malcolm about it one day at the Bulldog Café, when Malcolm—who'd been a pilot during the Great War—
stated that Hitler could blow hot air all he wanted, but
that he would never dare to start something really big
because the Krauts had learned their hard lessons back
in 1918. The world had kicked their tails and could do
so again at any time, and that knowledge would keep
the Germans in line.

Cliff, on the other hand, hadn't been so sure. There

was something in the pictures and newsreels he saw of Hitler that gave him chills. Chills and an uneasy feeling that the world was becoming a trickier place to live with every passing day.

As Cliff and Jenny seated themselves, the image on the screen changed as a zeppelin with a bold swastika painted on its tail descended from the skies over someplace or other. The announcer said with incredible cheerfulness, "And just to prove he's a swell guy, here comes the chancellor's latest goodwill gesture—the mighty airship *Luxembourg*, on a coast-to-coast friendship tour of the United States."

Jenny and Cliff divvied up the snacks as the zeppelin's captain and crew mingled with an excited crowd on the screen. "First stop, New Jersey," said the announcer, "where the locals turn out in droves to meet Captain Heinrick and the crew. Winning friends the old-fashioned way—with good German chocolate!" Sure enough, the German airmen were handing out candy bars to eagerly grabbing children.

Cliff shook his head in disgust. Kids would do anything for a few slabs of candy, and here this stupid newsreel was making that seem like a good thing. To top it off, the Heinrick guy turned and waved to the camera as the announcer said, "Welcome, boys! Look us up when you get to Hollywood!"

There followed afterward a trailer for a new Errol Flynn picture, *The Adventures of Robin Hood*. There was a quick shot of Olivia de Havilland saying to Flynn, "You speak treason!" Cliff chuckled to himself. She'd said the exact same thing to him in *Captain Blood*. Apparently Errol never tired of talking treason, and she never tired of hearing it. Flynn seemed like a decent enough duck. Anybody was better than that Sinclair creep.

After that came a trailer for a new cliffhanger entitled *The Return of Milo Flint*, which looked to be a two-fisted detective flick, and then Cliff settled into the seat as the movie began and Neville Sinclair's name appeared on the screen in huge letters.

Jenny nudged him. "You'll love this."

"I love it already," muttered Cliff. "If I loved it any more, I'd be in the hospital."

The nurse emerged from the patient's room and walked toward the police officer who was seated at the nurses' station, adjusting the dials on a radio. Spooky music came on, followed by the sounds of ominously creaking doors and hollow, evil laughter. He looked up and asked her, "How's he doing?"

"I just gave him a sedative," said the nurse. "He'll sleep like a baby."

Inside the hospital room, Wilmer, in heavy traction, lay dozing in bed. The only sounds in the room were his gentle snoring mingling with the creepy radio organ music filtering through the door.

Then, slowly, the window slid open, the breeze billowing in the curtains. A massive figure crept into the room, moving with a quiet that was in remarkable contrast to its size. It approached the sleeping form of Wilmer and then, with a large thumbnail, cracked a match and held the faint illumination up to Wilmer's face.

The man—if such a word could be used—who peered down at the sleeping gangster, looked like something out of a Boris Karloff film. A neanderthal brute in a badly fitting pinstripe suit. His massive jaw was distended, his cheekbones were flat, and he didn't have eyebrows so much as a heavy ridge that sat over small, sunken, piglike eyes.

He reached up and clutched one of Wilmer's traction cords in a meaty hand, and gave it a sharp yank.

Wilmer's groggy eyes fluttered open, and then his pupils dilated in horror.

He recognized the creature looming over him, even in the poor light. He'd seen him once, but that one time was more than enough to make an indelible impression. He'd been called Lothar by that Limey fruit that Eddie had been contracting with. Lothar—a name out of a horror flick. Went with the face.

"It's you," muttered Wilmer. "Tell your boss I don't answer to nobody but Eddie."

Lothar eased his massive hands beneath Wilmer's body and then lifted him easily.

Wilmer gasped, having no control of the situation at all. The eeriness of the moment was heightened by the creepy music that was pouring out of the radio in the hallway, and suddenly Wilmer was even more afraid than when he'd been staring down the front of a plane that was hurtling toward him. More frightened than when the feds had been firing on him. More frightened than any time he could remember in his life.

"Okay! Okay! Ease off," he gasped. "I pulled a switch, see? I got the dingus stashed good . . . at the airfield. Hangar three. Some old plane . . ."

And then he felt a horrible pressure begin to be exerted on him, a pressure as horrible as the satisfied, evil grin that played across the man-monster's lips.

"No!" gasped out Wilmer, and for the umpteenth

time the thought went through his head, *I was going to quit! This was my last job!*

At the nurses' station they heard the screams but thought they were coming from the radio. They sounded a bit too loud, and the cop reached over to lower the volume, but before he could do so the program went to a commercial . . . and the screams kept on coming.

It was then they realized what was happening, and the cop charged the door of the room where Wilmer was supposed to be sleeping. Wilmer, the man whom he was supposed to be guarding. Wilmer, who had talked endlessly of this being his last job and going straight.

The cop shouldered open the door, his revolver drawn, with the nurse directly behind him. Her hands flew to her mouth and she screamed.

The cop winced at the sight.

This had indeed turned out to be Wilmer's last job. However, he had not gone straight. In fact, he was just the opposite: he was hanging suspended above the bed, dangling from the traction gear, his body bent backward in half. His eyes were dead and staring.

The cop rushed to the open window, where curtains were fluttering like ghosts. He peered out into the darkness. Nothing.

He pulled back into the window, turned, and went to call his chief. His superior was not going to be the least bit happy to hear this.

And on the ledge above, a massive pair of wingtip shoes shuffled off into the night.

8 The Bulldog Café was a stone's throw from Chaplin Airfield and the second home—some would say the first—to a number of the fliers in Bigelow's Air Circus.

There had never been a café more accurately named than the Bulldog, for that essentially was what it was. It had been done up to resemble a large white and black canine, a full story high, sitting on its haunches. Its eyes were wide open in a perpetually surprised expression, as if amazed that anyone would actually come there to eat. A pipe stuck out of its mouth with a sign reading OPEN hanging down from it. The exterior had the word EATS painted in big letters on either side, and down the front of its left and right front legs were the words, respectively, TAMALES and ICE CREAM, which, so claimed some cynics, were indistinguishable from each other the way that Millie, the owner and head cook, prepared them.

The door to the café was situated smack in the fake animal's belly, and at that moment a large, genuine bulldog was scraping at the door, asking to be let in.

Millie, wearing a gingham dress with white apron, came to the door in response to the animal's pathetic whining, but her face was stern. "Forget it, Butch," she said. "I'd let you in, but that genius over there"—she pointed in annoyance in the direction of Cliff Secord, who was seated opposite Jenny in a booth—"had to go and feed you some beef jerky. You know what that stuff does to you. I can't have you in here stinking up the joint."

Butch whined for sympathy and lay down on his side, looking pathetic and questioning.

"I know, I know," said Millie in irritation. "Was up to me, I'd've thrown Cliff out with you. Thought he was being funny, Mr. Secord did. But he's here with his girl and all and, well, you know how it is."

Butch looked up at her and obviously didn't know how it was.

Millie sighed. "Wait here." Moments later she returned with a large soup bone which she tossed to Butch, and the obnoxiously homely dog caught it in his large mouth and trotted away, satisfied with the transaction.

Millie walked back to behind the counter, but not before stopping to give Cliff a quick rap on the head with a frying pan. This drew amused laughter from Skeets, Goose, and Malcolm. "Hey!" Cliff protested.

"That's for giving Butch the beef jerky," she said.

"I could get amnesia or something!" Cliff told her, rubbing his head. "Forget how to fly, or where I live or my phone number or something."

"Phone number!" said Jenny suddenly. "Oh, thanks for reminding me, Millie. I've got a new phone number."

"Wish she'd picked a way to remind you that was easier on my noggin," Cliff said.

"They changed the number on the pay phone at the boardinghouse," she said. "We were one digit off from a movie theater, and people kept calling and asking us for the times."

Cliff patted himself down. "Anybody got a piece of paper Jenny can write her new number on?" he called out.

"Oh, don't worry about it," she said, and she got up

and went to the wall next to the café's phone. Nearby were framed photos and other aviation mementos. And around the phone was a series of various phone numbers written right on the wall. Jenny pulled out the pen she always kept with her, not wanting to be caught short the first time someone might ask for her autograph, and wrote 'Jenny' on the wall, followed by her number and, as always, her trademark heart with the arrow through it. Then she put the pen back and returned to the table.

By this point Cliff had recovered enough from the unexpected visitation on his skull by a skillet to remember what he'd been in the middle of saying. "Oh, the Sinclair film!" he said.

"Yeah, you were tellin' us about it," Goose said.

"Right. Right. So . . . get this, fellas! At the end of the movie he flies over the enemy trenches and drops a bottle of champagne!"

"Let me guess!" said Goose. "It hits the general and we win the war, right?" This drew a chorus of guffaws from the fliers. They were used to the Hollywood depiction of themselves as all-powerful heroes, but giving good booze to the bad guys . . . uh-uh.

Privately, Jenny had thought it was a bit much herself, but she was the one who had chosen the movie and talked it up, and she felt constrained to defend it. "It was symbolic!" she said. "He was being chivalrous!"

"Where'd he get it?" asked Skeets. "The champagne, I mean. They didn't have liquor stores at the front."

"Not that I can recall," Malcolm said thoughtfully, giving the impression that he was actually trying to remember if there had been liquor stores. "Would'a been nice. . . ."

"It doesn't matter *where* he got it, the point is . . . oh, forget it," Jenny said in exasperation. She turned to Millie, figuring a woman would understand. "It was so romantic, Millie. I cried and cried. Neville was wonderful."

"'Neville'?" said Cliff, making no attempt to hide his irritation. "Guy's never been *up* in a plane, much less flown one."

"Who cares?" said Millie. "He's a living doll."

At that moment Patsy, Millie's ten-year-old daughter, approached Malcolm. With her brown hair in braids and her general tomboyish attitude, she reminded Millie so much of herself at that age that she found it hard to believe she wasn't staring into a mirror that showed the past. Patsy, wearing a plaid shirt and blue overalls, was carrying a little tin airplane with a broken wheel.

Malcolm smiled down at her. He'd remembered the day she was born, and now here she was, more like a genuine person every day.

"Malcolm, the wheel came off," she said.

"Lemme see, princess," said Malcolm. "Give it to me, we'll fix it up."

"Give it to Cliff, he'll fly it," laughed Goose. Jenny looked at him in mild confusion and Cliff shot Goose a look that immediately shut him up.

Malcolm, meantime, said to Patsy while studying the plane, "Did I ever tell you about the time I got shot down by the Red Baron?"

Patsy innocently began to nod her head, rather emphatically. But then she caught her mother pointedly shaking her head and giving her the "be polite" stare. So Patsy instantly shifted gears and started shaking her head just as Malcolm looked up.

"No?" he said, pleased. He could've sworn he had. Well, so much the better. As he began fiddling with the toy, he said, "Well, there I was, flying patrol over the Ardennes, when all of a sudden he came screamin' out of the sun, guns blazing!" Behind him, unseen, Skeets was miming the actions, to the amusement of the other fliers. "I tried to loop, but he stuck to my tail like a dirty diaper. 'Fore I knew it, my bird was shot to tatters. I musta fell for half an hour, and then *smack*—!"

And the wheel from Patsy's plane shot out of Malcolm's grasp and landed with a splash in Jenny's soup. Droplets sprayed all over her blouse.

"Bull's-eye, ace," said Cliff in annoyance.

"I'm sorry, Jenny," Malcolm apologized as Jenny dabbed at her blouse with a napkin.

Cliff fished the wheel out of the soup for her as she said, "That's okay, Malcolm." Then, lowering her voice, she said to Cliff, "Elegant dining here at the Bulldog. Once in a while it wouldn't hurt to try a new place . . . away from the airfield."

Cliff felt as if he'd had this conversation a hundred times before. "What'll it be? The Copa or the Brown Derby? How 'bout the South Seas Club while you're dreaming?"

She nodded eagerly. "Yeah! Someplace an actress can get noticed."

"And a guy can get skinned!" Cliff protested. "For the cost of dessert in one of those joints, I could overhaul an engine."

"I'm not saying all the time . . ." she began, and then she sighed. She smiled in that way that she had, and Cliff simply melted and they took each other's hands. "Okay," she said, offering a compromise. "How about this? We'll have a *real* night out on the town after you win the Nationals."

There was a dead silence from the other fliers as they traded uncomfortable glances. Cliff tried to nod unconvincingly, and now Jenny knew that something was definitely up.

But it was Malcolm, oblivious to anything unless it was spelled out for him, who swiveled around on the stool and said, "You're flying in the Nationals after all? I'm glad to hear it, after that landing today."

Millie quickly stepped in with a pot of coffee. "How 'bout a warm-up, Malcolm," she said, hoping to distract him.

Jenny looked accusingly at Cliff. "You said there were a few bumps."

Before Cliff could respond, Malcolm laughed loudly. "Boy, I'll say! You shoulda seen it. Folded like a kite when she hit the pavement. We thought ol' Cliffie's number was up, what with the fire and all."

Realizing that subtlety was a lost cause, Millie whacked him with a spoon. He stopped in confusion, looked at the faces of the others, and suddenly realized that his big mouth had just landed Cliff in a barrelful of trouble.

"I was going to tell you," said Cliff.

Jenny's voice could have steamed wallpaper off the wall. "When? After the milkman found out?"

"Jenny, losing his plane isn't something a pilot goes bragging about!" said Cliff. The heads of the other pilots bobbed up and down in confirmation. "I . . . didn't want to spoil our evening."

"That's very thoughtful," she said. "Thank you. You'd rather make a fool of me."

"I'm sorry, I—"

"I don't want you to be sorry!" she said in frustration. "I want you to stop treating me like a china cup! Cliff, when something goes wrong, I should be the first to know, not the last."

"Honey, everybody else knows because they were there!"

Immediately Cliff knew that hadn't sounded right. It came out sounding accusatory, and that was exactly the way Jenny took it before he could clarify. "I had an audition! It was important!"

But now her use of the word *important* irritated Cliff, sending him from defensive and guilty to annoyed on his own behalf. Resentments he had thought long gone bubbled up. "Yeah, just like the time I flew the Regionals. You had a big part. You stood behind Myrna Loy with a bowl of grapes."

Jenny threw her napkin down, leapt up, and grabbed her purse. " 'Night, Millie. Thanks for the soup," she said, her voice trembling with embarrassment and fury, and then she turned and stalked out of the café.

Cliff sat there, all eyes on him, hating himself for blowing it so badly. And finally Millie broke the silence by waving her spoon and shouting, "Well, go after her, you dope!"

Realizing she was right, and knowing what a dope the others thought he was, Cliff immediately bolted from the table and out the door.

He ran out into the street just in time to see Jenny hopping a bus. "Jenny!" he called out.

The bus pulled away and Cliff pounded after it, but it disappeared down the street. He stood there, shoulders sagging, and sighed. "Dammit," he said.

There was a heavy footfall behind him. "Cliff, I'm sorry," said Malcolm. "I really put my foot in it, didn't I?"

"It's all right, Malcolm," sighed Cliff. "It's not your fault."

He walked back to the Bulldog, leaving Malcolm alone and miserable on the street.

In the simple house that Cliff and Peevy shared, the old mechanic was seated at the dining room table, which was covered with tools, rivets, and scraps of metal. To his right was a simple metal shell that he'd measured off Cliff's head hours before so that the helmet he was working on would fit just right.

He couldn't get over it. When the thing was finished, Cliff would have a hard head and Peevy's was still undeniably soft. And yet . . .

In his career, Peevy had worked with the best fliers around. Everybody knew Peevy. When Wiley Post had wanted someone to check over his equipment five years earlier before launching his epic world flight, who'd he called in for a consult? Peevy. To whom did Jimmy Doolittle attribute his success? Peevy. And when that lanky redhead, Amelia Earhart, prepared to fly alone across the Atlantic in 1932, who checked her engine over? Peevy. In fact, in his heart of hearts, Peevy still blamed himself for Amelia's being lost a year ago in the Pacific— she had invited him to be a permanent part of her staff. But Peevy had been too involved with Cliff's career at that point, and besides, hell, he was getting too old for flights from New Guinea to Oakland. To this day he still hoped that somehow, through some miracle, that gutsy little woman would turn up.

There was a lot in Cliff that reminded Peevy of all those great fliers, those phenomenal pioneers. It was remarkable when Peevy considered that his grandparents had crossed the country in a covered wagon, and here he was working on devices that they would have considered flights of fantasy.

Cliff could be one of the great ones. Cliff could be *the* great one. Peevy prided himself on spotting young talent and helping it develop, grow, and blossom. Yet it was difficult with someone like Cliff. On the one hand, you didn't want to extinguish that enthusiasm and guts that made him what he was. On the other hand, you had to temper his moxie with the common sense that only years of experience could bring.

Of course, when you thought about it, common sense said that flight was impossible unless you were a bird. Certainly Peevy's father had believed that the first time, the first time that seven-year-old Peevy jumped off the roof with feathers tied to his arm, flapping furiously. If only his father could see him now!

It was hard to tell where to draw the line.

As the first strains of "Begin the Beguine" filtered over the radio, Cliff stormed in, threw down his jacket, and went straight to the phone. In those motions Peevy read the probable outcome of the evening with Jenny, but he simply said neutrally, "You're home early."

"Jenny had a seven A.M. call," said Cliff.

Peevy smiled in amusement. The first time Jenny had said something like that to Cliff, he demanded to know who was phoning her so early in the morning. She had to explain, without laughing, that it meant she had to be on the set of a movie at that particular time of the morning. So now Cliff was tossing around that same lingo with no problem.

Of course, that wasn't the real reason Cliff was back so early, and Peevy figured he might as well be straightforward about it. "What was the fight about?"

"I don't know, Peev," said Cliff in exasperation. "I can't figure her out." He stood with the telephone to his ear, letting it ring and ring before he finally hung up. He stood there for a moment and then said, "Maybe she just needs a little more time."

He walked off down the hallway, leaving Peevy quietly working at the table and saying to himself, "Don't give her too much time. 'Cause somebody's gonna figure that girl out."

The radio was broadcasting nothing but dead air as Peevy dozed in an easy chair. Clad in a worn bathrobe, yawning after an uneasy night's sleep, Cliff shuffled toward the kitchen, stopping only to turn off the radio and toss a blanket over Peevy.

The amount of debris on the dining room table seemed to have grown exponentially, and in the middle of it was something covered with a large polishing cloth. Cliff reached over and removed the cloth, and then whistled softly at what he saw.

He picked it up and held it at arm's length. It was something right out of *Metropolis*. The morning sunlight glinted off the burnished metal of the helmet, creating a soft and yet powerful glow. An aerodynamic fin curved from the helmet's crown. Amber lenses were set in the eye sockets, and vents had been cut into the mouth area.

He whistled and looked at the sleeping mechanic in amazement. "Onward and upward," he said.

9 On the curving stairway of the castle, two expert swordsmen were locked in mortal combat.

Sir Alec of Trent, dressed in the finery of the English court, parried a thrust from the man who was before him, the man who had the temerity to run about in a dashing, form-fitting black mask and go by the absurd name of the Laughing Bandit. Noblemen and women in the court below gasped in appreciation of Sir Alec's skill and yet their faces seemed torn in their loyalties. The Laughing Bandit was so heroic, so mysterious. . . .

The bandit leapt down from the stairway directly into the midst of the amazed audience. They backed away to give him room as Sir Alec duplicated the feat. The two men paused, taking a breath, as if sensing that this was the final engagement. Then they came at each other, their footwork unerring, their swords a mutual blur. To those watching it was amazing, two blades practically invisible.

The bandit pressed the attack, driving Sir Alec back, back, and suddenly Sir Alec was amazed to find that he had run out of room, his back against a stone column. The momentary lapse was potentially fatal against an opponent of the Laughing Bandit's skill, and the masked man did not miss it. The sword flashed out and knocked Sir Alec's rapier to the ground. An instant later the point of the bandit's sword was at the throat of Sir Alec.

The nobleman drew himself up and radiated disdain, even now, when his demise was imminent. "What, kill me as I stand? I thought you were a sporting man."

"True," said the Laughing Bandit with his famed insouciance. "I would hate to stain my legend on a villain such as you."

The bandit's swordpoint stabbed forward to a different target—the red rose on Sir Alec's tunic, which he flicked through the air to land in the hands of a beautiful noblewoman.

Sir Alec's face purpled with rage as the Laughing Bandit then, in an utter show of self-confidence, flipped the nobleman's sword to him with the toe of his boot.

It was clear at that moment that Sir Alec knew he could not beat the bandit man to man, but that wouldn't stop him. Alec immediately bolted, and the bandit took off in pursuit.

Sir Alec charged up another winding stone stairway, running higher and higher as the bandit unhesitatingly pursued him. Just as the bandit was about to catch up with him, near the top, three guards appeared practically out of nowhere.

The bandit hesitated, and then realized that he was in trouble when two more guards advanced from behind, blocking his escape.

Sir Alec now stood five steps in front of him, a smug expression on his face. "Prepare to die, that we may learn the true identity of the Laughing Bandit!"

"Why wait?" shot back the Laughing Bandit.

He ripped off his mask and there was a collective gasp from the noblemen upon seeing those fierce eyes and sculpted features. "It's Sir Reginald!" cried out a nobleman.

"None other!" declared Sir Reginald and, using the moment of surprise, thrust forward with his sword. The point struck home and Sir Alec gasped, clutching at his chest. His eyes rolled back and he tumbled off the stairway toward the castle floor below.

With a roar of fury the troops of the late Sir Alec charged Sir Reginald, a.k.a. the Laughing Bandit. The bandit leapt off the stairway, grabbing a lanyard that was anchoring a chandelier, and swung in a graceful arc to the banquet table below.

He swept up a goblet of wine and downed it in one gulp. A noblewoman rushed to his feet

She opened her mouth to speak and what came out was, "*Oh,* my prince, *would* dat *you* drinka *my* lips *so* deep!"

And from nearby, a frustrated and angry voice called out, "Cut! Cut! *Cut!*"

Immediately the noblemen and women looked in full disdain at the woman who had just spoken. Sir Alec sat up on the mattress he'd landed on and shook his head, and the Laughing Bandit shook his head in amazement.

Technicians from all over now emerged onto the set, preparing to recheck the lights and sound equipment. Cameramen leaned back and chatted with each other, comparing notes on how the master shot looked through their respective lenses.

In the meantime the director, a generally patient but easily frustrated man named Victor Brannon, approached the noblewoman who had delivered her line so abominably, and said, "Honey, you're a lady of the court, not a barfly from Philly!"

Still lying on the mattress, looking nonchalant, Sir Alec called, "Victor, how many times we gonna *do* this?"

Brannon ignored him, instead concentrating on the actress. "Now, look, acting is acting like you're *not* acting. So act—but don't act like you're acting. Get me?"

The actress, who until two weeks ago had been a barfly from Philly, looked at him blankly.

On the side of the movie set, Jenny and Irma—dressed as servant extras—looked at each other. Irma rolled her eyes.

"Boy oh boy, is *she* a block of wood. Your audition was *so* much better."

"Irma, *everyone's* audition was better," said Jenny. "It doesn't matter when you're the producer's 'niece.' "

Irma sighed loudly. "So *she* gets to play a scene with Neville Sinclair while we play scenery. I love Hollywood."

Jenny was glad that Cliff was nowhere nearby. He'd sure be having a laugh at her expense.

Cliff wandered around on the studio lot, feeling hopelessly lost.

He'd had a tough enough time sneaking in. The guard at the front gate had not been particularly inclined to let him in . . . to be specific, he'd told Cliff that if he saw him hanging around again, he'd personally boot the flier from here to Pasadena. Still, through dedication, Cliff had gotten past him. He'd simply waited for the right moment and it had presented itself: While hiding in the bushes, Cliff saw Mae West drive up to the gate in a low roadster.

She pulled up and immediately began to engage in what was clearly some sort of teasing banter with the guard. Maybe he was asking her what she'd said in that Adam and Eve sketch she'd done with Don Ameche on the radio a few months before. Whatever it was, it had gotten the FCC so steamed that they'd issued an official scolding. Or maybe Mae West was just being her usual sociable, slightly bawdy self.

Whatever it was, Cliff couldn't hear from where he was hiding, but he knew now was the moment. He bolted for the far side of the gate to which the guard had his back turned. Mae saw him go, but clearly the blond bombshell thought he was just an autograph hound or some other harmless guy, and she did nothing to tip the guard of what was going on. Cliff grinned, waved, and squeezed through the gate and onto the lot.

Once he was there, though, he knew he was going to have a problem. All around were large buildings that he knew, from Jenny's descriptions, were soundstages. But they all looked alike. There were people walking past him or riding past him on bikes, all clearly with someplace to go and something to do, and his attempts to get their attention failed miserably.

There was a woman standing a few feet away, and she didn't seem to be going anywhere. She was wearing what appeared to be a large black dress of some kind with large, puffy black sleeves. He walked up to her and tapped her on the back. "Excuse me," he began. . . .

She turned and Cliff jumped back three feet with a yelp of alarm.

Her face was pea green, and her nose was long and ugly. Her entire face seemed to be filled with evil.

"Jeez!" exclaimed Cliff. "I . . ."

She put up her equally green hands. "I'm sorry. I was just catching some fresh air. I'm here for makeup and costume tests. That's all. I don't normally look like this."

"I . . . I didn't think so," said Cliff, already starting to feel foolish. "It's . . . effective, I'll tell you that."

"You think so?" She examined her hands. "It's not too much?"

"No, it's fine. What are you supposed to be? A troll?"

"A witch, actually."

"Look, uh . . ."

"Margaret."

"Margaret, I'm looking for where they're filming some movie. Something with Neville Sinclair, I'm not sure what it's called."

"I'm sorry," she apologized. "I'm not sure. I wish I could be of help. Say, I've been practicing my laugh. Want to hear?"

"Yeah, sure," said Cliff, looking about distractedly.

She laughed, a nasty, brittle-sounding cackle. Cliff listened carefully and then said, "Try it a little higher pitched. And put more of an *eh-eh-eh* sound into it. Like a plane engine revving up."

She paused a moment, taking it in, and then let loose with a laugh so hideous that Cliff felt chills up and down his spine. He flashed her a high sign and started off, calling over his shoulder, "Good luck with your movie!"

"Aw, it's some kids' film," she said with a dismissive wave. "But, y'know, what the hell . . . it's a job, right?"

"All right!" shouted Victor Brannon, clapping his hands sharply. "Everybody back to first position! Let's see if we can get it right this time!"

"Quiet on the set!" shouted the assistant director, who happened to be Brannon's son, Fred. "We're rolling!"

The clapper boy stepped forward, clapper at the ready. "*Sword of the Avenger,* scene 114. Take twenty-eight!"

"And . . . action!" said Brannon.

Cliff saw a man dressed in what appeared to be Civil War-period clothes pacing back and forth near one of the soundstages. The man was muttering to himself, and then Cliff's eyes opened wide and he cried out, "You're . . . you're him! Clark Gable!"

Gable barely afforded him a glance. "Please . . . I'm trying to get my lines down."

"I thought you were great in *Night Flight*!" Cliff gushed. For clowns like Sinclair he had little patience, but this was Gable, for pity's sake!

"Fine. Great." Gable went back to muttering to himself.

"Look, uh, I'm looking for a film that Neville Sinclair is making—"

Gable pointed distractedly to the soundstage directly across the way. "In there. Now, please, this is an important line, and I have to make sure the delivery is right," and he went back to muttering.

"Okay, thanks. Uhmmm . . ." He felt like a rube, but when was he going to get this kind of opportunity again? "Look . . . I have a friend named Cliff who'd really like your autograph. He thinks you're just about the best, right up there with Cagney, and—"

Gable, his back to Cliff and, at this point, oblivious of his presence, tilted his head and said loudly, "Frankly, my dear, I don't give a damn!"

Cliff took a step back, surprised and embarrassed and then angry. "All right! Forget it, then! And you know what? *I* don't give a damn either! And for that matter, you couldn't come close to Cagney on your best day!" And he turned and headed for the sound-stage.

Gable, surprised at the sudden outburst that had interrupted him, turned and watched Cliff go. "Wonder what *his* problem is?" he murmured, and then shrugged and went back to rehearsing.

Cliff ignored the red light bulb that shone brightly just above the door and opened it, stepping into an alien world of darkness and cables and strange props. He might as well have been walking around on the moon.

Somewhere off to his right he heard shouting and the sounds of swords clanging together. He tripped over a cable and then quickly righted himself. Walls of a castle towered nearby, and he felt hemmed in by the labyrinth of stone walls. Someone on the other side was shouting something about a "Sir Reginald," but Cliff had no idea how to get around to where the shouting was coming from. The wall was an immense barrier, and it was so dark he was sure he'd trip and kill himself.

He decided the only thing to do was wait for somebody to turn on the lights so he could see where he was going.

He leaned against the sturdy castle wall.

On the set, the suave Sir Reginald had just downed his twenty-eighth glass of fake wine that day. Poised at his feet was the noblewoman from Philadelphia, and her little fists clenched in that way she had just before she would deliver her line.

The director, who was not looking forward to take twenty-nine, held his breath. His eyes, along with those of everyone else on the set, were glued on the noblewoman.

And to their utter shock, she said with breathless wonder, amazement, precision, and absolutely no trace of any accent except a perfect British one, "Oh, my prince! Would that you drink of my lips as deeply!"

It was all the director and crew could do not to give a collective yelp of joy. As if galvanized by the hope of finishing the damned master take already, Sir Reginald leapt off the table into the midst of the palace guards, sword poised. . . .

And at that moment Cliff Secord discovered that the sturdy castle wall was made of plyboard. Overbalanced by his weight, the wall started to topple.

A grip saw it first and, with alarm, he shouted, "Heads up!"

The castle wall tore right down the middle and collapsed slowly but inevitably. Cast and crew dashed in all directions, screams filling the air, and the flat landed in the middle of the set with a massive *thwap*.

Cliff stood there, feeling incredibly exposed. The eyes of a hundred people were staring at him. Ninety-nine, actually—Jenny, standing behind a pillar, had closed hers in pain and mortification.

The confused flier looked around and then said, "Uh . . . sorry. Is Jenny here?"

Victor felt as if his temples were about to explode. But he knew that if he lost control now, it would mean, at the very least, a stroke.

"Jenny," he said with great quiet. He turned and raised his voice. "Is there a Jenny here?" he asked, sounding sweet as pie.

Jenny had been shutting her eyes even more tightly, hoping that when she opened them it would all turn out to be a bad dream. Such, however, was not the case. Slowly she emerged from behind the pillar and, wishing that she would simply die there and then because anything was preferable to this, she raised her hand.

Victor made an elaborately gracious bow to Cliff, sweeping his hands toward Jenny in a be-my-guest manner. Cliff walked toward her, noticing how ashen she had become, and it was at that point that the director suddenly realized that the camera was still rolling. He glared into the camera and with a throat-slashing gesture—which was what he felt like doing at the moment—he said, "Cut!"

A swarm of crew members were helping Neville Sinclair to his feet. He deflected their concern with good humor. "It's all right," he said. "I'm fine. Never let it be said that a Neville Sinclair performance failed to bring down the house!"

This generated a round of laughter while the assistant director, Fred, went to the sprawled Sir Alec. "Charlie, you can get up now. . . ." He prodded the actor with his toe. "Charlie?"

Charlie Middleton rolled off and groaned, and Fred's eyes went wide with shock. "Somebody call the nurse!" he bellowed, stumbling back. "Charlie's been stabbed!"

Immediately there was shouting and yelling as the crew rushed over. Sinclair and Victor pushed their way through the crowd, and Sinclair dropped to one knee next to Middleton.

"Charlie, my God, forgive me!" he said. "I had no idea!"

His voice gurgling with pain, Middleton nevertheless managed to force a weak smile. "Did you think I was stealing the scene?"

Even though the director was master of the set, it was Sinclair who jumped to his feet, immediately taking charge. "John!" he called out to the second assistant director. "Use my car and driver! Get Charlie to the Queen of Angels!" To the nurse who had showed up and was quickly working on staunching the flow of blood, he said, "Gladys, you ride along with him. I'll have my personal physician meet you there!"

Sinclair pulled the director aside as everyone around rushed to do as he had instructed.

And when Neville Sinclair had the director over in a private corner, the actor's face changed. His expression hardened, his eyes brimmed with fury, and all the compassion vanished, to be replaced by a cold and icy demeanor. He looked now, in every way, the way he had the previous night in his home in the Hollywood Hills, when he had been holding champagne in one hand and running through the sword motions that he would be using in this day's filming, when he had told Eddie Valentine exactly what was what.

When he had phoned Lothar and arranged for the murder of the helpless Wilmer.

That man was the one who now faced the director, and Neville Sinclair, swordsman supreme, ignored the director's apologies and said tightly, "Next time find me a worthy adversary. Someone who can fence." He paused only a moment to call out in a sweet, caring tone to Charlie, who was being carried away on his shield, "Chin up, old boy! You'll be all right!" The moment the others were out of earshot he turned back to the director, still seething. "And this is supposed to be a closed set. No visitors. I want that girl banned from the lot!"

Somebody waved to Sinclair, a sympathetic expression on his face. Instantly all warmth, he waved back and then moved off, giving one last significant glance at the director. It was not lost on him, and Victor quickly waved for Fred.

Standing safely off to the side, Jenny was shaking her head as Cliff tried to explain what he was doing there. "Jenny, I said I'm sorry. I want to patch things up."

"You're off to a great start!"

"But I had to see you . . . something big has happened."

"Couldn't it wait?"

"No! Look, you're always saying you're the last to know! This is important."

She couldn't understand why his sense of priorities was so warped. "So's this acting job!"

"Acting? Honey, c'mon, you're walking through scenery!"

"At least I'm not knocking it down! Cliff, you're not being fair! This is a good job. The director thinks I'm very talented."

At that moment Fred strode up and handed her a slip of paper. She looked at it in confusion. "What's this?"

"Pay voucher. You're off the picture. Director's orders. You know this is a closed set." They were not words he said easily. He didn't like firing people, especially lookers like this one. But rules were rules.

Jenny shot Cliff a furious glance and then stormed off. Cliff raced after her. He caught up to her in front of a free-standing section of castle wall and whirled her around. She was fighting back tears.

"Jenny, stop! Just let me explain! Me and Peevy found something that will get us back on our feet!"

She didn't really care, and tried to pull away. "What do you mean, you found something?"

"It's an engine! You wear it on your back. It makes you fly like a plane!"

He was hoping that his enthusiasm was infectious, but apparently she'd had her vaccine. "You got me fired so you could tell me about *an engine*!" She yanked away from him and ran off.

Cliff was about to follow her when Fred showed up, followed by two security guards. "Do you know what *closed set* means, pal?" he said, and the guards yanked Cliff by the arms and dragged him away.

And from behind the flat emerged an astounded

Neville Sinclair. There was a cigarette dangling from his mouth, and he was holding a copy of *Variety*, but he wasn't tasting the cigarette or reading the magazine. Instead, he was in absolute shock over what providence had just handed him.

That little twerp had his rocket pack!

Sinclair tossed aside the cigarette and the magazine, and he raced after Cliff.

It was an abortive attempt, for some grips were suddenly in his path, carrying a huge flat. By the time Sinclair managed to maneuver around it, there was no sign of the young man—of whom he had caught only a brief glimpse—or his escorts.

What he did find, however, was the assistant director talking intently with the director. He bolted over to them, grabbed Victor, and said, "Where's that girl I told you to fire?"

Victor and Fred stared at him in confusion. "I fired her!"

The girl.

She was his only chance. The girl, Jenny, was the guy's girlfriend. Or perhaps ex-girlfriend.

Muttering a furious curse, he turned and bolted back toward the set. And he arrived just in time to see the girl, with tear-stained face, gathering up her things. Another woman, probably this Jenny's friend, was standing nearby, looking on sympathetically. They both looked up in amazement as he walked up to them, oozing charm, warmth, and sincerity.

"Hello, I'm Neville Sinclair," he said unnecessarily. "And you must be . . ."

"Jenny Blake," she said breathlessly.

He saw her clearly for the first time and he was thrown momentarily off step. She was a stunner. "Er

. . . hello," he managed to say, and then he recovered. "I . . . I'd hate to think I may be responsible for your being dismissed. I'm sorry."

"It was my fault, Mr. Sinclair."

"Neville." He paused, and then said, "Er . . . have you read for the part of the Saxon princess?"

Jenny stood there in a daze until she was prodded rather forcefully in the ribs by Irma. "Why . . . no."

Realizing that three was definitely a crowd, Irma did a graceful fade from their immediate vicinity, but stayed in Jenny's line of sight.

Jenny, for her part, couldn't believe this was happening. She'd gone from desolation to ecstasy in a matter of seconds. The abrupt swing was dizzying. She saw now that Irma was frantically mouthing the words *Neville Sinclair,* and Jenny felt compelled to rise to the moment. She quietly maintained her composure as Sinclair said, "Well, I'll see that you do. I think you'd be marvelous."

Behind Sinclair, Irma was becoming completely unglued, egging Jenny on. For Jenny, it was as if she were vicariously letting out the frantic young woman who was going berserk in her own head. Irma's theatrics allowed Jenny to keep a poker face as she said, "Mr. Sinclair . . ."

He took a step closer toward her, still not releasing his grip on her hand. "Ah-ah. Neville. Perhaps we could talk about the part over dinner."

Irma's eyes bugged out, and she mimed a scream. Jenny didn't even blink.

"I have a regular table at the South Seas Club," he continued. "Unless you're bored with the South Seas—"

"No, no." *And I've only been asking Cliff to take*

*me there since forever, and he just complains about
the money, and . . .*

Sinclair was puzzled. Was she refusing? "No?"

Irma was coming out of her skin, mouthing *Yes!
Yes!*

"I mean, of course," said Jenny. "I'd love to, Mr.
Sin—" And on his look she immediately corrected
herself. "Neville."

Irma went berserk, miming a heart attack. Sinclair
somehow became aware that something was going on
behind him, but when he glanced back, he saw Irma,
in the acting performance of her life, fully composed
and giving him a warm smile.

"Well . . . tonight, then," he said. The moment he
was out of earshot, Irma grabbed Jenny's arm so hard,
it felt like it would break off.

"Oh, honey, the South Seas Club! With Neville Sinclair!" And through Irma's bubbling, all Jenny could
feel somehow was that she was doing something terribly, terribly wrong.

Clark Gable walked slowly along, mumbling, "I *don't*
give a damn. I don't *give* a damn. I don't give *a* damn,"
when another actor dressed in similar dashing Civil
War garb and playing dashing Stuart Tarleton in the
same film Gable was shooting, tapped him on the
shoulder and said, "Clark. They want you back on
the set."

"Oh. Thank you, George."

And at that moment, an angry Cliff Secord, propelled by the two guards, rounded a corner and
slammed directly into the actor named George. They

went down in a tumble of arms and legs, and Cliff yelped in protest. Gable stood there, shaking his head.

One of the guards grabbed Cliff firmly by the back of the neck. "I'm sorry, Mr. Gable, Mr. Reeves . . . we'll get rid of him."

"See that you do!" said Gable, helping the other actor to his feet. "You okay, George?" George nodded, dusting himself off and checking the costume for damage.

"I was leaving anyway, you chowderheads!" yelled Cliff as he was dragged away.

Gable glanced down at the ground and, stooping, picked up a garishly colored magazine. "Look what that fool dropped."

"Actually, it's mine," said George, somewhat embarrassed.

Gable looked at him skeptically and then down at the magazine he was holding. "Action Comics number one? Comic books, George? At your age?"

"Well, it's a way to pass time between takes," said George.

Gable flipped through it. "Superman?"

"He's superstrong. And he flies. And he's named Clark."

"Flying men in costumes," said Gable, shaking his head and giving it back to George. "Silliest thing I ever heard of."

"I couldn't agree more," said George Reeves.

10

Planes soared overhead as the spectators for the latest edition of Bigelow's Air Circus clapped and cheered and roared their approval.

Peevy was annoyed to see reporters and newsreels recording the action and was mentally kicking himself. They were there because he'd been enough of a chowderhead to anticipate that the previous day's flight of the GeeBee would be a smashing success, and he contacted them all the previous week so that there would be coverage of the racer's public debut. Then, in all the excitement of the previous day, he'd forgotten to call them back and tell them there would be no GeeBee appearance after all. So here they were, and all they were going to be covering was business as usual—or even worse, Cliff in that godawful clown outfit. Cliff was going to kill him for this.

Except at the moment it was all moot, because Cliff had still not shown up—a fact that was not lost on Bigelow, who stormed over to Peevy and said, chewing furiously on his cigar, "What's wrong with that kid? I told him nine o'clock!"

"He'll be here," said Peevy calmly. Privately, he wouldn't have blamed the kid if he were somewhere over Hawaii about now.

Bigelow, as he did so often and so annoyingly, waved a cigar in Peevy's face for emphasis and said, "If he ain't in the air in five minutes, the deal's off—and you boys can clear out your hangar!"

Now, Peevy had heard such threats before, but this time Bigelow sounded like he meant it. He stalked off and Peevy checked his watch nervously, already trying to figure out a new location that he and Cliff might be able to use.

And nearby, within earshot of what had just transpired, was Malcolm, holding a bag of programs and wearing a cap that read PROGRAMS—5 CENTS stitched on the crown.

Here was his chance. Cliff was in deep trouble, and here was a chance for Malcolm to bail him out. For Malcolm to make up for screwing things up for Cliff with Jenny the previous night, and also to show the young pilot the kind of support that the pilot had shown him so often in the past.

A plan was already going through his mind as he quickly made his way through the bleachers. He dropped down and ran around behind the bleachers, passing four men who were huddled together, muttering to each other. One of them gave Malcolm a quick glance and then ignored him, as did all the others.

Moments later Eddie Valentine strode toward the four men and said impatiently, "Well?"

Spanish Johnny turned to face the boss. The other three men, Rusty, Jeff, and Mike, stood nearby with their arms folded. Spanish Johnny had been with Eddie the longest and generally served as the spokesman, especially when not great news was about to be delivered. "I know what Wilmer told Sinclair's goon, but the rocket ain't in Hangar Three," said Johnny with certainty.

"There was an old plane all right," Rusty put in, "but the only thing in it was this."

He handed Eddie a photo of a stunning black-haired woman. On it was an inscription that read, "With love from Your Lady Luck, Jenny," and a heart with an arrow through it surrounded it.

Eddie nodded appreciatively. "Nice." Then he was all business again. "But that's *it*?"

"We searched the place from hell to breakfast," said Johnny.

"So start over!" Eddie was as angry as they'd ever seen him. "Check every building, every shed, every peanut wagon. And keep your eyes peeled for this dame. Maybe she knows the guy who found our package."

"Okay, Mr. Valentine," said Spanish Johnny. "Let's go, boys."

The boys moved off, and Eddie was left there feeling frustrated and angry. Wilmer had given Sinclair's goon the information they needed . . . except maybe he hadn't. And maybe Wilmer had been lying through his teeth, except Sinclair's pet ape had killed him. That still had Eddie burning. Eddie was sure that Wilmer would never have rolled over on him. And even if he had suspected Wilmer, it was up to him to order the hit. Not Sinclair. The guy was getting on his nerves more and more, and sooner or later he was going to have it out with him. And the results might not be what Mr. High-and-Mighty Neville Sinclair expected.

Cliff pulled up to Hangar Three on his motorcycle and hopped off in time to see Peevy running toward him as if his shoes were on fire. Peevy grabbed him by the arm and said, "Bigelow's been spittin' nails! Where you been?"

"I had to see Jenny!" said Cliff, chomping furiously on a wad of gum. "Give me a second to get into that stupid clown suit, and I'll—"

And at that moment he was interrupted by a cheer that erupted from the stands, and the announcer's voice boomed over the PA system, "Hold on to your hats, folks! Here comes Fearless Freep, aviator extraordinaire—ready to dazzle you with an exhibition of razor-sharp flying!"

And high overhead, waving and dipping precariously, soared the Standard. The crowd laughed with delight.

Running in the direction of the crowd, Peevy and Cliff's gazes were locked on the biplane. For an instant, as if doubting his senses, Peevy took a look to his left to confirm that Cliff was indeed on the ground next to him and had not miraculously mastered the feat of being in two places simultaneously. Then he looked back up and bellowed, "Who the hell's in *Miss Mabel*?!"

And from nearby, a high-pitched female voice called out, "Programs! Get your programs!"

The heads of Cliff and Peevy whipped around, and they saw, to their horror, Millie's daughter, Patsy, lugging Malcolm's heavy bag while wearing his cap, which was hanging over her ears. Clearly having the time of her life, she caught the two men staring at her and waved cheerily.

In the Standard, Malcolm, wearing a clown suit and red rubber nose, gasped in sheer terror.

It was not what he had expected at all. He had been so sure for so long that all he needed was a chance. A chance to get back up there, get the stick in his hands, get to show that he still had what it took. That the best years of his life weren't behind him.

Now, with the ground far below him, feeling naked and helpless and every inch the buffoon that he was decked out as, Malcolm came to the heart-stopping, soul-rending realization that he simply didn't have what it took anymore. He felt vulnerable and aware of the thinness of the string by which his existence was hanging, and he knew at that moment with utter and certain clarity that the best years of his life were indeed behind him.

The problem was that at the moment the way he was white-knuckling the stick and his blood was pounding through him in sheer panic, it didn't look like there would be too many years of his life ahead of him. Or, for that matter, too many minutes.

Shoving their way through the crowd toward the grandstand, Cliff and Peevy shouted at each other. "Is he crazy?!" demanded Cliff. "He hasn't flown in years!"

"If he drifts into the race lanes, he'll kill somebody!" Peevy shouted back.

On the observation platform, Bigelow was watching the proceedings. His initial pleasure—not to mention sense of satisfaction at watching hotshot Secord make a fool of himself—had quickly turned to annoyance and even a vague sort of fear. "That's not the routine! What the hell is Secord trying to pull?"

He turned, about to demand answers from someone, and immediately got one when Cliff and Peevy stepped up onto the deck. His big jaw worked for a moment, uncomprehending, and then he sputtered out, "Who's in the—"

"It's Malcolm!" said Cliff urgently. At first he'd been prepared to deck Bigelow, assuming that the circus owner had been so fixated on getting the clown act up there—it sold tickets, after all—that he'd given Malcolm the chance that the old pilot had been begging for. Given it to him even though he knew what could—and probably would—happen. But the distinct shade of white that Bigelow's face had turned upon seeing Cliff made the young flier realize that Bigelow was as shocked as anyone.

"Holy . . ." stammered Bigelow, and then he shouted to the flag man, "Signal that Standard down! *Now!*"

It wasn't necessary. Malcolm was already endeavoring to get down. But a landing was a tricky thing, even to a practiced pilot in top-of-the-line equipment. Malcolm, who had seen the inside of a cockpit only in his dreams for the last decade or two, was attempting to pilot a flying pine box.

The Standard drifted into the path of three oncoming racers. The two lead pilots barrel-rolled away in two different directions. The third plane climbed hard as Malcolm yelled with panic and jammed his stick forward and to the side. The Standard heeled over and angled directly at the flag man, who was flapping his flags as if he had some hope of getting airborne. The flag man hit the deck, as did everybody else, and the Standard clipped a banner from the observation tower.

The crowd had at first been cheering enthusiastically at the antics, but when they saw the consternation of the ground crew, their voices began to rise in a confused babbling as they realized Fearless Freep was in a Freep of trouble.

The Standard climbed, engine sputtering, and then smoke began to billow out.

"That piston just gave out!" shouted Peevy.

Cliff made a quick calculation of Malcolm's chances of being connected with the ground in any way besides winding up six feet under it, and came up with somewhere between none and none. He grabbed Peevy's arm and said in a low, intense voice, "Peevy . . . where'd you stash it?"

Peevy, his eyes still on the struggling plane, said distractedly, "Stash *what*?"

"You know!" said Cliff.

The rocket pack. That had to be it. Why was Cliff suddenly interested in that now? "In the tool chest," said Peevy, working on how he was going to explain to Patsy just why Malcolm wouldn't be around to fix her plane wheels anymore. "Why—?"

He turned but Cliff was gone, dashing toward the hangar.

And that was when Peevy understood.

Malcolm was not immediately forgotten by Peevy, but he certainly dropped to second place in the immediate scheme of things as Peevy dashed after the receding form of Cliff. The aviator had already vanished within the hangar and, by the time a huffing and puffing Peevy had finally made it there, Cliff was struggling with the rocket's harness. He had already put on his leather flight jacket and his gloves.

"What the hell do you think you're doing!" demanded Peevy.

"What's it look like? Give me a hand with this thing."

Even as he tried to talk Cliff out of it, Peevy was readjusting the harness. He knew perfectly well he wasn't going to be able to dissuade Cliff, but he was going to be damned if Cliff fell out of it. Still, he had to say something. "But we ain't had a chance to test her right!"

"Cut it out!" shot back Cliff. "I'm scared enough as it is."

Peevy was thunderstruck. He'd never, not once, heard Cliff talk about being scared. Hell . . . for the first time, Cliff was obviously contemplating the idea that he might not be coming back. It was enough to make Peevy immediately use the few moments they had for coaching rather than remonstrations. "Okay, listen, I reworked the throttle!" he said, snapping shut the buckles. "Just give her pressure like a gas pedal. You wanna shut her down, punch the button and let go."

"Anything else?" asked Cliff, reaching for the helmet.

Peevy yanked the wad of gum out of Cliff's mouth and said grimly, "Yeah. A little luck." He slapped the gum on the top of the rocket's injector housing.

Cliff put the helmet on his head and buckled the final strap. He stepped back and presented himself for inspection. His voice sounded tinny from inside the helmet as he said, "How do I look?"

It was a dramatic moment. It was as if someone from the future had stepped back through time to present himself to the past of aviation as a preview of the future.

"Like a hood ornament," said Peevy succinctly.

Cliff stepped out of the hangar into the sunlight. The amber lenses did a nice job of protecting him against the glare of the sun, but he could hear his breath resonating inside the helmet. He took a deep breath then, angling his gleaming helmet toward the sun.

His fingers hesitated momentarily over the buttons, and he thought, *This is either going to be a quick ticket to hell . . . or the wildest ride of my life.*

He tapped the buttons, and there was a roar from all around him, and the acrid smell of something burning. He hoped it wasn't him.

Then he felt as if his body were elongating. He felt the power thundering through his torso, lifting him skyward, and the lower half of his body was left behind. Then, as if it were an afterthought, the rest of him came along for the ride.

Cliff rocketed into the sky, leaving behind a concussive blast that knocked Peevy off his feet, sending him tumbling ass over teakettle.

In the grandstand, the crowd was now in a full-throated cacophony of babbling, having come to the conclusion that something had definitely gone wrong. And then there was a sound like a thunderclap that snapped around heads everywhere.

The first thought that leapt to many minds was that a man had just been shot out of a cannon and was coming directly at them. People screamed, clambering over one another to get out of the way as the human cannonball hurtled toward them.

And then suddenly his angle changed, something that should have been flat-out impossible. He whistled over their heads like a torpedo, having corrected his course so that he missed them by inches rather than plowing into them. And a split instant later, he arced upward, and there was the briefest glimpse of something on his back, propelling him with the speed of a bullet. Bigelow almost swallowed his cigar as the flying man barreled upward, on a direct intercept course with the Standard and the helpless Malcolm.

Eddie Valentine caught barely a glimpse of the speeding man, but he saw enough—enough to make him react

in total amazement. No less stunned were the press, but
the news cameramen had the presence of mind to follow
the flight of the jet-propelled man.

"Tell me you're getting this!" shouted one reporter.

"I'm gettin' it," shot back the cameraman, "whatever
it is!"

The reaction of the crowd went from fright to shrieks
of amazement to cheers of pure unadulterated wonder.
There was now sweeping through the people a conviction that this had indeed all been a setup, all part of the
show. And what a show! And Bigelow took it all in, his
eyes wide, his brain working, adding up potential gate
receipts if he could only . . .

And while Bigelow contemplated how he could make
it all serve for his personal gain, Cliff zipped past a racing
plane as if it were standing still and went after the smoking Standard, which was a couple of hundred feet above
him.

But the concept of moving at two hundred miles per
hour with a rocket on your back was, understandably,
a new one for Cliff. As a result, the distance had been
covered in barely an eye blink and Cliff was unable to
stop in time. He smashed headfirst into the underside of
Miss Mabel, and if it hadn't been for the strength of the
helmet, Cliff Secord's career as the world's first flying
man would have been as short as Malcolm's odds of
landing the plane solo.

As it was, Cliff's head remained intact, even if the
Standard didn't. His helmeted head erupted through the
floorboards right at Malcolm's feet.

Malcolm looked down in horror and screamed. This
was too much. In hysterics, he kicked at the helmet before Cliff could catch his breath to get a word out, and
the intrepid flier's head was suddenly ringing, his brain

sloshing around in his head—if he had a brain, that is, as he kept telling himself. Malcolm, in the meantime, acting out of sheer, gut-wrenching panic, reflexively yanked on the control stick with everything he had.

The stick, mounted in the floorboard that had been shattered by Cliff, was barely attached as it was, and then it wasn't attached at all. It came out with a rending of wood, and Malcolm smashed himself square between the eyes with it. The world became hazy and dark, and Malcolm's thoughts drifted back to the Red Baron. And that was where they stayed as Malcolm lapsed into unconsciousness.

Cliff, for his part, didn't realize that Malcolm had passed out. All he had was a good view of Malcolm's feet. He'd cut the rocket thrust, not wanting to be plowed straight through the entire plane, and now was struggling like mad to disengage himself. Slowly he managed to pry his helmeted head out of the hole and dropped free. The landing gear broke his fall, however, and he threw his arms around it, holding on for dear life in the pull of the slipstream.

The air roared around him and Cliff fought down his urge to rush. Instead, he made sure he had a firm grip before he reached out and snagged the lower wing. He took a deep breath and then climbed up onto it. The airplane was shimmying beneath his feet, but Cliff was anchoring himself on, clutching on to the wing struts. Slowly, agonizingly, he dragged himself forward until he was only inches away from Malcolm. His plan was to try to calm the old flier down, maybe actually talk him through a landing. It was then he realized that the clown was out cold.

He shifted his weight to try to shove Malcolm's shoulder, hoping to jostle him awake. But the shift caused the

Standard's wing to dip sharply. Cliff fell backward, slid on his ass down the length of the wing, and tumbled out into empty space.

For the briefest of moments, flailing about in midair without a plane or even a parachute, he panicked. And then he remembered how he had gotten up there in the first place and felt a little sheepish even as he punched the ignition buttons. He angled around and zoomed back toward the plane, now knowing his problem was going to be tougher than he thought.

This time he didn't overshoot the plane but snagged the fuselage. His hands, however, were flat against the plane's surface, and he wasn't able to touch the control button to shut off the rocket. As a result, the rocket's thrust, which had only moments before been his salvation, now were proving to be his damnation. It began to push him, slowly but inexorably, headfirst toward the scything propeller of the plane.

Suddenly Cliff realized he was in a real jam. If he lifted a hand so that he could shut down the rocket, he'd lose his grip and go flying straight into the propeller, shoved into it by his friend, Mr. Rocket Pack. But he couldn't resist the thrust of the pack much longer.

Desperately, he reached out with the toe of his boot and just barely managed to hook the open cockpit, halting his progress perhaps an inch from the whirring blade. His full length stretched along the fuselage, Cliff held his breath as the fin on his helmet sparked as the edge of the propeller struck it. He lifted a hand and shut the rocket down, and then sighed in relief. His problems were over.

The plane abruptly lurched toward the heavens, practically standing on its tail. Screaming, Cliff slid down the length of the Standard, smashing through the rudder and ripping half of it clean off.

He plummeted off, dazed and barely conscious, spiraling down in freefall toward the swirling clouds below, becoming smaller and smaller and then vanishing into them as the Standard flew higher. Seconds later there was the roar of the rocket engine and Cliff soared upward once more. Beneath his helmet his jaw was set and determined.

He sensed that he might be running out of both time and luck. He had already screwed up twice, and both times he had gotten off lucky. Who knew how fast the thing consumed fuel? How could he be sure, every time he clicked the ignition buttons, that they would start again? It wasn't like a plane where, if it ran out of power, you still had a chance to glide it down to a safe landing. With this thing, it either didn't work or it did, and either he didn't die or he did.

But he wasn't going to die. Not today, dammit.

Cliff reached the Standard and this time didn't overshoot it, and he didn't botch up turning off the rocket with the proper timing and didn't, well, screw up either. He snagged the cockpit, cut the engine, poised on the wing, and started to reach toward Malcolm . . .

. . . and just to make things interesting, the Standard—stalling at the apex of its climb—began to drop back to earth. The engine noise departed in a manner that, to Cliff's practiced ear, indicated that it had had more than enough for this lifetime, thank you very much.

Riding the spiraling Standard to its doom, he struggled frantically to unfasten Malcolm's seat belt. As he did so, he shouted, "Malcolm! *Wake up! Wake up!*"

Malcolm did the worst thing he could possibly have done in the situation as the Standard plummeted faster and faster: he woke up.

He saw the creature staring at him through buglike

amber eyes. Some sort of alien or creature or whatever the hell it was, and Malcolm screamed and started to pound at it. He didn't know what was happening—perhaps it was the middle of some hideous dream—but he was going to teach this creature from the pits of hell that Malcolm Willis still had a few good punches left in him, that was for sure.

Cliff batted away Malcolm's fists and snapped, "Don't fight me, dammit! *It's me! Cliff!*"

Malcolm marveled at the insidiousness of the creature, that it would usurp Cliff's voice. It terrified him even more than ever, because the nightmare monster might have even more tricks up its inhuman sleeves. Then Malcolm, in his panicked haze, remembered that he had the control stick gripped in his hand, and he swung it around and smashed the monster on the head.

Once again the world around Cliff took on the general appearance of the inside of a bell. And now he realized that the clouds were far above them, which meant that the ground was not especially far below them. They had maybe seconds left at most.

He could have just leapt clear, ignited the rocket, and have done with it. But then he'd have to live with the knowledge that he'd left Malcolm behind. Malcolm, who had been trying to do him a favor and paid for that attempted kindness with his life.

No. It was either together or not at all. But if it was going to be together, it was clearly going to have to be the hard way. So be it, then.

Cliff slammed his helmeted head forward and it smashed into Malcolm's unprotected cranium. That was more than enough to send the already-groggy Malcolm screaming back to dreamland. And then Cliff saw the ground yawning up at them and realized that he had under ten seconds to prevent that trip to dreamland from being one way.

Throwing his arms around Malcolm from behind, he shouted, *"C'mon, you tub of guts!"* He punched the rocket to life, and the jet pack blasted them skyward, with Malcolm going seat and all. They punched through the top wing in a shower of shattered wood and canvas, and barely a second later the Standard hit ground zero. . . .

Which just happened to be, in a turn of events that was cosmically just, Bigelow's brand-new fuel truck. The airplane and truck went up in an enormous explosion that rocked the airfield.

The spectators saw the blast first, and seconds later heard the tremendous noise and felt the skin-searing heat. Bigelow staggered back, almost knocked clear off the observation podium. On the ground, Peevy and the others were watching with breath-holding suspense, for from where they were sitting, *Miss Mabel* had made her final swan dive with all hands aboard.

And then, just when it seemed that there was no way that it could possibly happen, the helmeted flying man seemed to hurtle right from the midst of the fireball. He was firmly gripping Malcolm, who was unconscious and still strapped into his seat.

To small children it proved that Fearless Freep was so fearless, he was able to sleep through something as incredible as this. To the adults it proved that miracles could happen. To Peevy it seemed a final vindication of everything that he'd worked for up to that moment in his life. And for Bigelow, it was a meal ticket that could set his table for the rest of his life.

He stepped forward, starting to shout, but the rocket man never even slowed down. He angled upward toward

the clouds again as the crowd went absolutely crazy.
Malcolm, just coming to, looked around in utter confusion, not certain just how he had managed to get down
onto the runway, considering that he was supposed to
be dead along about now. But he heard the cheers and
then saw the adulation, and the reporters trying to shove
and get through to him, stumbling over each other, and
he did what seemed to be the most appropriate thing—
he grinned widely and raised the broken control stick
above his head like a scepter.

"Sister Mary Francis!" roared Bigelow, watching the
flying man soar against the blue sky. "What I wouldn't
pay for that act!"

As if holding a casual conversation, Peevy said, "Five
hundred bucks a show?"

"Easy!" said Bigelow.

And the tone of Peevy's voice changed immediately,
from casual speculation to hard-edged negotiation.
"We'll take it," he said.

Bigelow shot him a stunned look, picking up on the
tone that Peevy had suddenly taken. Peevy was already
in motion, heading toward his truck, and Bigelow came
right after him. The circus man was glancing around,
trying to ascertain Secord's whereabouts, as if he
couldn't believe what the exchange between himself and
Peevy signified. But Secord was nowhere around and . . .

"You mean to tell me that's—" began Bigelow, pointing to the horizon line.

Peevy turned and snapped, "You don't know *who* he
is! That's part of the deal, understand?" Without waiting
for an answer, he hopped into his truck and peeled out in
the direction of the flying man, leaving an amazed Bigelow
behind to cope with the flood of reporters.

Behind Peevy, Eddie and his men were also piling into

their cars. They pulled forward, honking at the crowds blocking their way.

The reporters, meantime, were surging around the pay phones, trying to call the story in. Fistfights were breaking out, and over the general shouting of the crowd could be heard the openings of stories being bellowed into the phone, orders being issued.

"You heard me! Hold the front page!"

"That's right, a flying man! And I got the pictures to prove it!"

One elderly woman, determined to tell her sister of this phenomenon, was saying, "Hello, Louise?" only to have the phone ripped away from her.

"Pardon me, toots," said a reporter. "Your time's up."

The old woman decked him with a roundhouse right, and went back to her conversation without missing a beat. "You'll never believe what I saw at the air show today. . . ."

11 The black sedan barreled along on the road, with Spanish Johnny leaning out a back window, clutching a pair of binoculars. "There!" he shouted. "I think I see him up there!"

Rusty leaned out of the other window and squinted. "Nah. That's a bird. No, it's a plane."

"I see the bird, I see the plane. Over there! Heading toward the plane! That's him!"

"Don't worry about him!" snapped Eddie to Mike, who was at the wheel with some popcorn balanced between his legs. "Don't lose sight of the truck. I got a feeling they're connected somehow. And when we find where they connect, we find the rocket pack."

High above the earth, Cliff burst through a cloud, trailing wisps of vapor. His arms were spread wide as if in thanksgiving, and a howl of pure joy burst forth from him.

It was incredible, beyond belief. As the rocket pack had proven consistently reliable, and with the pure accomplishment of having saved Malcolm from fiery death, Cliff's fears had fallen away to be replaced by a giddy euphoria.

118

It was like seeing the world through entirely new eyes. Here he had always thought that flying in a plane gave him freedom, even power. Now he felt as if he had been kidding himself all that time. Being crunched into a cockpit was crippling compared to what he was experiencing now. The wind whistled past his body, and he stretched his arms out like a plane, experimenting with directions by angling the fin of his helmet.

It was staggeringly easy. What had there been to be afraid of? He was doing what no man had ever done in history, what men had only dreamed of. Men had given their gods the ability to fly as free as birds, but not themselves.

Not anymore though. Now there was Cliff Secord, the flying man. He had come through his literal baptism by fire, and now nothing could stop him. The idea of ever returning to flight the way it had been was as unthinkable as an adult deciding that he was going to return to crawling as sole means of locomotion.

Up ahead he saw a Mercury Airways Tri-Motor, and they had most definitely not seen him. Inside were nice, ordinary passengers who were entertaining themselves with the notion that they were flying. They weren't flying. Even the pilot wasn't flying, not really. Cliff understood that now. The plane was doing the flying. The plane was feeling the wind rush beneath it, the plane was hurtling forward. The people were just along for the ride.

Time to show them that.

He hit the thrust and, seconds later, had overtaken the plane. He cruised past the windows as astonished

faces pressed against the glass, pointing and gawking.
A pretty stewardess peered out. Cliff boldly tossed her
a salute and tilted his head to see her better . . .

. . . and spiraled completely out of control. With a
scream he plummeted out of sight, dropping like a
stone.

On the ground, his truck racing, Peevy spied the tumbling speck in the sky and breathed a prayer as he
veered sharply onto another road.

Cliff was flying with all the grace of an anchor. Birds
flapped to get out of his way as he plunged down,
down, the ground coming up even faster than it had
when he'd been fighting to save Malcolm.

Gone were airy thoughts of gods and man's ulti-
mate destiny. Banished were notions of pilots not
really knowing what flight was. The only thing that
was pounding through Cliff's brain at the moment
was how mortified he would be if they found him
smeared into jelly against a boulder somewhere.

Cliff saw that he was plummeting toward a farm,
and corrected his worry. Now he was concerned that
he might literally hit the broad side of a barn and end
his life as a cliché.

He pulled out of it at literally the last second, angling off and roaring along the ground at an altitude
of a less-than-impressive five feet. He shot past a
woman who was hanging up laundry and, before he

could slow himself down, became utterly enmeshed in a sheet she had been hanging up. She screamed and he kept on going, trying to untangle himself and having zero success.

His next nonstop was an orchard, smashing into a pair of wooden ladders that were supporting a couple of fruit pickers. They grabbed on to the branches, narrowly averting falls, and watched in amazement at the ghost that soared away past the fruit trees.

Cursing and yanking, Cliff finally managed to disengage himself from the sheet. He tossed it aside and it fluttered away as he turned his attention back to trying either to stop or to get some altitude.

Before he could do either, he saw what he was zipping toward and screamed. He threw his arms up in front of his head reflexively, as if his helmet weren't going to afford him enough protection, and before he could slow himself down, he smashed through a fence that was bordering a cornfield.

Wood splintered and flew as Cliff shot straight down the middle of the cornfield, chewing up a furrow from one end to the other.

Two good ol' boys sat perched on another section of fence. They had not seen Cliff make his explosive entrance, nor his equally dynamic exit. What they did see, though, was stalk after stalk being uprooted and sent flying by something that was fairly low to the ground and moving with remarkable speed. There was a succession of cracking and thudding, of corn being smashed down as loudly as possible.

A scarecrow with the poor luck to be in the way of the unseen force blasted skyward, twirling through the air and landing a couple of feet away from the silent spectators. They watched the trail of destroyed corn work its way across to the far end, and then turned and looked at each other with surprising calm.

"Big gopher," said one. The other simply nodded.

Cliff burst out of the cornfield, and just had time to congratulate himself for surviving that debacle when he discovered he was on a collision course with Peevy's speeding truck. Screaming once more, and feeling as if his vocal cords had gotten one hell of a workout, Cliff veered in one direction while Peevy swerved in the other. The truck spun out and scudded to a halt in a ditch just off the road.

In the meantime, Cliff finally managed to cut his thrust. However, the laws of motion required that he keep moving forward until some outside force acted to stop him. In this case, the outside force turned out to be a duck pond. He skipped across it like a stone, sending alarmed ducks skyward and quacking as if they were saying, *Who's this idiot who thinks he can fly?* He didn't fly much longer, though, as he crashed headlong into a thicket of reeds, bringing to a rather inglorious end the maiden flight of Cliff Secord, rocket-propelled pilot.

By the time Peevy caught up with him, certain that he was going to find a corpse, he instead discovered Cliff sitting up in steaming water, looking rather dazed but otherwise in one piece. Having found Cliff to be alive, Peevy's natural and immediate inclination was to kill him.

"You damn fool, you had to show off!" He waved his arms around. "Lucky you didn't break your neck! And what were you gonna do, fly to Paris? How much fuel do you think she holds?"

Peevy pulled the helmet off Cliff, and was amazed

▲

Wearing the most secret weapon of World War II on his back, Cliff Secord readies himself for action as the Rocketeer. *(All photos by Ron Batzdorff)*

Risking his life daily in some of the most dangerous planes of his time is nothing new to barnstorming air-race pilot Cliff Secord (William O. Campbell), but things are about to get a whole lot worse.

◀

▶

Master mechanic Ambrose "Peevy" Peabody (Alan Arkin), Cliff's best friend, designs the helmet that allows Cliff to live out one of man's greatest fantasies.

◀

Would-be actress, owner of Cliff Secord's heart, and damsel-in-distress Jenny Blake (Jennifer Connelly), whose dreams of stardom in Hollywood are about to become a living nightmare.

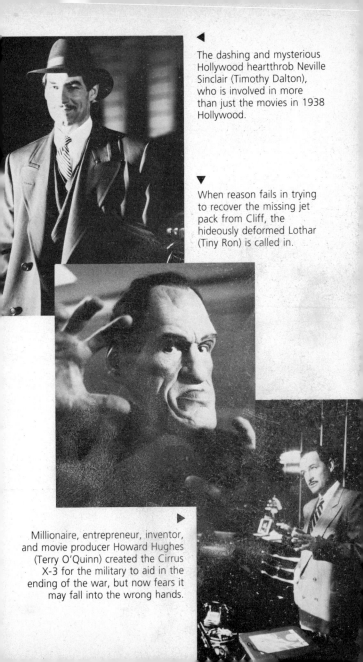

The dashing and mysterious Hollywood heartthrob Neville Sinclair (Timothy Dalton), who is involved in more than just the movies in 1938 Hollywood.

When reason fails in trying to recover the missing jet pack from Cliff, the hideously deformed Lothar (Tiny Ron) is called in.

Millionaire, entrepreneur, inventor, and movie producer Howard Hughes (Terry O'Quinn) created the Cirrus X-3 for the military to aid in the ending of the war, but now fears it may fall into the wrong hands.

Cliff Secord and his
prized GeeBee air racer,
one of the most
powerful planes of the
early years of aviation.
Cliff is one of the few
pilots to have flown the
plane and lived.

▼

Two of the most popular
planes of the era.

◀

The crew of
Bigelow's Air Circus.

▲
Nazi spies, having stolen the Cirrus X-3 from the military, engage in a gun battle in the hills near Chaplin Air Field . . .

. . . which cripples Cliff's GeeBee . . .

◀

. . . and leaves him in possession of a device that will change his life forever.

◄ Cliff takes flight for the first time as the Rocketeer.

► Using the jetpack at Bigelow's Air Circus to make money proves more than Cliff can handle . . .

◄ . . . as the press dubs him "the Rocketeer." This turns him into an overnight sensation and Bigelow (Jon Polito) into a very rich man.

The Bulldog Café and Butch, the diner's mascot.

Cliff and Jenny in quieter times.

Sinclair hatches a plan — to force Cliff to surrender the jetpack by kidnapping Jenny.

Atop a zeppelin bound for Nazi Germany, Cliff makes a last-ditch attempt to save Jenny and halt the Axis plans.

Neville Sinclair prepares to make off with the Cirrus X-3 as flames race throughout the helium-filled zeppelin.

Cliff and Howard Hughes talk, surrounded by onlookers and G-men.

Jenny gives Cliff and Peevy a very important piece of paper. Are the adventures of the Rocketeer over or just beginning?

to see the pilot grinning ear to ear. He looked up at Peevy with the expression of a child on Christmas morning and said, "I *like* it!"

For a moment Peevy stared at him, not sure of which way to cuss the kid out. And then, slowly, the success of Cliff's flight and the immensity of what they had accomplished began to sink in. The old mechanic grinned back and extended a hand. Cliff took it and Peevy hauled him to his feet with surprising strength for the old bones. The moment he was standing, the overjoyed Cliff threw his arms around him in an enthused bear hug.

Both of them were whooping and laughing, although Peevy managed to get enough breath to say, "Put me down, you lunatic!" Cliff complied by dropping him into the pond with a loud splash. Peevy tossed some water at Cliff, like a child at play, and Cliff kicked some back at his friend and co-conspirator.

With such horseplay did they quickly burn off some of the steam and enthusiasm of their remarkable achievement. But after a few moments of it they fell silent and serious, and Peevy said, "How was it, kid?"

Cliff tried to think of a way to describe it, tried to find a way to put into words all the thoughts that had been tumbling through his head when he had been airborne. Most of them had been pretty high-falutin', he now realized. Heady craziness inspired by the adrenaline-pumping thrill of the moment. Still . . .

He shook his head and said in awe, "Closest I'll ever get to heaven."

Peevy grinned. "Gotta work on those landings though."

They started back toward the truck . . . and then turned at the sounds of cars approaching.

It was a couple of black sedans and Peevy immediately said, "Must be the news boys. You really put on a show."

Cliff's immediate reaction was to want to go and shake their hands, pose for photographs, see his name splashed all over the papers. The thought of taking Jenny to the movies and watching himself soaring across a newsreel, propelled by the power of his rocket pack . . .

His rocket pack?

"They can't find out who we are," said Cliff in alarm. "Whoever owns this'll want it back, and I'm just getting the hang of it. Let's get out of here."

Peevy, who had already come to the conclusions that Cliff had just reached, hopped behind the wheel of his truck as Cliff started to shrug out of his harness. But when he turned the key, the engine refused to start.

Cliff heard the grinding noise, and both men threw panicked glances at the approaching sedans.

Cripes, thought Cliff, *what if it's not reporters! What if it's the feds! I'd be in the soup for sure!*

Tossing the helmet onto the passenger seat, Cliff hopped onto the truck bed and shouted, "Peevy, toss her in neutral!"

Peevy did so, puzzled, as Cliff braced himself against the back of the cab. "You steer," continued Cliff, "and I'll push!"

Not understanding what Cliff was talking about, Peevy leaned out and said, "You'll whaaaaaaaa—!!" The last word was elongated and drowned out in the rocket's roar as the truck blasted down the road at incredible speed. It was all Peevy could do to keep it on the road.

The strain on Cliff's arms was incredible. He thought for sure the bones were going to snap, and indeed for the next several hours his muscles were unbelievably sore. But he persevered, and within seconds the fire-breathing pickup truck had hopelessly outdistanced their pursuers.

Not, however, their pursuers' eyesight.

The sedans came to a stop, giving up the chase, but Eddie Valentine was now standing on the road, squinting at the dwindling truck. "Take this down!" he said, and Spanish Johnny began to scribble on a pad. "SJ two five seven."

Mike, the driver, stood and watched the distant smoke trail while munching on popcorn. Eddie gave him a look, slapped the box out of his hand, and said tersely, "Let's go."

Bigelow was loving every minute of it. His days as a two-bit air show operator were over. The proof of that was in the crush of reporters who were jamming into his office, occupying every inch of space, falling over one another, and standing on chairs or desks. They were all shouting, one atop the other, their questions overlapping, their pencils at the ready. Bigelow merely leaned back and put his feet up on the desk, his cigar—and he would be switching to a more expensive brand *real* soon now—sticking up into the air like a triumphant flag.

"How about some background on the flying man!" shouted one reporter, and the questions continued. "Yeah, where'd you find him?" "What's his name?"

Bigelow put up his hands. "Sorry, fellas, trade secret. Besides, it's part of the mystery, his background. As for the name, let's just call him . . . uh . . . Rocket Boy."

A hush descended and Bigelow suddenly felt nervous, as if he'd just stepped in something or said what a sweet guy Hitler was.

"That's lousy!" said one of the reporters, and they started echoing the sentiment, trying to come up with a better name themselves, keeping an eye toward the dramatic headline and what would sell papers. They were all shouting suggestions at one another and criticizing them.

"What about Human Rocket?"

"That's worse!"

"Missile Man?"

"Stinks!"

A few more seconds of that, and then they turned back to the proprietor of the show and said, "C'mon, Mr. Bigelow, give us a better name!"

Bigelow's mind raced. Here this godsend had dropped into his lap, and he was in danger of losing its shine because he didn't have a zippy enough name to sell it. And then, gazing out his office window, he saw a billboard for Pioneer petroleum.

Pioneer. And Secord was kind of a pioneer of rockets. The Piorocket? Incomprehensible. Rocketneer? Better, but . . .

"Uh . . . howzabout *Rocketeer*?" he said slowly.

The reporters looked at one another and their heads started bobbing approvingly. "Rocketeer, that's swell!" "Great handle!" "Rocketeer it is!"

Bigelow leaned back in his chair and inwardly breathed a sigh of relief. Easy street, here he came.

The newspapers were alive with it. You couldn't walk down a street anywhere without seeing the blazing headline, WHO IS THE ROCKETEER?

On a soundstage, Neville Sinclair stared at the headline and saw a photo of his rocket—*his rocket pack*—strapped to the back of some glory-seeking, helmeted fool. His eyes bulged and his veins pulsed, and it was all he could do not to scream and throw the paper across the floor.

There was another newspaper with a slightly different headline: ROCKETEER SAVES PILOT. This particular copy of the newspaper was spread out across the desk of Howard Hughes, and Hughes was staring at it in quiet incredulity as federal agents Wolinski and Fitch slowly entered the office with the air of a couple of kids being called before the principal. They carried an object bundled in an old, dirty blanket and laid it on the desk before Hughes.

Hughes tossed the blanket back and stared at the charred, twisted object that had been salvaged from the fuel truck explosion.

How in hell could he have trusted them? How could he have taken their word for it? Perhaps it was just that he couldn't stand to see the device he'd labored so long over reduced to a pile of burned junk. Perhaps he'd been an aviator for too long and the atmospheric changes had been turning his brain to mush. Perhaps he was just stupid. For whatever reason, he had not asked to examine the remains, and as a result was now as knowledgeable as whoever had been after the rocket pack in the first place, not to mention every man, woman, and child on the West

Coast—and probably the rest of the country, within a few hours.

Still, he had been holding out a vague hope. That it had all been some sort of bizarre coincidence. Such things happen. Perhaps there had been some brilliant genius mechanic laboring away in obscurity in a hangar who had developed a device the same as Hughes had. Stranger things had occurred. And indeed, if the object on his desk were in fact the Cirrus X-3, then that's what must have happened.

He nursed this hope for about three seconds. Then he shoved the object to the floor. Charred pieces went flying, and a cast metal brand name bounced across the floor and came to a stop next to Fitch's shoe. It was, by coincidence, the last name of the FBI's director, J. Edgar. It was also the maker of a well-known household appliance.

"Congratulations, gentlemen," said Hughes dryly. "Due to the diligence of the FBI, this Hoover vacuum cleaner did not fall into the wrong hands."

A bundle of newspapers slammed to the pavement as night fell over Hollywood. A newsboy slit the twine and began selling them as fast as he could hand them out.

"Extra, extra!" shouted the newsboy. "Read all about it! Man flies without plane!"

One of the people who snatched a copy was a young pilot on a motorcycle with more than just a casual interest. He grabbed up a paper, tossing the kid a nickel, and smiled at the headlines.

"Rocketeer," said Cliff Secord, running the name around in his mouth to see how it fit. "Not bad. Would make a great comic strip." And with that he stuffed the paper into his saddlebag and drove off.

There was only one thing Cliff regretted in all this, and that was that Bigelow was going to be attaining all the goals that his avaricious little heart could have dreamed of. Every single article that ran, every single word on the street, was to the effect that something spectacular had happened at Bigelow's Air Circus. And Bigelow left such a trail of ooze behind him, he sure didn't deserve the bounty that Cliff's sheer guts and fortitude had handed him.

Aw, what the hell. So Bigelow came along for the ride. In a way, they were all along for the ride. It was certainly nothing to get bent out of shape over.

Wooly and Fitch were beginning to feel as if they were spending their entire lives at this two-bit airfield that they had ever heard of before. It was the site of one of their most embarrassing moments, and if they never saw Chaplin Airfield again, that would've been jake with them. But no, here they were, back again, pulling up to Bigelow's office as a beautiful yellow full moon hung in the skies overhead.

Wooly pointed at the light that was burning inside the window and Fitch nodded in acknowledgment. "Seems Mr. Bigelow is working late."

"Counting up all the extra scratch takes time," Wooly seconded.

Moments later they were knocking on the door of the office. Wooly said authoritatively, "Mr. Bigelow. FBI. We'd like to have a word with you."

Fitch wanted to have more than just a word. He wanted a few words, along the lines of, "You're under arrest for theft of private property." But there was no answer from within, and immediately the hairs on the back of Fitch's neck rose. He looked at Wooly significantly, and they both pulled their guns from their shoulder holsters.

It was timing that they had developed from long practice. Fitch gave a quick nod and then Wooly kicked the door open, dropping immediately into a crouch position with his gun leveled. Fitch stood just to his right, also aiming his gun into the dimness of the office.

There was no sign of movement whatsoever. But there had been plenty of motion earlier, that was for sure. The place had been ransacked. As Wooly and

Fitch, guns still out, entered cautiously, they observed the emptied drawers, the papers scattered all over, the general disarray. A single desk lamp provided illumination.

The only thing left on the desk was a small pad of paper bathed in a pool of light from the lamp. Wooly started toward it and then tripped over something that was in the darkness. He fell against the desk, cracking his shin nastily, and then swung the desk lamp around to see what the obstruction was.

"Mother of Mercy," he gasped.

Fitch had been on the other side of the room, and now he turned in response to Wooly's shocked exclamation. His breath caught in his throat.

Bigelow was lying dead on the floor, his eyes glazed and bulging. Insanely, they were staring at the backs of his shoes.

"He's been folded in half," said Fitch, and he turned away to fight down the feeling of his gorge rising.

Wooly was thicker-stomached than Fitch—always had been—and he was already studying Bigelow's lifeless body carefully while Fitch was busy composing himself. He spotted a pencil gripped in the dead man's fingers and said, "He was writing something."

Fitch was now leaning against the desk, trying to look anywhere, and at anything, rather than the grotesque *thing* that was sprawled on the floor. When Wooly spoke, however, Fitch immediately noticed the notepad on Bigelow's desk. Quickly he picked it up and squinted at it, angling it toward the light. The sheet that had been written on was gone, of course, but Bigelow had been a big guy with big hands, and such men tend to lean heavily when they write.

Sure enough . . . numbers and letters had been indented onto the sheets under the top one, and when Fitch squinted, he was able to make out what had to be an address: 1635 Palm Terrace.

Lothar stood under a street lamp, checking the address once more that was on the sheet of paper in his huge hand. Then he glanced up once more at the house directly across from him. He saw someone move past a window in the house—an old man matching the description of the guy called Peevy that Bigelow had described . . . one of the last things that Bigelow had ever done, as it turned out.

Bigelow had squealed. Bigelow had poured his guts out. It had hardly required any effort on Lothar's part at all. In point of fact, he hadn't really had to kill Bigelow at all. The fat man hadn't even gotten a good look at Lothar, couldn't have even described him. And simply ripping the phone out would have prevented Bigelow from warning his pals that Lothar was on the way.

No, no reason at all, really. And yet he had killed him anyway.

Aw, hell. He'd needed the exercise.

Lothar crumpled up the piece of paper that read 1635 Palm Terrace, scribbled in a dead man's hand, and then started across the street.

Peevy returned to the kitchen table, the rocket pack sitting there patiently. All the dents had been smoothed out of the helmet, and Peevy glanced at the funnel that he had inserted into the rocket's fuel port. It had almost finished filling up with the alcohol that Peevy had tilted into it, and he smiled approvingly. Then he sat down and added the finishing strokes to a schematic drawing he'd been putting together that detailed the rocket pack's workings.

The radio was tuned in to Peevy's favorite dramatic show, *The Shadow,* and when Lamont Cranston gave that famous evil laugh, Peevy couldn't help but imitate it with a fiendish "Mwaaa-ha-ha."

The Shadow. All those guys from pulp fiction. Peevy had always considered that stuff to be pabulum, but now he wasn't so sure. Seeing Cliff airborne like that, doing things no one would have dreamed possible—it was like something out of those magazines that Street & Smith published. Hell, for all he knew, Doc Savage had invented the blamed rocket pack. Sure seemed like something the Man of Bronze might create. If the rocket pack was real, maybe Doc was real too. Any minute now, a couple of his guys— Monk and Ham most likely—would come pounding through the door, demanding it back. . . .

And then he heard a creaking from the back of the house.

His imagination already fired up, and fully aware that Cliff always came in through the front, Peevy was immediately on his feet. He grabbed the rocket with one hand and a ball-peen hammer in the other. If it was Cliff, and Peevy was prepared for trouble, he'd look like an old fool. But if it wasn't Cliff, and Peevy wasn't prepared for trouble, then he'd *be* an old fool.

"Cliff?" he called out.

Another creak, a heavy footstep, and a massive hand smashed in through the outside kitchen door.

With a yelp, Peevy dashed into the living room, clutching the rocket pack to his chest. He looked around frantically, trying to find someplace to hide it. And he knew why he was going to hide it too. Because if it was the feds, they would have announced themselves. They always blared out, "This is the FBI, come out with your hands up." If someone was plowing their way into the house unidentified, chances were they weren't going to be playing by the niceties of the law. They wanted the rocket pack, and they might just kill everyone involved once they had it.

Which meant that Peevy's sole shot at living long enough to give Cliff a good pounding for getting him into all this was to stash the rocket pack.

They'd look in the closet. They'd look under the couch. And there was nowhere else . . .

Except . . .

Cliff pulled up on his motorcycle and parked it just inside the driveway. Taking the newspapers under his arm—he'd found a copy of every one on the stands, including some in languages he didn't understand— he started up toward the porch.

It was then that he heard a heavy crash, the breaking of furniture, and glass shattering inside. Immediately Cliff dropped everything and lunged for the doorknob.

"Peevy!" he shouted, pulling on the doorknob. Locked. He continued to pound on it, push on it, pull on it. Nothing.

Peevy picked himself up from the floor as the massive shadow loomed over him. He was still clutching the ball-peen hammer and the feisty mechanic hurled it, like Thor the thunder god flinging his mighty war hammer at attacking frost giants.

This giant ducked the hammer effortlessly. It sailed past his head and bashed into a mirror on the wall, sending glass across the living room.

Seven years bad luck! Damn! flashed giddily through the mechanic's mind, even as he backed up toward the fireplace, looking around for a weapon. He started to make a motion for the poker, and the giant moved in that direction, but it was a fakeout. Instead, Peevy grabbed a large air race trophy from the mantel and threw it like a harpoon, like Ahab defying Moby Dick.

The great whale of a human being was struck squarely between the eyes with a satisfying thump. Peevy waited for the monstrous intruder to sag to the floor, unconscious, or at least fading fast, so that he could then make a dash for it. He heard Cliff's pounding outside and shouting. On the one hand, he was happy that Cliff was there to help. On the other hand, he was concerned that Cliff was going to get himself killed.

The latter seemed the more likely, for the giant, his back against the front door, was shaking off the ef-

fects of the heavy trophy. It hadn't even sent him to
one knee. A second later his head had cleared, and he
smiled coldly at Peevy.

But the shouting from outside was getting distract-
ing, and besides, it might be someone who could help
out with gathering information. The giant suddenly
turned the doorknob and yanked the front door open.

In hurtled Cliff with such speed that Peevy realized
the flier had just now been charging the door, ready
to knock it down with his shoulder. Instead, deprived
of a target, he stumbled in, and the giant put a meaty
paw on his shoulder and added to his forward motion.
He hurtled across the carpet and landed on a coffee
table.

Peevy leapt forward, landing squarely on the
giant's back. The huge thug reached around and
grabbed Peevy's collar as the mechanic pounded with
utter futility on the massive back, doing more damage
to his own fists than to the intruder. The giant flipped
Peevy aside like a poker chip. Peevy landed in an easy
chair with such force that the chair, and Peevy, top-
pled backward from the impact.

The giant turned back toward Cliff, who was just
trying to get to his feet. He grabbed Cliff by the face
and, for the second time that day, Cliff left the ground
through the force of a superior power. The giant held
him high in the air and shook him like a rag doll, the
flier's feet dangling above the carpet.

"*Where is it?*" snarled Lothar.

Cliff's voice was muffled since the giant's hand was
covering his face, and Lothar readjusted his grip so
that Cliff could at least see and speak. But he couldn't
breathe any too well, and he was still hanging several

feet above the carpet. Insanely, Cliff noticed that the ceiling needed cleaning.

"Where's what?" gasped the pilot.

"The rocket!" rumbled Lothar.

Cliff actually had no idea. He had assumed it would be on the kitchen table or someplace out in the open. It would—

His eyes widened as, just past Lothar's shoulder, he saw the rocket pack.

It was sitting on an end table with a very nice fringed shade atop it, and looked for all the world like an art deco lamp. Through pure audacity and a degree of luck—Cliff had accidentally broken the lamp that went with the shade just last week, and Peevy hadn't gotten around to fixing it, so it was sitting stuck in a closet somewhere—Peevy had managed to hide the thing in plain sight.

Cliff forced a ragged smile. "Sure you've got the right house?" he asked.

Snarling, Lothar shoved Cliff upward, slamming his head through the lath and plaster ceiling. Powder fell all around him and Cliff coughed and thought he was going to pass out. Peevy started to pull himself up from behind the easy chair, and it was at that moment that they were all suddenly transfixed by the glare of headlights coming in through the windows.

"Secord!" came a shouted voice. "Peabody! Open up! FBI!"

The giant hurled Cliff aside and drew twin .45s from within his jacket. Without hesitation he started firing through the windows and doors.

Cliff, to his horror, heard the thud of a falling body on the porch, and he saw shadows in the headlights diving and running for cover. Seconds later there was the sound of return fire, and bullets ripped through the windows, chewing up the walls and furniture.

The giant ran out of the living room and Cliff crawled across the floor to Peevy, shouting, "We gotta get outta here!"

"Let's just surrender!" Peevy yelled back.

"Aw, great idea, Peev!" screamed Cliff. "The rocket pack we could just make like we found, but that palooka was shootin' at them! They'll never believe it wasn't us! They'll put us away for a hundred years!"

Cliff looked at him expectantly, and Peevy tried desperately to figure out what was the right thing to do—right meaning the way that was least likely to get them shot or jailed.

Into the kitchen ran Lothar, not weighed down by any concerns heavier than putting distance between himself and the feds.

He paused only a moment, his attention caught by the diagram on the kitchen table. He grabbed it and glanced at it. He couldn't begin to understand it, but it looked important, and that was enough for him to shove it into his pocket. Then he turned and headed for the back door.

Agent Wolinski had made it around back while Fitch and the others had run to safer cover behind their cars.

Finding out the names and backgrounds of the occupants of 1635 Palm Terrace had been a snap. But the thing was, there was nothing in the backgrounds of either Secord or Peabody to indicate that they would put up this kind of resistance. They had no record of any kind. Where did they get this kind of hardware, not to mention the sheer nerve to engage in a shootout with the FBI? It didn't make sense.

But Wooly was convinced that he would have his answer in a moment. While they were preoccupied with a defense of the front, he would come in the back and—

—and that was the moment that the door burst free of the frame. It slammed Wooly to the ground, knocking the wind out of him as Lothar pounded across the door and down a nearby alleyway.

Wooly waited for the world to stop spinning, and was about to rise from under the door when two more sets of feet came stomping across it. This time the gun was knocked from Wooly's hand, and he lay there, dazed and helpless, as Cliff and Peevy—carrying the helmet and rocket—jumped a hedge and disappeared into the darkness.

13

The South Seas Club was, quite simply, the hottest spot in town. Huge palm trees festooned the orange and white exterior, which had a series of porthole windows in the facade, and the words *South Seas Club* blinked on and off in intermittent neon flashes on a large overhead sign. Stunning women in sarongs placed leis around the necks of various entering Hollywood gentry, whose admission was carefully monitored by tuxedoed doormen. Photographers and autograph hounds jockeyed each other for position at the velvet rope barricade, rubbernecking each new arrival.

A black limousine rolled up to the curb and a uniformed valet immediately hopped forward to open the door. There was a cheer from the crowd as Neville Sinclair stepped from the car, turned, and extended his arm. Jenny emerged with the beauty of Botticelli's Venus emerging from the clam shell. She was a bit more elaborately clothed than Venus, however, wearing a stunning evening gown so clinging that it looked as if it had been painted onto her. She looked around in wonder, her fantasy of an evening on the town being played out before her very eyes. She had wondered if this evening could be everything she had hoped. It never occurred to her that it could be more.

Sinclair's fans were shoving autograph books, napkins, body parts, everything they could at him for the purpose of getting his signature. One book was shoved into Jenny hands, and automatically she turned to pass it to Sinclair. And then, to her shock, the autograph hound shouted, "Not him, doll, *you*!"

Her face lit up. She couldn't believe it. Almost numb with delight, she scribbled her name and drew the signature heart around it. Her first autograph. She handed it back to him and he said, "Thank you!"

"Oh, thank you!" she said with a blinding smile, and then was swept into the nightclub by Sinclair.

The autograph hound, in the meantime, stared down at the signature. "Jenny Blake! Aw, nuts! Who in Sam Hill is Jenny Blake? I thought she was Paulette Goddard!" And with disgust he ripped the autograph out of his book and tossed it away, then turned back to watch for Hollywood types of more importance to come in.

Fortunately out of earshot, Jenny was inside the club. The decor was deco/tropical, with full-size palms and glowing lanterns. Sarong-clad cocktail girls walked past wearing gardenias in their hair. All around were pools of rippling water reflecting shimmering patterns. Incredibly, a woman dressed beautifully as a mermaid sat in a circular aquarium, smiling in a sultry manner to passersby.

At the moment, up on the stage, the orchestra was playing a lilting rendition of, of all things, "Smoke Gets in Your Eyes," with a stunning female vocalist standing in the midst of a giant clam shell and doing a very sultry rendition of it. For a moment it reminded Jenny that the previous night, that song had been playing on her radio just before she'd gone out on what was probably her final date with Cliff.

Now, why the devil couldn't she get him out of her mind? She forced his image away and instead smiled

engagingly at Sinclair, who in turn smiled back and
maneuvered her through the crowd with practiced
ease.

The moment they were seated at their table, Jenny's
eyes opened wide as a familiar gentleman with an
equally familiar martini in one hand approached.
"Neville, you old scoundrel!" he bellowed. "Fall off
any chandeliers lately?"

"Hello, Bill," said Sinclair with genuine fondness.
"Miss Jenny Blake, may I introduce Mr. W. C.
Fields?"

Fields took her hand, gallantly clicking his heels.
"Charmed, my dear," he said silkily, and rather ob-
viously allowed his gaze to linger on her cleavage.
"Doubly charmed."

Jenny tried not to laugh at the overtness of the com-
ment. Fields was so obviously lewd that it couldn't be
taken seriously . . . she thought. And then, to her surprise, she noticed that Sinclair was having something
whispered in his ear by a rather odd-looking man.
Sinclair nodded, then turned and said, "Forgive me,
Jenny. I've received an urgent call. I won't be a moment. Bill, look after the young lady."

"Thought you'd never ask. Scram!" He shooed
away Sinclair, dropping onto the chair just opposite
Jenny.

"I've loved all your movies, Mr. Fields," she said.

"Ah, my dear, I knew we had something in common," Fields replied. "And there are so many other
things we could have in common as well. The night's
still young, after all."

Overlooking the club from his office window, the club's owner—Eddie Valentine—peered down below in agitation at the evening's guests. As he did so, Stevie sat at the desk, phone balanced on his shoulder, mixing a bicarbonate of soda. "Yeah, okay . . . so long," he finished, and then hung up. Turning toward his boss, he said, "Spanish Johnny. Okay, get this: The license number was registered to an Ambrose Peabody, but when they went to check out the house, there were feds crawling all over it. So instead they went to the airfield to poke around there for info, and there were cops all over the place there! This Peevy guy is taking the law on some chase, I'll tell ya."

"So we want this Peevy guy, then?" asked Eddie.

"Maybe not," said Stevie. "Johnny found some fliers hanging around, and they told him—for a couple of sawbucks—that this Peevy's thick as fleas with some hotshot pilot named Cliff Secord. Peevy's an old guy, but Secord's a young flyboy. He might be this rocket jockey we're looking for."

"So where do we find Secord?" said Eddie, getting more and more irritated.

"Johnny's working on that now. He's checking on that hash house where the fliers hang out."

He handed the bicarb to Eddie, who downed it in one gulp. This whole business was getting nastier and nastier, and most of the nastiness seemed to be playing itself out on Eddie's digestive system. It was at that moment that Sinclair entered, without knocking and without much of an inclination to look even marginally polite. He stood there, glaring at Eddie as Valentine belched loudly and thumped his fist against his chest.

"Having a nice time, Sinclair?" said Valentine sarcastically. "Service all right?"

"Get to the point," said Sinclair impatiently.

Eddie slapped a newspaper onto the desk and pointed at the headline that was typical of those all over the city. "I got my boys tearing the town apart looking for this Rocket Head," he snapped, "and you're out steppin' with some dame!"

"That 'dame' " said Sinclair with icy calm, "happens to be the Rocketeer's girlfriend."

Eddie blinked in surprise, turned in his chair, and stared harder out at the young woman who was, at that moment, fending off the rather aggressive hands of W. C. Fields. "Holy crap!" he said, recognizing her suddenly from the picture his boys had found at the airport. "It's Lady Luck! Why'd you bring her here?"

"Because time is short," said Sinclair tightly. "The clock is ticking. I'll do whatever it takes to get my hands on that rocket."

It was that attitude that reminded Eddie why he'd wanted to see Sinclair in the first place. "Like having your goon break my man in half?"

"Just covering my bases. That's an American expression, isn't it?"

Eddie's mouth went thin and his eyes narrowed. "If that ape of yours lays a finger on any more of my men without my say-so," he said angrily, "you'll wind up kissing fish under some pier. Another American expression."

If Sinclair was the least bit intimidated, he didn't show it. "One word from Wilmer to the police," he said, studying his fingernails, "would have hung us both. Are you too stupid to see that?"

Bristling at the Englishman's arrogance, Eddie half

rose from behind his desk. "You don't know who you're dealing with, buster."

"Of course I do," rejoined Sinclair. "A small-time hood who made the big time by rubbing elbows with stars like me. And catering to our whims." His smile might have been made of steel. "Don't ever forget your place in the scheme of things, Eddie."

He crossed to the door, stopped, and shot off a final warning. "Now, do as you're told, or I'll demolish your shabby little empire with a phone call. I want that rocket. Tonight." He stalked out, leaving Eddie glaring across his desk.

"Boss?" asked Stevie hesitantly. "I promised my girl I'd get his autograph. This a bad time to ask?"

Eddie stewed for a moment, then snatched up the newspaper and hurled it at Stevie.

14 The giant mastiff form of the Bulldog Café sat serenely in the moonlight, warm light from within spilling invitingly through the doors.

Malcolm hurried into the Bulldog, anxiously looking for Cliff and Peevy, for Skeets, for anybody whom he could tell what he had just learned over at the airfield. But he couldn't get the words out, and instead just stood in the middle of the café, waving his arms, trying to signal that something big had happened. Skeets and Goose, seated at their customary table, watched him with curiosity, and Millie, finally becoming impatient, slapped the counter with her skillet and said, "Out with it already!"

"Where're Cliff and Peevy?" he demanded. "They gotta hear this too!"

"Hear what?" said Goose in annoyance, anticipating some new war story that Malcolm had just remembered.

Instead, he turned toward Goose with a pasty-faced look on his face that was the same kind of expression and pallor he'd had the day a year earlier when he'd barreled into the Bulldog to tell them about the Hindenburg blowing up in Lakehurst, New Jersey. And Goose knew immediately that whatever it was, it was pretty bad.

"It's Bigelow," said Malcolm darkly. . . .

The head of the Bulldog Café also happened to be the attic, and Cliff and Peevy were crouched in it now, listening to a radio that was perched on a small table. The announcer was saying, ". . . moments after the daring rescue. The masked hero has yet to step forward and identify himself, but air circus owner Otis Bigelow promises his birdman will return. Until then, all of Los Angeles is buzzing . . . *who* is the Rocketeer?"

Peevy snapped off the radio and turned to his companion. "Cliff, there's only one way out of this. Call the FBI and give the rocket back!"

"Nix, Peev! The FBI just tore our house in half! They think *we* were shooting at them. They'll lock us up!"

"But that gorilla tried to kill us," replied Peevy, having had time to compose himself and get a better handle on what was what. "Whoever these people are, they're playing for keeps. I'm tellin' you, somebody's gonna get hurt!"

There was a pounding on the attic trapdoor beneath their feet. Cliff and Peevy hurried to it, threw the bolt, and lifted it up. Millie and Malcolm were below.

"I just came from the airfield," said Malcolm. "It's Bigelow. . . ."

Cliff rolled his eyes. What did that blowhard want now? And Peevy said, with a trace of impatience, "What about him?"

"His office is crawling with cops. Somebody tore up the place like they were looking for somethin'." He took a breath. "They killed him."

The words flew through the air with the force of a hammer. Cliff rocked back on his heels and sat down, hard. All the blood drained from his face, and he looked at Peevy with pure horror.

All from the rocket pack. It had seemed like a game. Cops and robbers, us versus them. Keep one step ahead of the bad guys and the feds and show how clever you could be. And now Bigelow was dead. . . .

Millie sounded small and scared as she said, "Cliff . . . what's going on?"

With a new conviction in his voice, Cliff said firmly to Peevy, "I'll make the call."

Peevy nodded in approval and clapped Cliff on the shoulder.

Cliff and Peevy descended the ladder. The young flier could feel the gaze of Goose and Skeets, who had obviously already heard the news, on him. As Cliff went to the phone and picked up the receiver, Malcolm left the café to head back to the airfield and try to pick up more information.

"Operator? Please connect me with the FBI. Yeah, Los Angeles."

As he stood there, waiting for the connection, Millie went back behind the counter as if in a fog. Skeets and Goose looked at each other, each silently thinking about stuff they'd said to Bigelow that now they kind of wish they hadn't. After all, he was obnoxious and uncouth, but hell, he didn't deserve to die for it. Nobody did.

Cliff was concentrating on the ringing of the phone on the other end, trying to phrase just what exactly he would say when they picked up. So he did not hear the jingling of the bell on the café door indicating that someone else had just entered the Bulldog. At least, he didn't pay attention at first. But then he heard a set of heavy footfalls and he turned in that direction.

Four guys ambled in, and Cliff knew immediately, with no doubt at all, that they were thugs after the rocket. They wore expensive suits, shined shoes, and had an air of casual violence beneath their smiles.

Were they the ones who killed Bigelow? Cliff couldn't be sure. But there was no question that they were quite capable of murdering somebody . . . quite possibly, somebody in this café.

At that moment, a voice came on the other end, a gruff voice that said, "Federal Bureau of Investigation, Agent Gorman speaking." And then there was a pause, clearly waiting for some reply from Cliff.

Cliff licked his lips and said, as casually as he could, "Uh . . . yeah. I'll be home soon, honey. Love you too." And he quickly hung up, cutting off the confused Agent Gorman, who was saying, "Huh? Who is this?" before he was disconnected.

Cliff gave the four thugs a bland, pleasant smile and sauntered as best as he could over to the counter. Millie, not quite understanding what was happening, nevertheless knew enough to immediately put a plateful of food in front of him. She got the sense that in front of these men, no wrong moves could be made. And if Cliff was about to sit at the counter, there'd better be some food waiting for him.

Peevy, for his part, sat at the counter next to Skeets and Goose.

"What can I do for you gents?" asked Millie cheerfully.

Spanish Johnny smiled, glancing at his companions, Rusty, Jeff, and Mike. He chuckled inwardly. Oh, yeah, definitely gents. Gentlemen all. With an exaggerated drawl, Johnny said, "We're looking for a pilot, namea' Cliff Secord, ma'am. Anybody here know him?"

Millie thanked God above that Malcolm wasn't there. Malcolm couldn't lie if his life depended on it, and at that moment somebody's life might very well depend on it.

"Haven't seen him around," said Millie.

"We need a flier for a real special job," said Rusty. "There's a lotta lettuce in it. Hate to see the kid miss out."

No answer.

"Tell you what, we'll lay out a little finder's fee," said Rusty, and held a twenty-dollar bill up to Peevy. "How 'bout it, dad?"

"Yeah," said Peevy slowly. "Secord? Yeah, I know him. Little guy? Curly hair?"

"Didn't he moved to Cincinnati?" said Goose.

Spanish Johnny leaned down and put his face an inch from Cliff's. "Howsa 'bout you, bub? You know this Secord?"

Cliff glared at him and Millie said sharply, "If you boys aren't going to order, I'll have to ask you to leave."

Johnny turned to Millie, fixing her with a cold stare. "Oh, we'll order." He pointed at a rack of pies on the counter. "Those pies look good. They homemade?"

He suddenly seized the rack and sent the pies crashing to the floor. The pilots were immediately on their feet, but before they could make a move, they were gazing down the barrels of the guns that appeared in the gangster's hands.

"Don't," said Rusty with studied calm, "interrupt his meal."

Johnny sauntered along the counter, running his fingers along it. "Yeah. I like coffee with my pie."

He grabbed a full carafe and threw it against the wall, spraying glass and hot coffee across all the photos of fliers.

The radio was blaring "Pennies from Heaven," and Johnny turned toward it in annoyance and said, "It's funny. I just don't care for music when I'm digesting." And he fired two rounds into the radio. There was a burst of static and electricity, and with a sizzle and burst of smoke, the radio went silent.

Becoming more concerned by the second, Peevy said desperately, "I'm tellin' you, we don't know where he is!"

Johnny contemptuously wiped his hands on a counter towel, nodding slowly. "Okay, dad," he said softly. "Maybe we can refresh your memory."

He nodded to Rusty, who seized Peevy from behind, twisting his arm. Peevy grunted as Rusty dragged him around the counter toward the grill. He forced Peevy's head down so that it was a foot away from the hot surface and snarled, "Talk, or you get a facial!"

"Drop dead, weasel," Peevy shot back.

Rusty grabbed Peevy by the back of the neck and shoved his face slowly, inexorably, toward the grill. Beads of sweat trickled off the forehead of the struggling mechanic and dropped to the grill, sizzling and dancing across the surface.

"Leave him alone!" shrieked Millie.

Cliff desperately groped on the counter behind him,

and his questing fingers found a ketchup bottle. He grabbed it, about to whip it around like a club, and suddenly Mike's gun was in his face. Cliff froze as Mike yanked the bottle from Cliff's fingers. Mike made a *tsk* sound and said scoldingly, "Naughty boy."

Peevy's face was inches from the sizzling grill, and Rusty was chortling, "You're starting to smoke, old-timer." Within a second he was going to shove the old man's unprotected skin right onto the surface that was hot enough to fry hamburger.

Cliff couldn't stand it any longer. He opened his mouth, about to shout, *Here! I'm the one you want! I'm Cliff Secord!* and at that moment, Johnny suddenly said, "Hold it!"

Rusty kept a firm grip on Peevy, but lifted his face clear from the grill. Johnny, in the meantime, walked straight toward Cliff, and the flier realized that the thug must have known all the time. That he was sadistically toying with Cliff to see if he would own up. Cliff drew himself up, ready for whatever the thug might have in mind.

And Spanish Johnny walked right past him. Cliff frowned, confused. What was this guy playing at?

Johnny was walking straight to the phone, something on the wall having caught his attention. He nodded and pulled something out of his jacket, and Cliff gulped when he saw what it was: the autographed photo of Jenny.

Spanish Johnny held it up to the phone number that Jenny had scrawled on the wall the night before. On both photo and wall, the name Jenny had been written with the telltale heart around it. But the wall had something that the photo did not.

"Hey, lookee this, boys," said Johnny with satisfaction. "Lady Luck left her phone number."

Irma walked out to the ringing hall phone in the actresses' boardinghouse, wearing her bathrobe and curlers, and picked it up on the third ring. "Hello?" she said.

A clipped voice came from the other end. "Hello, this is the, uh, florist. I have a lovely bouquet for Jenny, but I can't read the address."

"It's the Stage Club, on Cahuenga."

"Oh, yes, where all the actresses room. I know it well."

She thought she heard snickering in the background, and wondered if this was some kind of prank call. "Who's sending flowers?" she demanded.

"Let me see . . ." There was a pause. "Cliff Secord."

Now it all was clear to Irma. There weren't any flowers. Secord was too cheap. He was calling and checking up on her was what he was doing. Well, he was going to fry when he got an earful of this. "Is that right! Well, he's too late, she's gone to the South Seas Club with Mr. Neville Sinclair!"

There was a click.

"Hello?" She grinned. That had certainly knocked Mr. Cliff Secord for a loop, and not the kind he turned in those airplanes of his. Maybe now he'd begin to realize just what kind of future lay ahead for Jenny, and just how far behind he was going to be left.

At the Bulldog Café, a chuckling Spanish Johnny hung up the phone and turned to his cohorts. "Rusty," he said to the man who had been laughing behind him, "this'll slay ya. Guess where the dish went? She's with the Limey . . . at the South Seas Club!"

Cliff shot Peevy a desperate look, but the thugs didn't notice. "Think fancy-pants is pulling a fast one on Eddie?"

"I dunno," said Spanish Johnny suspiciously. "I don't like it." He turned to Jeff and Mike and said, "You guys stay here. Watch what walks in. We'll call from the club." Then he announced to Rusty, "Let's go," and they exited the Bulldog.

As the sounds of one of the sedans faded in the distance, Mike sauntered over to the counter and sat down, swiping a doughnut. As he spun on the counter stool, he played with the lever action on his gun. Not for a moment were they letting the pilots forget just who was in charge.

Jeff, gun held loosely, strolled down the wall of photographs, and Cliff suddenly paled. A few feet ahead of the thug was a photo of Cliff with his arm around Jenny, the Standard in the background, and even these bozos would be able to put two and two together. He had about five seconds to come up with something.

Jeff paused at a picture of Peevy in his early flying gear. "Swell outfit, dad," he said sarcastically.

Now the others saw the imminent danger of Cliff's identity being revealed. Millie's hand strayed toward a large skillet on the grill. Cliff braced himself against the counter. Peevy silently, with his practiced mechanic's eye, gauged the distance to Mike and his gun.

The tension hung there. In a second all hell was going to break loose.

Jeff walked right past the picture without noticing it.

Cliff was about to let out a sigh and checked himself as Jeff suddenly leaned back and stared more closely at the photo. "Hey, there's Mr. Ketchup Bottle! That's quite a doll you got there. . . ." His voice trailed off and his mind started to work. He wasn't used to it, which was why it took a while. "Wait a minute! That's Lady Luck! So that makes you—"

He spun just in time to see Cliff's fist smash right into his face.

Jeff crashed back into the wall and was kept pinned there by a furious flurry of lefts and rights lobbed alternately into his gut and face.

Mike was momentarily startled, for it had happened so quickly, but now he jumped off his stool— doughnut still in his mouth—and swung his gun up. But Peevy grabbed his arm from behind and yanked backward as hard as he could. Mike's shot went wild into the ceiling as Skeets and Goose jumped on his back. He struggled in their grasp, blasting holes in the ceiling.

Cliff swung a fierce roundhouse punch that spun Jeff about completely, sending him crashing to the floor. He turned just in time to see the burly Mike shrugging off the combined efforts of Peevy, Skeets, and Goose. Mike once again aimed his gun at Cliff, who was too far away to do anything about it.

And that was when Millie swung her skillet in a manner that would have made Babe Ruth proud. It smashed into the side of Mike's head with a ringing *klonnggggg*, and the thug crumpled, out cold.

"Dirty bastards!" shouted Peevy, fists balled and ready for more. Skeets grabbed up the fallen gun and held it on the moaning Mike.

"Millie, I'm sorry about this!" Cliff said in a rush. "I'll take care of everything! I promise!"

And with that he raced up the ladder and hurried through the trapdoor.

Peevy followed Cliff up the ladder into the tiny storeroom, and there found Cliff swinging the rocket pack onto his back. Peevy grabbed his wrist. "Cliff, no! Not again!"

"Half the city's lookin' for us!" Cliff said, shrugging off the grip. "I can fly to that nightclub in five minutes and nobody can follow me!"

"Take a cab! The only place that rocket is goin' is straight to the feds. We agreed!"

"Peev." Cliff turned, taking the older man by the shoulders. He seemed desperately anxious to convince Peevy of what he saw as the only right course. "I'm sorry. I shoulda listened to you from the start. But Jenny's in trouble now . . . and that girl means more to me than—" He paused, searching for the right words, and suddenly he felt very helpless, in the grip of the only force he'd ever experienced stronger than gravity. "I . . . I love her, Peev."

Peevy was astonished. Cliff had never had the nerve to admit that before. "Does *she* know that?"

"I don't know." Then with certainty, he added, "But she's going to."

Peevy gave in to the inevitable. "Promise me one thing. When she's safe, we give this damn thing back."

"Brother, you got my word!" said Cliff fervently. "I'm sorry I ever laid eyes on it!"

He slammed the helmet on and raced onto the upper deck. "I'll meet you back here!" he called out.

Peevy wrinkled his nose. Something didn't smell right . . . or, rather, there was a familiar smell that shouldn't be there. He glanced at the floor and saw a trail of splattered fuel.

Fuel . . . leaking from . . .

Cliff, who stood ready to blast off, his finger poised.

"*Hold it!*" screamed Peevy just as Cliff was about to trigger the flight. Cliff looked back in confusion as Peevy said, "You're leaking fuel all over the place! Touch that button and we all go up!"

He rushed over to Cliff, who was shaking slightly at the abrupt close call, and fingered a crease in the rocket's housing. "She caught a ricochet! Musta ruptured a fuel tank!"

"Can you patch it?"

"Yeah, if I had two hours!"

"Peevy, we've got only minutes!" said Cliff urgently. "We need something quick!"

Peevy paused, thinking furiously. Then he spotted the wad of "good luck" gum that he had stuck to the top of the rocket's injector housing.

"How about a little luck!" said Peevy with amusement. He pulled the gum from where it was and jammed it over the fuel leak. Then, being cautious, he closed the door to the upper deck.

Cliff aimed his helmeted bronze face toward the sky. "Stand clear!" he called out in his muffled voice.

And Peevy, who was already standing clear and hadn't caught what Cliff just said, poked his head out and said, "What's that?"

There was the roar and a burst of light like an

exploding star, and the Rocketeer streaked into the heavens like a comet. And once again Peevy was knocked on his ass, slamming into shelves of canned goods and wondering for the umpteenth time what in the world he was getting out of all of this, aside from being knocked around and having guns shoved in his face.

And as Peevy picked himself up from the café's supplies, he heard the soft click of a gun's hammer being drawn back and turned to find himself having a gun shoved in his face.

The searchlights scanned the night sky over the Chinese Theater, where limousines were lining the curbs and stars and fans were packing the forecourt.

In the forefront of all of this stood the theater owner with a striking young woman next to him who had a high forehead, large lips, a round face, and unbelievable eyes. Her blondish-brown hair was carefully coiffed, as befit the occasion. "Ladies and gentlemen, please . . ." He gestured for quiet. Or, at least, as close to quiet as the mob scene would allow. "Welcome the lovely Bette Davis"—he gestured to the woman beside him—"who will become part of Hollywood history by leaving the prints of her hands and feet in our world-famous Courtyard of the Stars."

High overhead, on the theater's roof, a spotlight man noticed a fiery streak in the sky. "What the heck?" he muttered. He swung the heavy light on its pivot, attempting to spot the streak in his huge beam of light. . . .

And he saw a man. A flying man with a helmet.

"The Rocketeer!" he breathed, and kept moving the spotlight, trying to keep it angled on the soaring figure. . . .

His foot slipped over the edge of the roof. He stumbled, sliding down the steep roof and rolling over the brink. Frantically he clawed out and his fingers seized onto a gutter. He was left hanging precariously over the forecourt and his fingers started to go numb.

Down below, no one was paying any attention to anyone other than the lovely actress who was standing before a roped-off pad of wet cement.

"Thank you," said Bette Davis in that slightly breathless way she had. This ceremony couldn't have come at a better time for her. She was still incensed at losing the lead in Gone With the Wind to that British bitch, and she needed something to restore her self-confidence. "It's a great honor to be invited here tonight. I have all of you to thank, all my lovely fans—"

And then she was cut off by an alarmed scream from someone who, out of the corner of their eye, had noticed the dangling figure. "Oh my God! Look up there!" came the shout, and now all attention was upon the helpless man clinging to the theater's main tower for dear life.

The other spotlights now swept over to illuminate him, and the spectators held their collective breath as the man tried to put his feet up against the side of the building to shove himself back up onto the roof and comparative safety.

And then it was too late. His fingers lost their desperate grip, and the helpless spotlight man plunged toward the pavement below.

That was when the blazing fire trail descended from above, and literally from nowhere the Rocketeer snagged the falling man just before impact. The rescued man felt a sharp pain in his shoulder and knew that he had just wrenched his arm, but that sure beat wrenching his entire body permanently.

The Rocketeer angled downward, just barely able

to handle the additional weight, and dropped the man safely into the crowd.

A roar went up such as he had never heard in his entire life, and the Rocketeer decided to bask in the glory, just for a moment. He executed a loop and landed proudly, feet spread, hands at his side, cutting thrust with just the right timing to make it his best landing ever. The crowd went berserk and every spotlight, every camera, and every eye was on the Rocketeer.

It was then that he realized he'd landed in wet cement.

He looked down in annoyance at his smeared-up boots, and then there was nothing but shouting.

"It's him! The Rocketeer!"

"Lemme through . . ."

"Press!"

"Move it!"

"Mr. Rocketeer! Who are you? Where do you—?"

And the Rocketeer, faced close-up with his adoring public, decided that he liked them a lot better when there was some distance between them. Besides, what the hell was he doing hanging around here when Jenny needed him?

He blasted upward into the night, the rocket's thrust carving a crater into the cement between his footprints. In the twinkling of an eye he was gone.

"Miss Davis, Miss Davis!" shouted one reporter.

Relieved that the true focus of the moment was not going to be lost, Bette Davis turned and, smiling brilliantly, and giving a little toss to her head, said, "Yes?"

"Would you step aside, please?" He waved at her to move.

Surprised, the actress moved to one side as flash-bulbs exploded all around, photographing the cement slab for posterity. And Bette Davis shrugged, bowed to the inevitable, bent down with a pencil she took off one of the reporters, and scribbled, "The Rocketeer" into the wet cement.

There was far more than the wine that was intoxicating to Jenny as she sat across the table from Neville Sinclair. It was the people, it was the atmosphere, it was his presence . . . everything combined to give her a kind of light-headed feeling.

"It's all so . . . elegant," she whispered.

"You make it so," he said.

"It must be the dress." She leaned forward and whispered in a confidential tone, "I borrowed it from a friend in wardrobe. She tells me Marlene Dietrich wore this in *Desire*."

"She may have worn it, but it was made for you."

She basked in the glow of the compliment. Then she saw the way he was looking at her, and her conscience began to nag. "I have a confession to make. I've never been here before."

He laughed. "I'd be disappointed if you had."

"Usually I'm lucky to grab a sandwich at the diner."

"I know what you mean . . . I used to live on bologna on rye." He was amazed that he was actually saying this. It was the truth, something he rarely if ever told. "You know what my first role in a movie was?"

"What?"

"I played a dead body on a battlefield."

She was astounded. "You were an extra?"

He smiled at her reaction. It was hard for him to imagine it himself. It seemed a lifetime ago. "I'll tell you what—let's close our eyes and imagine we're in a diner having a sandwich."

She was taking in his gaze, the atmosphere, everything. "I don't want to close my eyes."

He raised his glass. "To you . . . and the extraordinary way your face catches the light."

Jenny felt as if she were melting through the floor as she sipped the champagne. Sinclair couldn't take his eyes off her. "You must let me have this dance," he said.

She looked around, confused. The band wasn't onstage. "But . . . there's no music."

"Really? I hear music."

He took her hand, pulling her gently but firmly to her feet. Puzzled and even a little embarrassed, but game as long as she was with Sinclair, Jenny went with him as they walked out onto the vast, empty dance floor. People started to notice them and a hush fell.

He took her in his arms and started to dance. Waiters stopped serving food. Wine ceased to flow. The only noise to be heard was the soft whisper of their shoes on the dance floor.

Up on the balcony, the puzzled follow-spot operator turned on his light. He pinned them in the beam and followed them across the floor.

Backstage, the bandleader noticed the total silence that had enshrouded the South Seas Club, and he peered out from behind the curtains to learn the cause.

When he saw what was happening, and who was on the dance floor, he quickly turned and said, "Break time's over, boys!"

The musicians ditched their cigarettes and straightened their ties. Taking the stage, they all stared at the couple that was moving across the dance floor. Then they glanced at one another and, shrugging, picked up their instruments and settled in to start playing "The Shadow Waltz" from *Gold Diggers of 1933*.

Sinclair smiled down at Jenny. "You see? It worked."

Buoyed by the return of the band, other couples started drifting on the floor, and the whole scene acquired a soft, romantic haze for Jenny. She gazed up at Sinclair as he said, "If you have a dream, Jenny, you must act on it. Dance . . . and the world will follow."

She laid her head on his chest and became swept away in the dance.

In the alleyway outside, a single rat, foraging for food, was frightened into hiding by the sudden flash and arrival of the Rocketeer, who alighted with such confidence that he felt as if he'd been doing this all his life. He peered around the corner and, seeing no one, removed his helmet and pulled the folded duffel bag from his jacket flap. Seconds later, having stuffed the rocket and helmet into the bag, he sneaked around to the front of the club.

He saw the black ties and evening gowns of the people going in, and glanced down at his own meager clothes. There was no way they were going to let him just waltz in. He had a choice: he could either stop everything and try to find a tuxedo rental place, or he could fall back on plan B. Deciding that the latter course was preferable, he then realized he had to come up with plan B.

The arrival of plan B was announced by the breaking of glass near the service hallway of the South Seas Club. Cliff's hand snaked in through a hole in the transom window, and he pushed the latch over. He opened the window and dropped inside.

Where the hell am I? he wondered, and then he heard footsteps and ducked into a room to his right as busboys walked right past where he had been.

He only had time to think quickly that the way things were going, the room he was running into now would be filled with gangsters or feds or someone else who wanted to pump him full of holes. But for once luck was with him. He found himself in the middle of a laundry room, filled with washing machines, sinks, and—lo and behold—a rack of waiter uniforms. There were no windows, but there was a laundry chute, beneath which was situated two large sacks of dirty laundry.

Cliff grabbed an empty sack off the shelf, shoved the duffel back into it, and added it to the two sacks on the floor. He made a mental note that it was the sack on the right—the last thing he needed was to lose track of where he'd hidden the rocket pack. And then, having executed plan B brilliantly, he proceeded with plan C, and reached for one of the waiter uniforms. . . .

Jenny and Sinclair moved back to their table amid a great deal of warm applause that was, by and large, for them. Sinclair put up a hand in appreciation and Jenny felt herself flushing slightly with embarrassment. Embarrassment and something else . . .

"Was it something I said?" asked Sinclair, noticing her abrupt change in mood.

"It's nothing," she sighed.

"Jenny, I know that look all too well," he said firmly, and made it clear that he wasn't going to be satisfied with anything less than coming clean. "Is it your boyfriend? Beautiful girls always have boyfriends."

"I'm sorry, Neville. It's just that Cliff and I talked about coming here so often . . . and now that I'm here . . ."

In response, he checked his watch and said, "We can still make dinner at the Brown Derby."

At that they laughed, and Jenny was grateful for the good humor with which Sinclair was taking all her confessions and problems. Only a supremely confident man could react that way. Why, with Cliff, all you had to do was mention another man, and he'd go off like a rocket.

"Tell me about him," said Sinclair. "At least give me a chance to know my competition."

Jenny studied Sinclair closely, trying to discern how serious he was being. Competition? Was Sinclair really that interested in her that he felt he was fighting for her affection? Trying to sort it out in her mind, she said slowly, "Well . . . he's a little rough around the edges. He can be pretty thoughtless sometimes . . . then he'll turn around and be the sweetest guy in the world."

She held up her delicate wrist, and from it was dangling a charm bracelet. She picked out a tiny silver orange. "He gave me this little orange when we met. My family has a small ranch, and Cliff came through town dusting the groves. Dad was broke, but Cliff helped us out anyway. He gave me this little pilot," she continued, holding up another one, "when I complained he wasn't around enough."

"He's a flyer?" asked Sinclair, wide-eyed and apparently very interested.

She nodded and searched for a small silver plane on her bracelet. "He flies a racing plane like this one. At least he did until yesterday. There was an accident at the airfield. Cliff was almost killed."

It had been difficult enough for Jenny to put him out of her mind when she wasn't talking about him. When she was talking about him, she began to realize with dread how much she missed him. Missed him! Seated across the table from Neville Sinclair, at the most glamorous restaurant in Hollywood, and all she could think about was that pilot!

Sinclair, in the meantime, was studying the miniature GeeBee with great intensity. "Really!" he said. "What happened?"

Suddenly an empty bowl was placed in front of Sinclair with such force that it shook the table. He looked up and said, "We haven't ordered anything!"

"Yes sir," said the waiter in a nasal voice. "One of your fans sent the soup over."

Another empty bowl came down in front of Jenny, and her eyes widened as she saw a piece of paper in it that read, *Meet me by the big fish. Now!*

She looked up, unable to believe her eyes. It was

Cliff, dressed in an ill-fitting waiter's outfit, motioning toward a large sculpted dolphin surrounded by thick foliage.

Jenny drew her hand away from Sinclair as if he'd been prodding her with a hot poker. Cliff ladled hot soup into Jenny's bowl, covering the note.

"Go on," said Sinclair, deciding to ignore what was clearly some sort of demented joke on the part of Eddie Valentine. "You were saying . . . ?" When Jenny stared at him blankly, he prompted her. "The accident on the airfield?"

She shot Cliff a furious look. He was motioning vigorously toward the dolphin as he filled Sinclair's bowl. Her blood began to boil hotter than the soup. He'd been spying on her! She was actually feeling guilty over ditching the little creep, and he'd followed her! Seething, her entire demeanor changed and she said lightly, "It's kind of silly when you stop to think about it. He missed the airstrip altogether. Hit the only tree for miles around. It's surprising the *real* pilots let him use the runway!"

Cliff clenched his teeth and looked in anguish at Jenny, moving his head so frantically in the direction of the dolphin that he looked palsied.

Sinclair, oblivious, chuckled. "Sorry to laugh, but I'm feeling better about the competition already."

Jenny smiled sweetly at him, and Cliff shot Sinclair a look with an eye toward decking him. All the while he continued to place glasses and silverware on the table while insistently looking at Jenny with as much urgency as he could muster.

Sinclair suddenly frowned and stared at Cliff. "Have you worked here long?" There was something vaguely familiar about him. . . .

"Oh, yes, sir. I waited on you the last time." *Two can play at this game, sister,* he thought smugly, and added, "You were with the redhead with the, uh . . ." He cupped his hands under his chest to indicate bounteous female endowments. "Very nice," he finished.

Sinclair and Jenny exchanged an embarrassed look, and Cliff chortled inwardly. Pure guesswork on his part, but boy, did he nail that Sinclair creep! He looked significantly at Jenny in a way that said, *Now! Come on!* And she looked back at him with equal significance in a way that said, *Drop dead.*

"Ah . . . where is he now?" asked Sinclair.

"I don't know," she said, trying not to look at Cliff. "He's probably hatching some harebrained scheme. He's working on an engine that a man can strap on—"

Cliff's eyes widened in alarm. He picked up the champagne bottle and began to pour champagne into Jenny's glass. He missed it by the length of a football field and instead "accidentally" inundated Jenny's lap with icy champagne. She let out a yell and leapt to her feet, a pair of actions that was mirrored by Sinclair. "You idiot!" he bellowed, as suave as a bison.

"Sorry—I'm sorry!" exclaimed Cliff, who was only sorry that he hadn't managed to spill some ice cubes as well.

"Get something to clean this up!" Sinclair ordered.

Cliff promptly headed off in a circuitous route toward the dolphin sculpture, and Jenny knew when she was beaten. As Sinclair said in aggravation, "I'm sorry, darling!" Jenny waved him off and said, "It's all right, Neville. I'll just go to the ladies' room. Excuse me."

She headed off toward the ladies' lounge and,

when she was sure that Sinclair wasn't watching, doubled back toward the island of foliage around the dolphin. When she was near enough, Cliff's hand reached out and yanked her in. She landed on top of him, and they both fell to the floor. Cliff yelped from the sudden chill and wetness of her dress against him, and angrily she got to her knees and pushed him away.

"It's not a fish, it's a dolphin! That's a mammal!" she snapped, which wasn't vaguely important but, for some reason, seemed the perfect symbol of Cliff's incompetence.

"I'll tell you what's fishy!" replied Cliff heatedly. "I saw you dancin' with that creep and giving him the fish eye, is what's fishy!"

"Are you out of your mind!" cried Jenny. "What are you doing here?!"

"Will you just listen for a minute?"

"You're jealous!" She didn't have to listen to anything. She didn't have to be an athlete to know what the score was. "You found out I was here with Neville—"

"Jenny!" He took her firmly by the shoulders and practically shouted in her face, "Bigelow's been murdered!"

She had expected protests, vituperation, accusations . . . anything but this, which came completely out of left field. She blanched and whispered, "Murdered?"

He nodded. "Remember what I told you at the studio?" At that moment he was so grateful for listening to what Jenny had told him earlier about filling her in first when something important happened. It sure saved a lot of explanation later on if things got hinky.

"The rocket we found . . . the people looking for it killed Bigelow to get to me, and now they're after you! They've got your picture . . . the one from the GeeBee."

He could see from her face that she didn't know if she believed him or not. He couldn't blame her. It sounded like a movie.

He took a deep breath and said, "Honey . . . get ready for a shock. I'm"—he paused dramatically—"the Rocketeer."

Her eyes went wide. "The Rock—!" Then her eyebrows knitted together. "Who?!" she said in exasperation.

It was somewhat ego-deflating. Crowds of people shouting his name, and a city singing his praises, and his own girlfriend didn't know him from dirt! "Haven't you seen the papers?!"

"I've been locked away on a soundstage all day!"

He shook his head. "It doesn't matter. Just get in a cab and go to your mom's in Redlands. Stay there until you hear from me!"

She searched his eyes, wanting to believe him. And yet, part of her was still nursing the notion that this might be some elaborate ruse to get her to ditch Neville. But would even Cliff be so driven that he would have the poor taste to lie about someone being murdered? But—

"Give me one good reason that I should believe a word of this."

He spoke from the heart with words that could be motivated only by genuine fear for her safety, and a fervency that spoke volumes of what he felt for her. "Because if anything happened to you, I'd go out of my mind, I swear to God I would."

She melted faster than the half-ton snail ice sculpture that was nearby. "Oh," she said softly.

Cliff grabbed her and kissed her hard, and then he released her as if she had suddenly become charged with high voltage. For he had spotted, entering the club, Spanish Johnny and Rusty.

To play it safe, he dragged the astonished Jenny down to the floor, completely out of sight, as the two thugs walked to the head of the stairs overlooking the dance floor. Johnny entered the room at the top, which left Rusty standing four feet above Cliff and Jenny, looking around the room.

"That's them!" he said in a harsh whisper. "The ones with the snapshot!"

Moments later Johnny emerged, and the two of them strolled down the stairs onto the dance floor, casting watchful eyes through the crowd. The dance floor was crowded with happy, swinging couples.

"Go! Right now!" said Cliff urgently.

"What about you?"

"I'll be okay, I promise. Go on! I'll call you as soon as I can!"

She clung to him a moment more. Then, giving him a brave smile, she rose and made her way toward the main entrance.

Cliff parted the foliage to make his getaway . . . and then saw that there was no way he could make it to the service hallway without passing in view of the two thugs who were . . .

Standing at Sinclair's table, talking to him.

To Sinclair! And the way he was talking, he seemed to know them!

Cliff sank back down behind the foliage, now more interested in watching than getting away. Something was definitely going on, and whatever it was, Sinclair was up to his neck in it.

Jenny fought her way through the crowd at the coat check, waving her ticket and keeping an anxious eye out for the two men that Cliff had pointed out. "My wrap, please!" she called.

After what seemed like an endless struggle, like a salmon swimming upstream, she finally managed to get her coat and head for the doors. She gave one last, longing glance around the South Seas Club, hoped that somehow Neville would be able to forgive her—Irma was going to kill her when she found out that Jenny had ditched Neville Sinclair!—and exited through the nearest door.

At precisely the same moment that she left, Lothar entered. He wasn't wearing a tux, but somehow the bouncers saw fit to let the walking land mass into the club.

Cliff watched Sinclair apparently issuing orders to Rusty and Spanish Johnny, and the two thugs nodded in understanding and walked off to do his bidding.

The thugs who were after Cliff.

Who wanted Cliff because he had the rocket.

Which meant that whoever they worked with wanted the rocket.

Which meant Sinclair was in even deeper than Cliff had surmised.

He knew it. He knew from the moment he'd seen

that Limey creep drop a bottle of champagne to the enemy in that stupid film that he had to be no good.

Sinclair was seething as Spanish Johnny and Rusty filled him in on what they had learned. It was madness that all this was taking so long. He had been working one end of the operation, that moronic Valentine had been working the other, and Sinclair had assumed that when they met in the middle, the rocket pack would be sitting waiting for them.

And what did they have? That damned "Cliff" of Jenny's, the one who had to have the rocket pack in his possession, kept managing through the sheer luck of the stupid to stay one step ahead of them.

Meantime Sinclair had opted for the next best course of action: to wine and dine the young woman, genteelly prying information about this Cliff Secord— as Johnny said he was called—out of her. It hadn't exactly been a hardship—she was an unbelievably striking young woman. Indeed, another hope of his had been that his courting of Jenny would draw Secord out of hiding in some sort of jealous . . .

All the blood drained from Sinclair's face.

"The waiter!" he spat out.

Rusty, not understanding, turned and called, "Waiter!"

"It was Secord!" snarled Sinclair.

"What? Where?"

"Here, you imbecile!" he snapped at Spanish Johnny. "And more the fool I! I saw him only from the back before, so I didn't recognize him immediately! But Jenny must have . . ." His voice trailed off, and he suddenly realized that Jenny should have been back from the women's room by now.

He forced himself to maintain a polite smile, but when he spoke, his voice was laced with iron. "Secord's here," he said. "Somewhere around. He's dressed as a waiter. He has sandy hair and the belligerent attitude of a bulldog. Find him. And find his Lady Luck. . . . I think she may have tried to make a dash for it."

"And what will you do?"

"Keep up appearances." Sinclair smiled thinly. "It wouldn't do to have Neville Sinclair dashing about like a headless chicken. People will know something's up, and I think it best for all concerned if we keep a low profile, don't you?"

As soon as the two thugs moved off, Cliff saw his way was clear and seized his chance. He left his hiding place and started in the direction of the service hallway. He kept watching over his shoulder and saw that miraculously, the thugs were looking in every direction except his. He had only a short distance to cover until he reached safety.

And he bumped smack into Lothar.

" 'Scuse me," he said quickly, and stepped around, hoping that the giant didn't have enough brain power to realize where he'd seen him before. This hope lasted for about a half second as the animal growl from Lothar alerted Cliff and he jumped frantically away from the long and grasping arms.

His exit cut off, Cliff turned and dashed out onto the dance floor, disappearing into the crowd. While

Cliff wormed his way between the dancing couples, Lothar felt no such need for social niceties—he plowed through the people like a bulldozer, shoving them aside and eliciting screams and curses. Male escorts who felt the dignity of themselves or their dates had been trod upon would turn to chastise the perpetrator, but when they saw the size of him, they quietly turned back to their dates, exasperation clearly on their faces.

Sinclair looked up from his table in reaction to the disturbance and saw the head and shoulders of his henchman cutting a wide swath through the crowd like the dorsal fin of a shark. Immediately he knew what was happening and he half crouched in his chair to try and get a better look.

"Please," he muttered, "let something go right."

Cliff saw the swinging doors of the kitchen just ahead and barged through them, squarely nailing a waiter with a tray. Dishes went flying and Cliff spat out a quick apology as he kept going. He had an infallible sense of direction, and that told him that a right turn would bring him back and around to the laundry room.

The waiter, who was on the floor and trying to pull himself together, shouted a curse at Cliff's departing form as he bent down to clean up the mess, at which point Lothar barreled through like an express train, sending the waiter bellysliding across the floor to get out of his way.

Just up ahead was the laundry room, and Cliff, heart pounding, was congratulating himself. He had done it. He'd used the rocket pack, gotten there in time, gotten Jenny out of there—and even scored major points on their relationship—and now he was going to make a clean getaway as soon as he had the rocket pack. The image of that giant and that creep, Sinclair, standing in the alleyway in helpless frustration as the Rocketeer blasted skyward, free and out of their creepy clutches, was a pleasing one indeed.

He burst into the laundry room, spun, slammed the door, and bolted it. It would take just a few seconds to get his gear on, and even if that behemoth caught up to him, Cliff would simply give him a blast of rocket exhaust right in his ugly mug. Then he would . . .

He turned and screamed.

Where once there had been only three laundry sacks—with his rocket pack securely in the one on the right—there now sat at least two dozen. The place was lousy with laundry sacks, and buried somewhere in that mountain of burlap was his only means of escape.

There came a furious pounding on the door behind Cliff's head and he moaned softly, "Why me?"

16 Jenny stood on the curb and waited for a cab to pull up. And as she headed for it, her wrap pulled tightly around her shoulders and her mind working furiously over what Cliff had told her, somebody beat her into the cab. "Excuse me!" she called out, but the cab's occupant paid her no mind and a moment later the cab pulled out.

She turned, saw another arriving, made a beeline for it, and another couple practically swiped it out of her hands.

She knew what it was. Cabbies made no effort to take single women as fares because they figured single women didn't tip much, if at all. Men were the ones who showed what great guys they were in front of their dates by tipping generously. If Jenny was going to get a cab, she was practically going to have to throw herself in front of one.

Damn. There was never a big, strong man around when you needed one.

Lothar threw his big, strong shoulder against the door of the laundry room, annoyed that it had taken him a couple of tries to get through. What the hell were they storing in there anyway? Gold? After another moment, though, it didn't matter as Lothar smashed through, tearing the door from its hinges. Panting, Lothar charged in like an enraged bull and found . . .

178

Nothing.

Not exactly nothing. There was laundry all over the place, piles and piles, as if someone had gone tearing through the laundry bags and yanked out some of the contents of practically every one.

Was the little creep hiding somewhere in the midst of all this? Was that his plan? If so, it was a damned stupid one, and Lothar started shoveling through the piles looking for some lump that was more solid than the others, some . . .

Then he spotted a pair of boots in the laundry chute. Boots just like the type that punk was wearing. Just like the type he was probably wearing at that moment.

With a roar Lothar leapt for them, and then his roar was drowned out by the ear-shattering explosion. Lothar was blown backward off his feet as the Rocketeer hurtled straight up the laundry chute, out of reach.

In the second-floor ladies' lounge, several women were checking their makeup in the mirror. A towel girl brought towels to the ladies from a low cart, and then swung around and dropped the used ones down the laundry chute.

Enjoying a peaceful and dignified evening out, away from the insanity that working with Julius and the others entailed, Margaret Dumont primped in the mirror and said in an amused voice to the woman next to her, "This place is really going to the dogs. A few minutes ago"—she thought back to the spectacle of that young couple wrestling behind the dolphin statue—"I saw a couple making whoopee in the bushes."

Abruptly there was a rumble in the wall behind them, and for a moment all the women thought the same thing—that they were about to be subjected to an earthquake. And then the laundry chute door burst open and out hurtled a jet-propelled, bronze-helmeted man.

As one, the women screamed as the Rocketeer blew out of the chute, moving so quickly that he couldn't immediately navigate in the unfamiliar surroundings. And when he tried to look around, his finned helmet sent him in the direction of wherever he was looking. As a result, before he could react he smashed directly into Margaret Dumont. The matronly woman let out a yelp and was thrown backward onto the towel cart, her unwilling assailant right on top of her, completely tangled up in arms and legs and dress.

A second later the Rocketeer, Margaret Dumont, and a towel cart blasted out onto the upper mezzanine, plowing through tables and bowling over a couple of men waiting for their dates. People dove out of the way as Margaret Dumont kicked and screamed and demanded to be treated in some manner in accordance with her status.

The cart slammed to a stop against a railing, ejecting the Rocketeer out over the club as he lost his grip on Dumont. The embattled actress sailed in a rather impressive arc before impacting with one of the full-size palm trees that gently broke her fall. It also gently broke at the base with a rather loud snap, and Margaret Dumont was deposited into one of the pools of water.

She sat up, sputtering and spitting up water, and noticed that people were laughing and pointing and actually even applauding. They probably thought it was funny. Julius would have thought it was funny too. She never did understand Julius's sense of humor and now, looking around at the amused faces, she decided she didn't understand anybody's sense of humor anymore.

Meantime the Rocketeer, barely in control, zoomed over the heads of musicians, bouncing off a wall and ricocheting back across the room like a pinball.

Now the speeding rocket man couldn't help but draw attention away from the drenched Dumont, and people were shouting and pointing, a few diving for cover. More, though, were standing and pointing and crying out, "It's the flying man!" "The guy in the papers!" "The Rocketeer!"

The Rocketeer caught a glimpse of that Sinclair creep and darted toward his table. He was eminently pleased to see the actor fall to the floor to get out of his way and then high-tail it toward the mezzanine. Let him know who was boss, that was for sure. But then he realized that he couldn't just keep buzzing around the inside of the club. Someone might get hurt—either clubgoers, or himself, if someone got lucky with a gun. He was fast, but not bulletproof.

Cliff, desperate to find a way out, cut his thrust by half and did a series of touch-and-go hops across a group of tables, scattering dishes and setting fire to napkins and tablecloths.

It was at that point that patrons realized that the flying man either might not be in control, or, worse, that he might be dangerous. That was when panic began to set in, and the fickle crowd, rather than hang around and admire the pyrotechnics, leapt to their collective feet and began to stampede for the exit.

Eddie Valentine, up in his office, heard the alarmed screams and shouting. He went to the window and all he could see was a surge of people, his nice, sedate club transformed into an orgy of chaos. "*What the hell?!*" he snarled.

He ran out of his office and was immediately caught up in the floor of panicked patrons. He fought his way back toward the main room, gasping and shoving, his feet being mashed into the ground and his ribs and stomach being pummeled. He was going to be black and blue the next morning, he knew, and as far as he was concerned, whoever had caused this nightmare was going to be blacker and bluer.

Jenny stood on the curb in utter frustration, about ready to give up and just hoof it home, even though it was miles.

And then a cab pulled up.

And no one was in it.

And no one was around.

She couldn't believe it. She looked around one more long moment, unable to accept that finally, after umpteen tries, she wasn't going to be shoved, pushed, manhandled, or tossed to one side.

She started for the cab, triumphant, and then a tidal wave of people poured out of the South Seas Club, all shouting and screaming and all wanting cabs. Jenny was lost in the crush.

The Rocketeer made another pass over the musicians, who were now trying to flee along with the patrons. He bumped into the giant plaster clam shell, tipping it shut. Six musicians were trapped in the mammoth mollusk, their arms and legs protuding and flapping around helplessly. "Sorry!" called Cliff, not that he could be heard through his helmet or over the sounds of his rocket and the screaming.

Sinclair shoved his way through to Rusty and Spanish Johnny, who were helplessly watching the Rocketeer zip around and make a shambles of things. They were thugs, that was all. They could function perfectly if given orders, but if a new situation arose, they were paralyzed until someone told them how to handle it.

That someone was now Sinclair, who snapped to Rusty, "Get those doors closed! We'll trap him like a fly!" And then he spun toward Spanish Johnny and said, "Shoot him down! *Now!*"

Spanish Johnny, relieved at having been told what to do, pulled out his .45 and started firing into the air, trying to draw a bead on the Rocketeer. Stevie and yet another thug, Monk, took the shots as a signal and they also opened fire. A hail of lead now filled the air of the South Seas Club.

Outside the club, Jenny heard the shots and ran to one of the porthole windows. Then she ducked back reflexively as a helmeted man buzzed past, a blur propelled by some sort of rocket on his back. . . .

"Oh, my God," she breathed, remembering everything that Cliff had told her and realizing just who that blur was. "Cliff—!"

She ran for the main door, oblivious of the bullet that blew out the window she had just been peering through. She got to the doors just as they were slammed shut and locked by some thuggish man with red hair. Her pulling on them did nothing.

Cliff rocketed around the club, bouncing off walls and tearing through decorations. Everywhere he went there would be another of the thugs, sealing off another possible escape route. They were also blocking off the handful of patrons who had not managed to get out before the main doors had been sealed, and Cliff felt anger and mortification that more innocent people were getting caught up in this crazy game of his.

The cloths that the rocket had ignited began to smolder and burn, and smoke began filling the club.

Below, Cliff could see a man in a suit arguing with Sinclair. The man was shouting, "Goddammit, Sinclair! Stop!" At least the guy seemed concerned about the welfare of others, and had the moxie to shout at the crazed actor.

But Sinclair bellowed back, "Keep out of this, Valentine!"

"You're wrecking my club!"

"Put it on my bill!"

The Rocketeer angled down and then up, and a stray bullet shattered Eddie's mermaid tank. It was exactly the wrong move. A thousand gallons of water cascaded forth like a tidal wave, and riding the crest of the wave was a startled and somewhat terrified little mermaid. Sinclair leapt adroitly out of the way, but Valentine was bowled off by her and sent tumbling to the floor.

Cliff spotted, out of the corner of his eye, the giant emerging from the service door with clothes singed and hatred in his piglike eyes. Knowing that he had to stay out of the grip of those massive arms, the Rocketeer angled in the opposite direction, swooping under the mezzanine and sliding the length of the bar, knocking glasses and bottles in all directions. Glass shattered all around like a series of grenades going off.

At the end of the bar was an escargot buffet table, the centerpiece of which was that snail ice sculpture. The Rocketeer slammed into it at full speed, tipping the table, and snagged the eye stalks of the half-ton ice snail. His mind moving even faster than his rocket, Cliff immediately saw the possibilities, and an instant later had transformed the snail into an icy rocket sled that was anything but sluggish. Clutching firmly onto his escargo-cart, the Rocketeer shot toward the main exit, which no one was watching because it had been locked and bolted. He left an icy slime trail behind. Anything or anyone getting in his way was going to be mowed down in a very ignominious fashion.

"He's got a battering ram!" shouted one of the gangsters.

Sinclair, his patience taxed beyond endurance,

tossed aside all notions of discretion and grabbed the
.45 out of Stevie's hands. He opened fire on the speeding snail, bullets chewing into it and spraying crushed
ice into the air.

The eye stalks that served as the Rocketeer's han-
dles snapped off, and Cliff veered, swooping out from
under the mezzanine and arcing high across the floor.

The snail kept going, hurtling on its own. It
smashed through the doors, unstoppable in its half
ton of velocity. The grateful remaining patrons now
streamed through the reopened door. . . .

And unseen by the Rocketeer, one plucky young
woman, shouting, "Cliff!" shoved her way in and
ducked behind a column, searching the smoke for
some sign of him.

In the meantime, the Rocketeer spotted another potential escape route, a window situated toward the
top of the club. Sinclair looked up, saw the means of
escape, and also saw the fishnet hanging over the ceiling. Not wanting to take the time to explain what he
wanted done, Sinclair grabbed the tommy gun from
Monk and opened fire on the support ropes as the
Rocketeer swooped to make his escape.

Cliff glanced down disdainfully in the direction of
the machine gunfire. Figures that it was Sinclair aiming the thing, he thought smugly. The Limey creep
hadn't even come close to hitting him.

And that was when the net, severed of its supports,
fell on the Rocketeer, snaring him and bringing him
crashing to the floor, completely entangled.

Cliff immediately cut the engine. Hogtied as he
was, he might very well set himself on fire in a matter
of seconds. And then he heard the shouts of "The
rocket! Get the rocket!" It was Sinclair, and leaving

concerns for his own life behind, Cliff boiled at the thought of the no-good bum getting the last laugh at his expense. This was more than life and death. This was personal.

Lothar converged on Cliff just as the Rocketeer thumbed the ignition buttons. Like a rocket-powered wrecking ball, the Rocketeer leapt off the ground, shrouded in the net. He collided head-on with Lothar and gave it everything he had, but the giant had a grip on him and couldn't be shaken loose, even though the Rocketeer dragged him in circles around the dance floor.

They rolled to a tumbled stop, and the world was swirling so much around Cliff that he was forced to cut the ignition once more. Even if he'd managed to get off the ground again, he was so dizzy that he would have just smashed headlong into something. Maybe even driven his head down to somewhere around his hips.

And as he waited for the few seconds he needed for the world to stop spinning, Lothar very graciously did not provide them. Instead, the behemoth came up behind him and threw a massive bear hug around the Rocketeer, pinning his arms at his sides. Cliff felt such power in those huge arms that it seemed as if the giant could break him in half without serious strain.

Cliff gasped and tried to struggle free, but there was nothing he could do. He couldn't even draw a breath, much less the strength he needed to liberate himself— and he doubted he would have had that strength, even with air in his lungs.

Suddenly there was the sound of a crash, and the giant moaned and sank to the floor. Released of the choking grip, Cliff hungrily sucked air into his lungs and spun in time to see the giant falling to his knees. Lying next to him on the floor was the shattered remains of what appeared to have been a plaster sea horse. It was as if someone had appeared from behind and beaned the giant a good one.

Cliff had no time to speculate further, for he saw more of the goons moving through the thickening smoke, weapons at the ready. As they closed in, Cliff jabbed the ignition buttons once more.

The engine fire and the Rocketeer arced upward, propelled by the screaming rocket pack. Directly overhead was the skylight, and the Rocketeer threw his arms over his head and smashed through it like a linebacker.

He struck the skylight with the impact of an artillery shell, every bone in his body shaking. The stained glass tropical scene exploded, dropping rainbow shards onto the dance floor in a deadly, jagged hail.

There were the sounds of machine gunfire once more, but the skies were beckoning to the Rocketeer and he knew that he had made it. . . .

And then, as if issuing a reminder to him of just how close things could be, a bullet caught him a glancing blow to the helmet, creasing the bronze. The Rocketeer spiraled away, leaving a twisting curl of flame across the Hollywood sky.

Within the South Seas Club, smoke all around her, Jenny emerged from a line of potted palms, brushing the dust from the plaster sea horse off her hands. She felt a small sense of accomplishment. Cliff had risked life and limb to warn her and save her from dangerous men—not the least dangerous of which, it seemed, was the man who had attempted to wine and dine her. Well, she was going to have a lot to say to the police, to the director, to anyone who would listen. As she dashed for the door, she thought to herself, *We'll see who's the patsy, Mr. Neville Sinclair!*

A shadowy figure stepped from the smoke and grabbed her by the arm, just a few feet shy of her escape. She started to struggle and then gasped as a small automatic pistol was pressed into her ribs.

And into her ear breathed a voice that mere hours before would have made her swoon had it been whispering the selfsame words in a different setting. "Don't go," urged Neville Sinclair, jabbing the pistol farther into her side. "Our evening has just begun."

17 Dressed in a smoking jacket, looking the picture of elegance, Neville Sinclair moved down a hallway of his Hollywood Hills home, satisfied with the way things were going. He had just emerged from his radio room. This communication had been far more satisfying than the previous one—especially when he had been able to tell the recipients that he would be able to come through with the rocket pack on time after all. He stopped at a door, smoothed his hair, unbolted the lock, and entered.

He stepped into his richly furnished guest room. It was dimly lit, but the casual eye could make out a large mirror poised above the bed, and large portraits of nudes decorated the walls. This particular guest room had hosted a number of female luminaries that would dazzle even the most casual of autograph hounds. Now, though, it was occupied by someone who was a virtual nobody—to everyone except Sinclair. To him, she had become the most important individual in the world.

Well, the second most important. The first was cutting through the skies of Los Angeles somewhere. But she could bring the Rocketeer down to earth.

He switched on the lights and smiled at Jenny, who was lying on the wide, opulent bed. She was still dressed in her evening gown, her image reflected in the mirror. Her eyes were shut, her head lolling to one side.

He crossed the room to a cabinet, from which he removed a decanter of brandy and a snifter. He carried them to the bedside table, put them down, and studied her unmoving form for a moment. Then he sat down next to her on the bed, ran his hands along her thigh, over her hip. She moaned softly, stirring.

He reached into his pocket for a vial of smelling salts, which he uncorked and passed beneath her nose. That brought her around immediately, coughing and sputtering. Sinclair smiled down at her. "Welcome to my home," he said. He proceeded to pour the brandy. "Here . . . drink this." When she put a hand to her head and looked dizzy, he continued calmly. "The affect-effects of chloroform. It'll pass in a moment."

He held the brandy up to her lips for her to drink. She sniffed it suspiciously. How quaint. She thought it was poisoned. He could have just as easily shot her and no one would have heard. What made her think that he had to resort to such parlor tricks? Undoubtedly she had seen too many movies.

"Don't worry," he said calmly. "I wouldn't spoil a fifty-year-old brandy."

"Do you have to drug your women to seduce them?" He laughed at the absurdity of the suggestion, and then her eyes widened as she remembered. "Oh! Those awful men!" She turned away as if to physically remove herself from the memory.

He touched her shoulder, comforting. "Shhhh. It'll be all right. I promise you."

She turned back, glaring at him with frightened eyes. "You're involved in this! You kidnapped me!"

He'd anticipated the response from her and already had his lines prepared. "Against my will, believe me. I'm as much a victim as you."

She looked at him suspiciously. Perfect. Already the seeds of doubt had been sown. Now all he had to do was spread a little more manure to help them grow. "It's true!" he said, desperate for her to believe him. "They've used threats, blackmail. The tools of their gangster trade. I've been forced to cooperate. I'm not proud of it."

He reached out and touched her hand. At first she resisted, but then she let him hold it.

He lowered his voice in a perfect approximation of fear. "These are brutal, ruthless men"—then he added a touch of hope—"but they can be reasoned with. As long as they get what they want."

"Oh, Neville," she said forlornly, "I'm so frightened."

He pulled her into his arms and said, "There, there. I won't let any harm come to you. I swear it on my life."

She gazed up at him, clearly wanting to believe. "You feel that way . . . about *me?*"

"Earlier, when we danced"—here he used the full force of his thespian prowess—"I felt something move inside me . . . I felt it tear loose . . . and take flight . . ."

Her eyes lit up and she said, "That's what you said to Greta Garbo in *Napoleon's Mistress.*"

He was momentarily taken aback. He wasn't accustomed to women nailing his lines that quickly, if at all. Then he recovered and said, "You'd have been fantastic as Lady Catherine. You have beauty, grace, and a certain raw talent. With the proper nurturing you could become a great star." He approached her and sat mere inches away. "If you would put yourself completely in my hands, I could teach you, mold you

THE ROCKETEER   193

into a leading lady . . . clay in the hands of a master sculptor."

He leaned forward, attempting to kiss her. They drew closer and closer and then suddenly Jenny put a finger against his lips and frowned. Then she brightened, snapping her fingers. "*Moonlight on Broadway* with Carole Lombard! The scene at the top of the Empire State Building."

He was almost ready to belt her, but he forced himself to maintain his gentility. "But that was make-believe. This only seems like a dream. A dream from which I hope I . . ."

Then he saw the concentration in her eyes that indicated she was about to nail yet another source of what he was saying. He quickly changed gears. He ran a fingertip along the strap of her dress. "You can't be comfortable in that gown."

He crossed to an armoire and opened it with a flourish. A dozen negligees hung inside.

He turned to face her, once again the picture of elegance. "Oh, come along. Don't be shy."

Jenny rose from the bed and went to the wardrobe. She fingered the fine laces and silks and said in a hushed and breathy voice, "They're beautiful. . . ."

He selected a sheer black lace gown and passed it to her. "This one, I think," he said with finality.

Jenny held it against her body, studying the reflection in the armoire's mirror. He stepped behind her, eyeing her hungrily.

And then she lowered the negligee self-consciously and said, "What am I saying? You kidnapped me! I don't know what to think, you've got me so confused . . . !"

Seeing the moment slipping away, Sinclair took definite action. He spun her around, crushing his mouth to hers hungrily. He felt her hands tremble for a moment and then slide up his back, grasping and flexing urgently.

With what seemed a supreme effort of will, Jenny pulled away and said in a deep, hoarse voice, "Don't you want me to put this on?" She looked up at him with pure desire in her eyes.

"Desperately," he said.

Then she looked down with an utterly charming moment of modesty, and said, "I'll be back."

She went into the bathroom, leaving the door ajar. Sinclair smiled and started to unbutton his shirt while attempting to sneak a glance into the bathroom. It was all, all too easy.

In addition to having his sport with her, he could not wait to tell Secord—and he would catch him, sooner or later—of how his girlfriend had been utterly and completely Sinclair's, body and soul . . . but especially body. Oh, that would strike at the core of the Rocketeer's pride. That would begin to even the score for how much inconvenience and frustration Cliff Secord had caused him. He looked forward to the expression that the pasty-faced pilot would have when he learned of Sinclair's exploits. Sinclair made a mental note to make sure that Secord wasn't wearing that garish Rocketeer helmet when he learned the news. Couldn't see his face that way.

"Neville?" Jenny's voice floated from the bathroom. "Would you come in here, please?"

Eagerly he headed toward the door. He entered the gilt and marble bathroom and smiled in anticipation. Jenny's evening gown was open down the back, exposing a wedge of smooth, pale skin. She looked demurely at him over her shoulder, her glance then going to the zipper on her back that was down to her waist.

"Can you help me?" she said with an annoyed little pout. It looked scrumptious on her.

Sinclair stepped forward, more than eager to assist.

Jenny suddenly turned, a ceramic pitcher in her hand. Using the same form and style that she'd employed to bring the formidable Lothar to his knees back in the club, she brought it down on Sinclair's head. It shattered satisfyingly, and Sinclair dropped to the floor, unconscious.

Jenny shuddered in revulsion, looking down at the unconscious actor and quickly zipped up the back of her dress. Still, the bleak humor of the moment was not lost on her. Pretending so convincingly that she was interested in the advances of the hypocritical thug validated her own acting skills for all time.

"I finally played a scene with Neville Sinclair," she said.

Moments later Jenny was creeping out to the stairway landing, and then she came to a halt. Crouching low, she peered between the banisters and saw that escape down the stairs was impossible. A big, hulking, brute of a man who looked like a leftover from a B horror flick was seated in the foyer below. Incongruously, he was delicately eating a plate of cold chicken as *Amos 'N' Andy* played on the radio. Once, just once he uttered a laugh that sounded like a wheezing freight train.

Then she heard Sinclair's voice, bellowing and filled with pain and fury from the bedroom. *"Lothar!"*

The giant got to his feet, and she could hear his heavy shoes ascending the stairway.

Afraid of remaining exposed up there on the landing, Jenny ducked into another room, praying that there would be no one inside.

She found herself in what appeared to be a library, and there was a balcony on the other side. She ran to it and opened the large double doors, but a glance outside confirmed her fears—she could make the drop to the driveway below only if she didn't mind having two broken legs, not to mention probably the rest of her body shattered as well. Either way, once she landed, it seemed unlikely she would have a chance at a getaway, much less a subsequent film career.

She had one advantage though. She knew about the hidden room.

When Sinclair had emerged from the room in the wall a few minutes earlier, he had not been unobserved. Jenny had already recovered from the chloroform. She had gotten up from her bed and found that she was locked into the bedroom. As she had tried to find a way out, she had gone to a window and discovered she could see into the library across the way through the balcony entrance. And she had been amazed to see Sinclair emerge through a sliding wall panel in the library.

It was that clandestine activity that had confirmed for her that Sinclair was willingly in on this up to his eyeballs. But she also had been able to make out Sinclair's casual dress—he was clearly intending some romance, and one did not have to be a rocket scientist to figure out who was the intended romancee. So she had quickly retreated to the bed and lay down, feigning unconsciousness. It took all her strength not to scream when he had had his hands all over her, but now at least her subterfuge had enabled her to have the last laugh.

Except, unless she managed to hide quickly, Sinclair would be the one laughing.

Suddenly she heard voices in the hall, and from the sounds of them the owners were coming her way. Turning quickly, she went to the bookshelf. She had seen what shelf his hand had gone to in order to trigger the sliding panel, but not which book he had pulled.

She scanned the shelf, knowing she had virtually no time, and then spotted a book called *The Secrets of Casanova: Seduction Made Easy*. Somehow she had a funny feeling that that would certainly appeal to Sinclair's sense of humor, and she pulled on it, praying. To her great relief, the bookcase obediently slid out, revealing what seemed to be a small radio room.

Reasoning that any shelter was better than none, Jenny darted into the cubbyhole and closed the panel.

She crouched there, holding her breath, and the voices seemed to be pausing just outside the library. Whether they were arguing or what, she couldn't quite make out. What she could make out, though, as her eyes adjusted to the dim light, was the transmitter and assorted documents and code books piled on the radio table.

She saw a sheaf of papers clipped together, papers about aviation and speeches by FDR, articles about the Turrou spy inquiry, and cuts in the wages of steel workers. . . .

And clippings about the Rocketeer. She sifted

through them, amazed. Cliff hadn't been exaggerating; there were articles from every major newspaper. Here she was caught up in romances with creeps and nowhere parts in movies, and she was blind to her boyfriend making genuine banner-headline history.

Then she discovered some handwritten notes, and what appeared to be some sort of diagram that said *Ambrose Peabody—Aviation Mechanic* above it. Jenny studied it and frowned. It looked like mechanical drawings for some sort of rocket . . . and then her eyes widened. It must be for the rocket that Cliff had been wearing! Had Peevy actually invented the thing? Or had Peevy been making a diagram while studying it? Either way, the paper had no business being in the hands of Neville Sinclair. She folded the diagram and hid it in the bosom of her gown.

The voices grew louder now, having entered the library, and Jenny's heart pounded. She knew now that any second she risked discovery. If she kept her mouth shut, it was possible that whoever was outside wasn't going to look in here for her. On the other hand, if she kept mum and was discovered, she'd blown her only chance to improve her situation.

It was a desperate gamble, but one she felt she had to take. She grabbed the radio microphone and blindly hit switches until the transmitter lit up and static crackled over the speaker.

"Hello, hello!" she called. "This is an emergency! Can anyone hear me? Please send help, I've been kidnapped—"

To her joy, a voice—male and guttural—began to reply. And then her heart sank as she realized that she couldn't understand a thing he was saying. Moments later, a chill seized her spine as she realized just precisely why the voice was incomprehensible.

It was speaking German.

The dawn rose in her brain, bringing revelation, and as the light reached her mind, so did the dim light in the room also reach her eyes enough to find a code book with a swastika emblazoned on the cover.

"Oh, my God!" she said in a louder voice than she would have liked. "Neville Sinclair is a—"

"A what?" asked a snarling voice.

She whirled to see Sinclair in the doorway of the radio room, a handkerchief held to the back of his head. The brooding giant was hovering ominously at his elbow.

"A spy?" continued Sinclair. "A saboteur? A fascist?" And he reached out, grabbed her by the elbow, and dragged her to him, practically spitting in her face. "All of the above."

18 The hulking shape of the Bulldog Café squatted in the silver moonlight. The neighborhood all around was dark and quiet, as if holding its breath. Not a soul was in sight.

Cliff had been watching for several minutes to make sure no one was around. He felt exhausted, as if he hadn't slept for a week and could sleep for twice that time. Still, he didn't want to just go waltzing into the café and be a sitting duck with the rocket pack if someone was in there waiting for him. So he'd taken care to stash it before coming over, in a place that he hoped was clever—and yet simple—enough to avoid detection.

Now he poked his head into the back of the Bulldog Café and whispered, "Peevy? Millie?"

No response. Maybe they were in hiding. He climbed up a few steps of the storeroom ladder and looked cautiously into the attic room. "Peevy? Millie?"

"Hey, Cliff!"

He was so startled he dropped the trapdoor on his head and slipped off the ladder, landing heavily on the café floor. He looked up in confusion to see the bathrobe-clad Patsy emerging from a shadow.

"I couldn't sleep." She pointed next door, to where her mother and she lived in a small, modest frame house. "An' I saw you sneak in."

"Patsy," he gasped. "You scared the livin' ... heck," he said, amending his original word, "outta me."

"Sorry!"

He took a breath to steady his jangled nerves. After surviving bullets and thugs, he was getting rattled by a kid. "Where's Peevy?"

"Some men took him away," she said worriedly.

No less worried was Cliff as he looked at her in shock. Men? What men? Which men? There were so many people involved in this thing, it seemed, and they all had guns or badges or both, and none of this was doing Cliff a shred of good.

Suddenly the phone rang loudly. Catlike, Cliff was on his feet and snatched the receiver. "Peevy?!" he practically shouted into it.

"Wrong," came a guttural voice. "This Secord?"

Cliff's mind shifted into overdrive. This didn't sound like a fed. Didn't sound like Sinclair. It sounded kind of like the guy Sinclair was shouting at in the restaurant. The one he'd called Valentine.

"Who is this?" said Cliff slowly.

"Wanna talk to your girlfriend?" said Valentine.

Cliff sighed in relief. Whoever it was, it was somebody who didn't know how to bluff worth a damn. "You're fulla crap! She's safe outta town by now!"

"Yeah? Get a load of this, smart ass!"

There was a brief pause, during which Cliff wondered what sort of lame trick they were going to try now. And then his blood ran cold as the unmistakable voice of Jenny came on. "Cliff ... is that you?" She sounded tentative and terrified.

"Jenny!" he shouted in alarm. "Where are you? What are they—?!"

"Ah-ah," the voice of Valentine cut back in. "Just a taste, lover boy. So you know we're serious."

"You bastard!" hollered Cliff, feeling more helpless than ever. "If you touch a hair on her head, I swear I'll . . ."

"You want her back?" Valentine had gone from silky and even amused to hard-edged nastiness. "Bring us the rocket! Now, write this down."

Cliff grabbed a pencil and a paid bill from a spindle by the cash register and scribbled quickly as Valentine continued. "Griffith Observatory. Exactly four A.M. By the statues. We'll be waiting. And, Secord?" There was a dramatic pause and Cliff knew what was coming. He'd seen it in films, and sure enough: "Come alone or the girl's dead." And, as if in preview, the phone went dead.

Cliff hung up and stuffed the bill into his pocket. Patsy, frightened by the conversation that she'd just heard, said urgently, while tugging on the leg of his jodhpurs, "Cliff, what's happening? What are they doing to Jenny?"

Short-tempered, angry, Cliff snapped, "Quiet, Patsy! I have to think!"

Patsy fought to hold back tears, and immediately Cliff felt remorseful. Hell, the kid hadn't done anything. He knelt down next to her and said softly, "I didn't mean to yell at you. Listen . . . can you keep a big secret?" She nodded. "You know the flying man who saved Malcolm today?"

Immediately all thoughts of tears were forgotten. Patsy remembered the awe she'd felt when she'd seen him swooping down, the sunlight sparkling off his helmet as he soared through the air like a bird. "The Rocketeer!"

"He's going to help me get Jenny back," said Cliff firmly.

She looked excitedly at him. "Then it'll be okay! He'll save her! The Rocketeer can do anything!"

He stared at her, unsure of what to answer, unsure if it even needed an answer. Obviously it did, because Patsy immediately picked up on his uncertainty and said, "Can't he?"

Cliff put his hands on her small shoulders and looked into her eyes. "Yeah." He said it as much for his benefit as for hers. "Yeah . . . maybe he can."

She threw her arms around his neck and hugged him tight.

And that was the moment when the front and rear doors of the diner were kicked in. Four large men with guns rushed in and surrounded Cliff before he could move so much as an inch. He froze, afraid that any kind of play would cause a hail of bullets and a severely perforated little girl. Not to mention himself.

He waited for what seemed eternity to learn whose side these new gunmen were on.

The front door swung open and a familiar man stepped into the wash of lights. He smiled lopsidedly.

"Remember me?" said Agent Fitch.

19

In the office of Howard Hughes, Peevy sat across from the millionaire aviator, holding a cup of coffee and eating a sandwich. "Gotta admit," said Peevy to Hughes, who was listening intently to the old mechanic, "I always thought if I met you, I wouldn't know if I'd want to shake your hand or punch you."

"Why?" asked Hughes, amused.

" 'Cause I helped out Wiley Post."

"Ah," said Hughes, understanding immediately. "And I broke Wiley's record for circling the globe. His record stood for five years, Peevy. A hell of an accomplishment. And he was alone. And he flew a slightly longer course."

"And he had plane trouble!" added Peevy, his annoyance resurfacing. "Talk about all the trouble he and the *Winnie Mae* had . . ."

"And all the advantages I had."

"Why, if Wiley were alive today," bristled Peevy, and then he realized that he was being impolite to his host. He settled back and said, "Still . . . little under four days. You did pull off one hell of a stunt, Mr. Hughes."

"Thank you, Peevy," said Hughes. "And be aware that I've always tried to be helpful and supportive to those fliers who don't have my . . . advantages. For example, did you hear about Corrigan?"

Peevy frowned. "Doug Corrigan? Nice guy. Kind of quiet. If you're gonna tell me he flew nonstop from California to New York, I heard about that. . . ."

Hughes leaned back and smiled. "He's not in New York anymore. He's in Dublin."

"Dublin, *Ireland*? How'd he get there?!"

"Illegally," said Hughes. "He wanted to get permission to fly the Atlantic but was hampered by the permit procedures. Government apparently was reluctant to let him go. So he went anyway. Landed in Baldonnel Airfield just yesterday. Claims he intended to fly from New York to California and his compass got stuck."

Peevy roared with laughter. "His *compass*? You mean he says he went the wrong way?"

"That's right," agreed Hughes, a twinkle in his eye. "State Department was ready to hang him out to dry. But I placed a call to Secretary of State Hull on Corrigan's behalf. Pulled a few strings. He'll be back here in California in no time."

"Yeah, but the next time I see him, I'll be sure to call him 'Wrong Way,' " said Peevy.

"The point is, Peevy, I admire men like Corrigan. And Secord. The times we're living in are among the most exciting in the history of mankind. Between air flight and radios, the world is shrinking before our eyes. It's becoming smaller and smaller, and what frightens me is that if we don't get more accustomed to living with each other, we're going to choke each other to death."

"Yeah," said Peevy darkly. "Like that Hitler guy."

"Like Hitler," agreed Hughes. "Which is what the rocket pack was built with an eye toward. So tell me how you got it up and running, Peevy. I've seen the photos of the Rocketeer. It flies. I can't believe it."

"I'll tell you," said Peevy slowly, "if you tell me what Katharine Hepburn is really like."

Hughes grinned. "Deal. You first."

"Well," said Peevy, leaning back, totally at ease, while a man who could buy and sell him a million times over hung on his every word, "all I did was bypass the pressure valve, and that solved your throttle problem."

"But adding a rudder to the helmet. That's ingenious."

"Nah." Peevy waved off the compliment. "Just basic aviation."

At that moment the oak doors swung open. Peevy turned in surprise as Cliff was led in by several extremely annoyed-looking federal agents.

"Cliff! Am I glad to see you!"

"Same here, pal." He glanced up at the huge model of the sea plane hanging from the ceiling. Jeez, what a monster.

Fitch dumped an envelope onto the desk—Cliff's wallet, coins, pocket knife, chewing gum, and a folded restaurant bill. He turned and looked at Cliff in annoyance but addressed Hughes. "No sign of the rocket, and he's not talking."

Hughes rose and faced Cliff. The young aviator, for his part, didn't look remotely intimidated. It was surprising. If death and the laws of gravity didn't faze him, certainly a simple millionaire wasn't going to do it. "Do you know who I am?" he asked.

"What pilot doesn't, Mr. Hughes?" replied Cliff evenly.

"I designed the Cirrus X-3, the rocket pack. It was stolen from me."

"*I* didn't steal it," Cliff bristled.

"I told him the whole deal, Cliff," Peevy said. "He believes us. Give him the rocket." He knew that Cliff would be thrilled to hear it. After all the trouble they'd landed themselves in, Peevy had managed to save both their hashes and get everything squared. Boy, was Cliff going to be thrilled.

So it was with considerable shock that Peevy heard Cliff say, "I . . . can't do that. Not yet, anyway."

Peevy's eyes widened, and he said nervously, "Cliff, we agreed to give the rocket back to the right guy. That's him!"

Cliff's only response was an anxious, tight-lipped stare.

"Secord," said Hughes easily but dangerously, "I don't think you know the game you're playing." He tapped an intercom and said, "Go ahead, roll it."

Cliff didn't know what to expect upon hearing that, but the last thing he anticipated was what happened . . . namely, a screen lowered and a projector fluttered to life behind a wall port.

A grainy, silent black-and-white film unspooled on the screen. Adolf Hitler was seen shaking hands and exchanging *"heils"* with various high-ranking German military officials.

The Germans were busily adjusting a crude rocket pack—heavier and bulkier than the one Cliff had used—onto the back of a test pilot. As they did so, Hughes narrated. "The German prototype had the same problem as our first design. The combustion chamber would overheat and . . ."

On the film, the pilot fired an ignition button as the other Germans stood clear. He shot into the air about twenty feet, and then the rocket sputtered, pitching the pilot toward the earth. Cliff winced as the rocket then fired again, slamming the pilot into the ground.

Others ran toward him now as the pilot writhed helplessly, one pant leg on fire. Just before they could reach him, the rocket fired once more, blowing them back. The action, of course, prompted an equal and opposite reaction, and the pilot spun across the ground, striking the side of a bunker. The rocket then burst into flame, engulfing the unfortunate man's tangled remains.

". . . explode," Hughes finished somewhat dryly. "My boys finally figured it out. A double-walled chamber through which the fuel is pumped. Cool the chamber and preheat the fuel at the same time."

Inwardly, Cliff was shuddering. How close he had come! What if he'd glommed onto a rocket pack that was an earlier design, or had some other defect. He could've been blown to kingdom come. Despite all the bullets he had dodged in the last twenty-four hours, both literal and figurative, this, he felt, was the closest call of all.

"The German experiment didn't seem like much to worry about," continued Hughes. "But when we got our hands on this next film, we realized the scope of their plan."

The image on the screen abruptly changed to an animated map of Europe, swarming with flying soldiers. Rocket-powered storm troopers. Rocket men blanketing the skies, flying in formation above burning, ruined cities. The unstoppable winged commandos swept across the continent.

Cliff and Peevy stared somberly at the animated film, and then came the bleakest image yet.

A map of the United States appeared, suddenly assaulted by dark arrows that spread from points east. Rocket-borne assault troops advanced on Washington, D.C. As the Capitol burned, searing flames leapt up to engulf a proud federal eagle. The symbol melted like wax, and then reformed into a Nazi eagle.

To Cliff and Peevy, who had been watching newsreels and hearing reports for months now, with Hitler spouting words of peace and even FDR talking of disarmament . . . these were the most chilling, terrifying images that anyone could have presented. Naked aggression, bald-faced lying exposed to reveal a plan of worldwide domination.

As the film ended and the screen rose, it was almost too much for Cliff to take. He stared somberly at the toes of his boots as Hughes said quietly, "Where's my rocket pack, Secord?"

The immensity was so overwhelming, Cliff couldn't find the words. And his hesitation was misinterpreted by Fitch, still smarting from looking like a fool for his efforts, as more stonewalling. Angrily Fitch snarled, "I'm tired of square-dancing with you! I can slap you with grand theft, espionage, treason—and that's just my short list. Wooly, cuff this punk!"

The threat of incarceration immediately spurred Cliff into action as he remembered why he couldn't be imprisoned. Someone's life depended on it. "They've got my girl!" he said.

"Holy Moses!" exploded Peevy.

"They've set up a rendezvous, to swap Jenny for the rocket."

"Cliff," said Hughes with almost paternal familiarity, "I understand your concern. But you've got to let us handle this."

"They'll kill her if I don't go alone! And if anything happens to Jenny, I don't much care about the rest of the world. I swear I'll return the pack . . . tomorrow."

Even the more patient Wooly was starting to get exasperated. "This ain't a negotiation! Those guys are playing for keeps—"

"I can deal with Valentine and his boys," said Cliff confidently.

"The Eddie Valentine gang is only hired muscle." Hughes waved off the notion. "They work for a Nazi agent." He shot a look at Fitch and Wooly. "Someone our intrepid G-men have been unable to identify."

"It's Neville Sinclair!" Cliff exclaimed.

"What?" Fitch looked at him in disbelief.

"Sure! It makes sense." Cliff was speaking faster and faster. "He was ordering Valentine's guys around at the South Seas Club . . . and that's why he was so interested in Jenny!"

"Nice try, kid," said Wooly in amusement. He turned to Hughes. "We're taking them downtown and locking 'em up."

Cliff looked desperately to Hughes for some sort of support, but Hughes was shrugging. "Sorry, Cliff. If you won't cooperate, it's out of my hands." He raised his hands as if surrendering.

Cliff's gaze followed the hands, and his eyes lit on the huge airplane model. The model looked pretty damned sturdy.

Moving with speed that was fueled by pure panic, Cliff leapt up onto the desk. Wooly lunged for him and Cliff's legs snapped up as his arms snared the understructure supporting the large wings of the model.

The support wires snapped and the model rolled forward on the overhead track, heading straight for the window. Fitch and the other agents ducked as the *Spruce Goose* smashed through the windows, dragged off the track by Cliff's added weight.

The model sailed out over the canyon with Cliff Secord hanging on for dear life. The agents were already drawing their guns, but Hughes, astounded and fascinated by what he was seeing, shouted, "*No guns!*"

Cliff dropped down, down and away out of sight, the air current supporting him and his own skill and nerve enabling him to dangle from beneath like a hang glider. The ground blurred beneath him, but compared to rocketing along at two hundred miles per hour, this was slow motion.

The others watched him go, getting smaller and smaller, and then they turned slowly, with great trepidation, toward Hughes. They were sure they would be on the receiving end of more anger, more sarcasm.

Instead, Hughes was grinning ear to ear. "The son of a bitch *will* fly!" he said in amazement. They thought he was talking about Secord and didn't understand. He was, in fact, talking about "Hughes's Folly." The *Spruce Goose*. The rapidly dwindling model bespoke great achievements to come, and even more potential miracles.

In the meantime, the wind blew the folded-up restaurant check onto Peevy's shoe. He glanced down and noticed the writing on the back: *Griff Obs—4AM—.*"

Darkened Chaplin Airfield had had all manner of aircraft land on its weather-beaten tarmac in its time, but never had a sight such as this one graced the skies overhead.

The *Spruce Goose* swooped downward, its nerveracked pilot trying to gauge perfectly the speed and distance he had left. Cliff's arms were throbbing, his muscles quivering from the strain, and he knew that he was going to have only one chance to pull this landing off.

He started running in midair, to get his legs moving, and the runway came at him fast, so damned fast. In no time at all he was there, and he tried to keep his feet moving as fast as his airspeed was taking him. But he mistimed it, and the weight of the model overbalanced him, sending him tumbling end over end across the tarmac. The model splintered and shattered into a thousand wood fragments, and Cliff Secord rolled, banging up his elbows and knees still more as he tucked his head under his arms and tried to bring his headlong roll to a halt.

Finally, finally, he skidded to a halt, and he lay on the runway, his breath slamming against his lungs and his heart pounding so hard he thought it would break a rib. Hell, maybe he'd already broken a couple.

He stood on uncertain legs and then stumbled in the direction of where he'd hidden the rocket pack.

Moments later he was in the office of the late Otis Bigelow. It had seemed the perfect hiding place. The police had already gone over it with a fine-tooth comb, and so it seemed unlikely that they would go back over where they had been—especially in the middle of the night. Nor would other pilots be especially eager to enter the office; a man had been murdered there, and no one wanted that kind of jinx hanging on them.

It was a gamble that, apparently, had paid off big, for there was the rocket, in the duffel bag and secure as ever under Bigelow's desk. Cliff pulled it and the helmet out and checked a clock. He started to check his pockets for the piece of paper, but then remembered that the feds had taken it.

It didn't matter. He remembered where and when. He checked the clock and realized he had just under an hour to get from Chaplin Field to Griffith Observatory.

Not a major problem for the Rocketeer.

It was close to four in the morning, and the sky was clear over a sleeping Los Angeles. Diffused moonlight splashed over the white walls, curved parapets, and copper domes of Griffith Observatory. Behind the domes, the cliffs dropped off sheer and straight, and city lights glimmered like a jeweled carpet.

The forecourt was a dark lawn crossed by wide concrete paths. In the center of the lawn, a tall stone obelisk was surrounded by statues of famous astronomers who stood solemn watch.

Three Valentine gang sedans were parked at the base of the steps. Eddie, Rusty, Spanish Johnny, and several others of his gang waited impatiently on the lawn, tommy guns in hand.

Sinclair's car rolled up, and Eddie flashed a dark look of "about time" at his boys. The first one to emerge, naturally, was Lothar, who then pulled open the passenger door and dragged Jenny from her seat.

Sinclair then stepped out, stopping to take a tuxedo jacket from the backseat. He handed it to her. "Here," he said. "Put this on."

"I'd rather freeze," shot back Jenny.

He looked her over and smiled at the way the steady wind was blowing the tight dress even tighter, and her exposed skin was becoming even whiter in the chill air. "Quite right," he said appraisingly. "I prefer you that way."

214

Jenny immediately snatched the jacket and put it on. Sinclair smiled as he turned and walked toward the obelisk. Lothar followed, pulling Jenny behind, and Eddie approached them, scowling.

"Cheer up, Eddie," said Sinclair with that joviality that Jenny had once thought was so charming. "You're about to make a fortune."

"Good," said Valentine tightly, "because I've got a club to repair and an ulcer to plug."

"Hey, boss!" shouted Johnny. "Here he comes!"

Everyone looked up toward the heavens and, at first, it looked like a comet streaking across the night sky. It grew larger and brighter, and soon they could hear a roar becoming louder and louder. Eddie signaled his men, who quickly formed a loose circle around the lawn, tommy gun barrels swinging up.

Jenny felt a stark surge of terror. It looked like a firing squad. The only thing that gave her any comfort at all was that they wouldn't open fire on Cliff because they wanted the rocket pack, and presumably not full of holes. But once they had it . . . then Cliff had had it too, and probably her as well.

The Rocketeer swooped down, then up, as if he were toying with them, before landing on the grass. He removed his helmet to defiantly face the surrounding thicket of gun barrels.

Eddie didn't like it at all. The kid sure wasn't acting like he was outmanned and outgunned. He was coming across like he had the drop on them. Did possessing the power of flight really give you that kind of confidence? He glanced around at his own men, as if to verify for himself that they in fact had the upper hand, and then he nodded to himself briskly. That kind of confidence could get you killed.

Cliff locked eyes with Jenny. "Jenny, are you all right?" he asked.

"She's fine," Sinclair replied.

With barely contained disdain, Cliff shot back, "I wasn't talking to *you*."

Sinclair ignored the tone. "Take off the rocket. Carefully."

"Let Jenny go. When she's driven down the hill, I'll—"

In a voice that could have cut diamond, Sinclair snapped, "I'm not here to bargain, Secord!"

Cliff was the picture of calm by contrast. "Then you don't get the rocket."

Sinclair pulled Jenny away from Lothar, drew a Luger from his coat, and pressed it to her temple. Jenny, for her part, was starting to feel more frustrated and helpless than ever. A piece of meat to be used for bargaining, shielding, and as a symbol of acquisition.

"You wouldn't kill her," said Cliff.

Eddie sounded almost indifferent. "Oh, yes, he would, kid. Take it from me."

"The rocket, Mr. Secord," said Sinclair in an even tone.

Eddie felt for the kid. He'd learned to dislike Sinclair enough to know how he would feel if the Limey had the upper hand in a bargain. "Come on, kid! Hand it over so we can all go home!"

And Cliff looked at Sinclair with utter contempt. Without addressing anyone but, at the same time, addressing all of them, he called out, "What's it like working for a Nazi? Does he pay you in dollars or deutsche marks?"

There was dead silence. Sinclair was stunned. He had warned Jenny that if she said one word about the radio room, he would kill Cliff and herself no matter what the outcome of the exchange. But Secord knew too—? Where was it going to be next? The *Times*?

"What's he yappin' about?" demanded Eddie.

"I heard it straight from the feds, Eddie," called out Cliff. "A Nazi spy ring, flying commandos . . . the works."

Sinclair, the consummate actor, had already recovered neatly, and said dismissively, "He's been flying where the air's too thin."

But now, emboldened, sensing a shift in direction of the "meeting," Jenny declared, "Ask him about the secret room, and the Germans on the radio!"

Sinclair glanced at Eddie's men, who had been listening intently. Several of the tommy gun muzzles began to drift in Sinclair's direction.

Lothar started to reach into his coat, only to find Rusty's tommy gun in his face. "Relax, Frankenstein," said Rusty dangerously. "You ain't bulletproof."

"Talk fast, Sinclair," said Eddie, stepping in front of him.

"Come on, Eddie," said Sinclair, trying to sound casual. "We all must serve someone."

"Adolf and his goose-stepping rats!" bellowed Eddie, bristling.

"You tell him, Eddie," said Cliff.

"Shut up!" Eddie fired back, not sure of what the hell was going on.

Deciding he had to take a firm hand in this, Sinclair said, sounding quite tough, "Now, listen—"

"No, *you* listen!" said Eddie, sounding tougher still. "I may not earn a straight buck, but I'm one hundred percent American, dammit!"

"Then you're one hundred percent doomed," laughed Sinclair. "You're just a slave to an outdated government that's going to be swept away by a rain of fire." His voice rose in volume and intensity. "With an army equipped with these"—he gestured toward the rocket pack—"we could rule the world!"

"Eddie Valentine," said Eddie in a voice as dark as the grave, "is nobody's slave. Let the lady go."

He nodded to his men, and suddenly Neville Sinclair was staring down the gun barrels of the gangsters. There was no director around to yell "cut," no prop man to gather the guns up and store them in the prop bin.

Which was why it was all the more surprising when Sinclair said, with simple conviction, "I'm still taking the rocket."

At that, Eddie laughed. "You and what army?"

And suddenly, to everyone's surprise, Sinclair hollered into the surrounding canyons. His voice echoed in words that were not English: *"Sturmabteilung! Angreifen!"*

Twenty German commandos in gray jump suits rushed from the bushes, or appeared atop the observatory's staircases and domes, surrounding Eddie and his men. They aimed their Schmeisser machine guns at the stunned gangsters.

Cliff could have kicked himself. If only he'd done an aerial survey of the area first. But the moment he'd seen Jenny he'd been drawn to her, moth to flame. And now they were both going to get burned.

Sinclair flashed a serpent grin at the gangster and said, "I believe it's your move, Eddie."

Realizing that he was outgunned and outmanned, Eddie signaled his men to drop their weapons. Slowly and reluctantly, they did so.

Curiously, Cliff saw that Sinclair was checking his watch. Now, who could he have had an appointment with—?

Then he heard something, something that had been faint but was now getting louder and louder. The sound of whirring engines, immense, bigger than anything Cliff had ever heard in his entire career of flying.

Everyone turned their gaze to the sky.

The sky turned silver.

21 It completely filled the night sky, blotting out the moon, blotting out hope of escape, blotting out everything. It seemed to have sailed out of a Movietone newsreel directly into the living nightmare that the lives of Cliff Secord and Jenny Blake had become.

The zeppelin lowered itself toward the observatory, gondola softly aglow with its running lights. Emblazoned on the airship's side was the name *Luxembourg*, and, as if it needed any further announcement of its loyalties or origins, a huge swastika decorated the rudder. It almost seemed as if the behemoth balloon weren't even there, but merely some deadly, spectral apparition.

The reality of the newly arrived zeppelin was testified to by Sinclair's sharp, barked commands to the German soldiers that surrounded them. *"Ergreifen die Rakete! Schnell!"*

Cliff didn't understand the entire command, although *"schnell"* he knew to be "Move it, buddy." But *"Rakete"* sounded close enough to "rocket" to make it pretty damned clear what their intention was, as if it weren't painfully obvious already. One of the commandos ran to Cliff and started to unbuckle the rocket pack. Cliff's mouth tightened as he restrained himself from swinging his fists, as much as he wanted to. He knew right where he would hit this Nazi clown too—smack on the upper lip, where he looked like he was starting to grow a mustache. In emulation of Uncle Adolf, no doubt.

"*Haltet sie in Schach!*" snapped out Sinclair, and if there was any question as to what that meant, it was clarified immediately when the commandos swung their Schmeissers at their captives. Switching back to his charming facade with the skill of a consummate actor, Sinclair said jovially, "So long, Eddie. Thanks for the memories. . . ."

And suddenly Sinclair was blinded.

Everyone was. Car-mounted spotlights stabbed out to illuminate the observatory. Tires screeched and smoked as police cars and FBI sedans pulled up. Wooly and Fitch, grabbing at the opportunity to vindicate themselves in high style, were in the lead, in position with tommy guns ready.

Fitch felt a degree of annoyance. Here he'd wished that for once they had automatic weapons so they'd be on par with the bad guys. So now they had tommy guns and what did the bad guys have? Schmeissers and a goddamn blimp. Still, at least he wasn't crouching there, facing armed German commandos while waving what amounted to a pop gun. Through a bullhorn he bellowed in a voice that echoed throughout the area, "This is the FBI! Throw down your guns!"

Cliff tossed a quick glance at the Nazi commando who had been in the process of unbuckling the *"Rakete."* He had been totally distracted by the goings-on, and even better, was acting as if Cliff were utterly helpless and to be forgotten. What he didn't realize was that as long as Cliff had the control brackets attached to his wrists and thumbs to hit the ignition, he'd never be helpless.

He hit them now.

Jenny saw him do it, and her alarmed scream was drowned out by the rocket's sudden flare-up. The force of the blast hurled the terrified Cliff—who was certain he was going to crack his skull wide open like a cantaloupe because he wasn't wearing his helmet— across the lawn, dragging the hapless commando behind. They disappeared over a ledge, falling roughly into the tangle brush.

The momentary distraction was all that was needed. Cliff's scream had not yet faded when Lothar yanked his twin .45s free of their holsters and, with a howl that seemed to hearken back to the Stone Age, started firing with reckless abandon. Cops and feds hit the deck as slugs punched through fenders and shredded tires.

It was an invitation to chaos, and nobody elected to miss the party. The feds started firing on the commandos in the forecourt, while Sinclair and Lothar headed for the stairs to the roof. Jenny almost made a break for it, but Lothar grabbed her firmly while continuing to fire with his other hand.

Seizing the opportunity, Eddie Valentine and his men snatched up the tommy guns that the Germans had so ingraciously—considering they were visitors to the country—insisted that Eddie's gang toss down.

Eddie Valentine decided to make his sentiments widely and immediately known, both for the sake of letting his own men know who to aim at, and because the last thing he needed was to become the next target should the feds decide they wanted some American gangster hot dogs to go with their Krauts. "Lousy Krauts!" he shouted. "Let 'em have it, boys!"

The feds were stunned to see the Eddie Valentine

gang abruptly on the same side, emptying their bullets into the commandos, and taking hits alongside the feds and cops. In short, having cast their lot on the side of the angels, they were fighting as valiantly as anyone could have asked.

Fitch was astounded, and then realized that there were other concerns besides Eddie Valentine's totally unexpected alliance. From behind the shelter of his bullet-pocked sedan, he called out to the men, "Watch the zeppelin! That thing's filled with hydrogen! One bad shot'll fry us all!"

He caught a brief glimpse of Sinclair—Damn! It *had* been Sinclair! Maybe they should recruit that Secord kid or something—Sinclair's hired gorilla, and a terrified girl who had to be a hostage, all heading up toward the observatory roof. But there was nothing he could do about it except take cold comfort in the fact that the ranks of Nazi commandos were thinning. If they were thinned sufficiently, they might have a shot at going after Sinclair.

He heard a burst of machine gunfire to his right, and he and Wooly glanced over, unsure of the origin of the fusillade. There, crouched behind a police car, was Eddie Valentine, blasting away at the Germans with patriotic zeal. He tossed a tight grin in the direction of two men who would gladly, five minutes earlier, have tossed his butt in jail and sent the key on a one-way trip to France.

"Now I've seen everything," muttered Wooly.

What Wooly was not able to see, at that moment, from his angle, was what was occurring on the roof of the observatory. Specifically, a ladder had been lowered from the zeppelin's gondola and snagged by the formidable Lothar. He had passed the struggling Jenny over to Sinclair and was now, appropriately apelike, scampering up the rungs toward safety.

"Please, Neville!" begged the desperate girl. "Let me go!"

Sinclair didn't even bother to reply as Lothar reached down and grabbed her, carrying her kicking and screaming into the gondola.

Her screams were covered by the steady firing of the machine guns from assorted countries; covered and unhearable to everybody but one person. . . .

Cliff, struggling to his knees, blood dripping from his forehead, looked up in alarm as he detected Jenny's piercing screams. His eyes were glazed over, and his mind kept wanting him to just lie down and sleep for a few minutes. He couldn't remember the last time he'd closed his eyes. . . .

But everything immediately snapped into focus as he saw the zeppelin lifting from the roof.

Jenny. The bastards had Jenny.

All right. If they were playing for keeps, then so was he.

He yanked a Mauser machine pistol from the holster of the unmoving commando beside him, and tried not to think about the fact that he had never tried to shoot a human being in his life, much less intend to take a life. But a line had been crossed and he was going to follow the people who had crossed that line, no matter where it took him. Gripping the pistol firmly, he struggled up the hillside.

Inside the gondola, a tense German wearing a dark suit and a swastika lapel pin saw what Sinclair was conspicuously not carrying and said harshly, *"Sie haben die Rakete nicht?"*

"I have her!" said Sinclair, pointing at Jenny. Upon the agent's confused glance, he continued. "That damned rocket will come to us! Now, get this ship above the clouds!"

Cliff, gaining strength with every step as adrenaline surged through him, reached the observatory lawn and snatched up the helmet that he had put down earlier. The cops were mopping up the last of the commandos, and the surviving hoods were aiding their wounded. No one was looking in his direction, and that was just fine with him as he raced up the winding stone staircase. He glanced up and saw that the gondola was already rising toward the clouds.

He heard the agent named Fitch shout, "We're losing 'em!" and then the other one, Wooly, suddenly cry out, "Maybe not! Look!"

He knew who they had spotted: him. But there were no shouts of "Halt! Stop!" No threats of arrest, no recriminations. Nothing except a sense of anticipation, of hope, of prayer, and the realization that all of a sudden he had gone from being patsy and victim to being their last hope.

He slammed the helmet on, and by God, as he paused atop one of the copper domes, for the first time he truly felt like he was what the papers had made him out to be. He was going to be the hero, the one who saved the day. All this time he'd felt like a fake, on the run from everybody, someone always coming after him.

Not now. Now they were doing the running and he was doing the chasing, and he wasn't just some idiot pilot who'd stumbled into something beyond his understanding.

He checked the Mauser's clip, ignited the rocket, and leapt into the sky, a blossom of fire and smoke carried upward by the power of one man's vision and the hope of several dozen agents of the law.

Finally, finally, finally, he felt like the guy he'd been reading about in the papers.

He was the Rocketeer, dammit. Time to show the Nazis just what that meant.

And boy, was Jenny going to be impressed.

The Rocketeer sailed upward toward the zeppelin. He had never dealt with anything quite so big, never had to judge distance between himself and something of that immensity. But he was utterly confident, carried away by the moment, that he could handle it.

That confidence almost cost him dearly, for the silver tail of the airship was rushing to meet him at a faster pace than he was prepared to make its acquaintance. He eased down on the throttle buttons, but he had completely blown his projected trajectory. As a result, his velocity carried him on a descending arc straight into the zeppelin's tail, and he smashed into the massive rudder with such impact that he tore the skin right off it.

He slid down the vertical stabilizer and landed hard on his back, shock slamming through his body, and not made to feel any better by the rocket pack's feelings as if it were going to be driven through his back and up through his chest. *Land on your chest if you're going to land badly, idiot!* he screamed at himself. Aside from the fact that he could snap his spine, the last thing he needed to do was burst the rocket pack and be stuck on this one-way ticket to the Fatherland.

In the meantime, the hole that Cliff had created in the rudder's skin was widened by the fiercely howling wind, causing the rudder to swing erratically. While that was of benefit to Cliff, the wind cut both ways, threatening to hurl him off. He pulled himself to his feet and crouched low, fighting the fierce gusts with everything he had.

They would know that something was wrong with the rudder. They weren't stupid. And they would undoubtedly send someone to check out the nature of the disturbance. Perhaps they would even assume that it was him.

Realizing that what all this added up to was that he didn't have tons of time, the Rocketeer started to move atop the airship toward an entrance hatch. A red beacon flashed on and off, bathing the bronze helmet in a weird light.

He was getting closer and closer to the hatch, now ten feet, now eight, now five, and the wind was trying its best to hurl him from his perch. But he resisted all the way and finally made it to within arm's reach of the hatch cover. He poised over it, gun at the ready.

Totally without warning, the hatch cover sprang open, and it knocked the Mauser from Cliff's hand. He watched in horrified helplessness as it bounced down the side of the zeppelin and fell away.

Lothar emerged from the hatch. And he just kept on coming and coming, like a flow of lava oozing from a volcano, massive and deadly.

The Rocketeer's foot lashed out to catch Lothar in the head, and the giant showed his lack of appreciation for that by grabbing the booted foot and shoving back as hard as he could, considering that he was off balance and not fully emerged from the hatch. All things considered, it could have been worse. The Rocketeer fell back, but landed on his shoulder and was immediately back up again, balancing lightly on the balls of his feet to compensate for the steady gusting of wind.

By this time Lothar had fully emerged from the trapdoor and had snapped a safety tether to his waist. The Rocketeer took some measure of cold confidence in this; the giant thus far had given every indication of being virtually indestructible. How nice to know that he was as concerned about falling off as mere mortals might be.

Lothar advanced on the Rocketeer, and the helmeted adventurer came in fast with everything he had. He gut-punched the giant, hit him in the chest, delivered a fast and furious volley of lefts and rights. Lothar's body quivered under every single punch, and the Rocketeer felt a surge of hope. The giant was helpless before his onslaught. The giant was stunned. The giant was—

Smiling. He had let the Rocketeer take his shots to show him that he posed no threat at all.

The giant swung a massive paw around and caught the Rocketeer on the side of the head. One punch to answer for the dozen or so landed, and it was more than enough. The Rocketeer went down as if pole-axed, the wind knocked out of him.

He tried to stagger to his feet, but now Lothar had gripped him firmly by the ankles and the scruff of the neck. He lifted the Rocketeer over his head and started to exert pressure. The Rocketeer felt an awful grinding in the area of his hips, a pressure deep in his spine, and then he realized what was happening. The monster was trying to bend him backward in half, snap his spine, kill him with as much ease as he himself would crumble a sheet of paper.

And he would have accomplished it too, except the bottom of the rocket pack jammed into the small of the Rocketeer's back, momentarily adding strength and, literally, stiffening his spine. The giant grunted, confused by the resistance, and then he realized what was causing it. By the time he had, though, the Rock-eteer had brought both his fists around and bashed Lothar in the skull, using the hand controls as if they were brass knuckles.

Lothar's brain, or what passed for it, slammed around inside the cranial casing from the impact of the metal-enhanced fists. Dazed, the giant lost his grip on the Rocketeer. The hero fell, struck the side of the zeppelin, and, unable to stop himself, plummeted down and away, his arms and legs waving madly like a puppet severed of its strings.

Lothar, shaking off the dizziness, stared down after where the Rocketeer had gone and suddenly realized, in a dim fashion, that he had screwed up. Sinclair had wanted the rocket, and now it was plummeting to earth on the back of an idiot who was no doubt unconscious from smashing against the zeppelin before falling.

Sinclair was going to be mad, and Lothar briefly wished that he could have another shot at the rocket pack.

His wish was granted, although not the way he would have liked, as the Rocketeer shot up and around from the opposite side of the zeppelin. He smashed into Lothar with the velocity of a missile and knocked the giant clear of the zeppelin. A safety tether he may have had, but suction cups on his feet he most definitely had not, and Lothar fell down the side of the zeppelin, completely and satisfyingly out of control.

In the gondola, the sweating pilot was fighting to control the zeppelin's flight. The Nazi agent, in the meantime, was still screaming at Sinclair, making it painfully clear that Adolf Hitler was not going to take kindly to a failed mission. Obtaining the rocket was not something about which Hitler had offered many options. He wanted it done, and therefore it had to be done. And now it wasn't done. Which meant the Nazi agent was going to be undone.

Sinclair, trying to ignore the torrent of German flooding his way, was holding Jenny firmly by the wrist as he snapped at the captain, "Do I have to fly the ship myself?! Keep us on course, dammit!"

"Do not worry, Herr Sinclair," said the captain with the calm that only a veteran could command. "My pilot is the finest in Germany."

Sinclair started to reply, "It's a pity we're not in

Germany." But all he got out was "It's," and then Lothar's body swung through the gondola windows, exploding into the gondola like a wrecking ball.

Totally out of control, he smashed into the best pilot in Germany. The pilot was sent flying backward into the door, and he hit it with such impact that it burst open, propelling him outward. He promptly was reduced to the status of best pilot in midair without benefit of propulsion systems, and then he became the best falling and, ultimately, dead zeppelin pilot in the vicinity.

Lothar, for his part, dangled for a moment like a broken marionette before drifting away into the darkness, still at the end of his tether.

The panicked Nazi agent whirled on Sinclair, wishing to hell he'd volunteered for something safer, like that endless dig for archaeological treasures in Tanis. "*Das ist deine Schuld!*" he babbled. "*Wenn wir ohne die Rakete nach Hause kommen, werden wir* beide *aufgehängt!*"

The captain, with a slight crack finally appearing in his professional demeanor, said worriedly, "We're losing altitude! We must drop some weight from the gondola!"

With no trace of hesitation, Sinclair pulled out his automatic and blew the Nazi agent backward out the open doorway. He allowed a small smile. He wasn't going to miss that idiot one bit.

Abruptly the roof hatch opened and the Rocketeer leapt down. The remaining German crewman jumped at him, and the Rocketeer dodged his punch, grabbed his wrist, and, blood pumping with excitement, threw him against the gondola wall. The crewman was knocked senseless.

"Jenny!" Cliff shouted.

Sinclair pressed the gleaming muzzle of his automatic pistol beneath Jenny's chin. His eyes were wild. "I've had a bellyful of you and your cheap heroics. You hand over the rocket"—he yanked back on Jenny's hair for emphasis, eliciting a squealed cry of pain—"or I'll blow her brains all over the cabin!"

Jenny couldn't stand the thought of Cliff being helpless once again because of her. In as brave a voice as she could muster, she cried out, "Cliff, don't give it to him . . . you can't!"

The Rocketeer looked deeply into her eyes.

"I have to," he said.

His shoulders sagging in frustration, Cliff Secord slipped the rocket's straps from his back as Sinclair said, "Slide it across to me." But as he obeyed, he pulled the wad of good-luck gum from the creased fuel tank.

Sinclair brutally pushed Jenny to the airship's captain and handed him the automatic. "If she moves, kill her."

As for Jenny, her nerves were utterly frayed to the breaking point. She was sick and tired of being a liability for Cliff, for the government, for the entire free world, it seemed. She muttered, "If one more man puts a gun to my head . . ."

The captain put the gun to her head.

"*That's it!*" howled Jenny, and in total disregard for her own safety—and frankly, the captain hadn't expected her to move anyway—she slammed her sharp heel into the captain's instep. He grunted in pain and she whirled free of his grasp, pushing him hard against the control panel.

Jenny completely lucked out. The captain smashed

his head against the upper portion of the panel and slumped to the deck, the gun falling from his hand. Instinctively she lashed out with her foot and kicked it across the floor and out the open door. It was only then that she realized that picking it up and pointing it at, say, Sinclair, might have been the sharper move.

Cliff lunged at Sinclair, throwing a punch that knocked the actor to the gondola floor. The pilot stood over him, fists clenched and poised, and he snarled, "Where's your stunt man now, Sinclair?"

Abruptly, Sinclair leapt to his feet and threw a punch that connected squarely with Cliff's jaw. Cliff staggered back, the lower half of his face tingling from the impact.

"I do my own stunts," Sinclair informed him.

Cliff, his face a mask of grim determination, charged him, and the two men slammed together. They pounded each other, all the anger and frustration that each of them had caused the other in this brief span of time now driving them to try to reduce the other into bruised slabs of meat.

Cliff felt his left eye starting to swell shut, and his upper lip was split, but Sinclair's nose had crunched satisfyingly under one of his jabs and he wasn't sure, but he thought he'd knocked out one of Mr. Wonderful's teeth. He didn't know which would be better—if Sinclair died in an out-of-control zeppelin, or if he had to live with a puss that had been battered by yours truly.

Then Sinclair knocked Cliff back, and the pilot stumbled hard against the cabin wall. Cliff's head bashed against an emergency case, and the contents spilled out across the floor—including a wide-barreled pistol. Jenny, seeing it sitting there, took the opportunity to make up for her tactical error of eighty-sixing the other gun.

Bruised and bloodied, Sinclair seized Cliff by the front of his jacket and slammed him hard against the cabin wall. He drew his fist back and Cliff was about to try to muster what defense he could when suddenly Jenny's voice rang out with authority, "Stop! I'll shoot. . . ."

They turned to see her aiming the wide-barreled pistol directly at Sinclair. "I swear I will," she said, and there was no trace of indecision in her tone. Her hands, however, were trembling.

Cliff, shaking the sweat and blood from his eyes, saw what Jenny was holding. Sinclair might not realize what she had, but any pilot knew it immediately. "Jenny—no!" he shouted.

And just as he did, Sinclair lunged at her. She screamed and yanked the trigger and, much to his credit, Sinclair was nimble enough to dive out of the way.

It was not a bullet he dodged, however. It was a signal flare.

The last thing anyone could possibly want anywhere near a vehicle filled with hydrogen was a berserk incendiary device, but that was exactly what the occupants of the gondola had. The flare ricocheted, leaving fire wherever it touched. And then, as if to spitefully make sure that they didn't have a hope in hell, it finally buried itself in the control console, where it burst into flame.

Cliff looked around frantically and spotted a fire extinguisher on the wall beside the smashed windows. Wrenching the cylinder from the bracket, he sprayed the liquid on the flaming console. The flames laughed at the extinguisher and continued to spread, and smoke was filling the cabin.

Insanely, Jenny thought that if somehow they lived through this, that definitely, beyond all shadow of a doubt, "Smoke Gets in Your Eyes" was definitely going to be "their" song.

"Sinclair!" shouted Cliff. "Help us get this fire out!"

And then he heard a distinctive click, and spun just in time to see Sinclair fastening the rocket pack's waist belt. He poised in the open gondola door, frantically adjusting the harness.

"Good-bye, my darling!" he called, the height of drama. "I'm going to miss Hollywood."

Cliff watched the fuel leaking from the rocket pack as Sinclair leapt from the gondola and fired the rocket.

"Don't be so sure," Cliff said with astounding calm.

Sinclair rocketed away from the doomed zeppelin, the Hollywood Hills spread below him. The wind rushed past him, the rocket roared on his back, and for a brief moment he understood why Secord had fought so hard to hold on to the rocket pack. This was truly a taste of what it meant to be totally divine.

He didn't notice the fuel spraying through the now-unplugged hole until it ignited the rocket pack's contrail. The fire was immediately sucked into the rocket pack, and the brainchild of Howard Hughes burst into flame.

Sinclair twisted around, trying to control his first and last flight. It was no use. The flame was spreading across his back, and he felt a heat so overwhelming, he thought he was in hell. As it turned out, it was a preview.

Rocket man became comet man became human torch as he blazed through the sky, heading toward gigantic white letters that loomed before him like a greeting card from the netherworld.

He smashed into the right-hand side of the sign that perched on the hillside overlooking the motion picture capital of the entire universe, and there was a tremendous explosion that removed both Neville Sinclair and the last four letters of the sign from the face of the earth. The air crackled and burned, sparks flying everywhere and shards of white letters falling all about.

And when the dust settled, the flaming ruins illuminated the spy's memorial—a gigantic sign which now simply read, HOLLYWOOD.

While high, high above, the doomed zeppelin with its last living passengers embarked on what was going to be its final journey, with a very imminent terminal point.

22

Cliff and Jenny emerged from the maintenance hatch atop the zeppelin, and he helped her up onto the fuselage. Cliff held her tight, protecting her from the wind, although he bleakly realized he didn't know what he was protecting her for.

She looked up at him with utter trust, and he realized, with dark humor, that she was finally getting her wish that he tell her first when something important cropped up. "This thing's full of hydrogen," he shouted over the wind's roar. "When the fire hits the envelope . . ."

She heard and nodded and didn't even flinch, but instead said simply, "I love you, Cliff."

She threw her arms around him and kissed him, hoping that they would be kissing when the end came because perhaps that meant they would spend eternity that way. It was romantic and corny and she wouldn't have had it any other way.

Below them, flames completely consumed the gondola and proceeded to work on the envelope of the zeppelin. They had seconds left.

And then Cliff's practiced ears heard engine sounds that he knew were separate from those of the zeppelin. And the flap of rotors . . .

He twisted his head around and his jaw dropped in amazement. Jostling the confused Jenny, he pointed.

"What is it!" she shouted.

237

"An autogyro!" Cliff couldn't believe it. He'd heard about them but never seen one before.

But there it was, an odd-looking aircraft with both a conventional prop and a blade like a helicopter. In the craft's pilot seat was none other than Howard Hughes. In front of him, guiding Hughes into position, was Peevy leaning over the edge. Hughes fought to keep the craft steady as Peevy tossed down a rope ladder.

Clutching at Jenny with sheer joy, not believing their miraculous salvation, Cliff started toward the rope ladder with his arm firmly around his overwhelmed girlfriend.

And that was precisely when the hulking form of Lothar blocked their way.

Cliff and Jenny stepped back, stunned. He had simply materialized in their path, like a spontaneous brick wall. Cliff saw the tether trailing downward and realized, to his amazement, what had happened. The behemoth had not only survived the impact of the fall earlier, but now the near-indestructible creature had pulled himself up, hand over hand, using the tether as rope and anchor and means of ascension. Now he loomed between Cliff and Jenny and their means of escape, and he started toward them, snarling and furious.

Without a clue as to what he was going to do about it, Cliff moved Jenny behind himself, interposing himself between the oncoming Lothar and . . .

And . . .

And Lothar's eyes widened in shock as he looked straight past the terrified couple. At first Cliff thought it was a trick, but Lothar had no need for subterfuge. He probably couldn't even spell it. Cliff's and Jenny's heads snapped around, and they saw, at the far end of the zeppelin, a churning ball of flame.

The zeppelin shuddered as the pockets of volatile hydrogen began to ignite. Lothar, knowing just how far he could push his invulnerability, turned and ran like hell toward the tail of the zeppelin, where the rope ladder still dangled invitingly. Right on his heels, but being outdistanced by the second, were Cliff and Jenny.

Like a chain reaction the explosions rippled along the airship's body. A huge fireball was surging toward the tail, hungry to swallow the fleeing trio.

Their breath was ragged, their legs aching, and once Jenny almost stumbled and fell. Cliff grabbed her, not especially gently, and pounded after the giant, who was rapidly outdistancing them.

It looked hopeless. Either the giant would reach the rope ladder, climb up, and kill Peevy and Hughes, thereafter sailing off into the sunset, or he'd keep Hughes around to pilot it and then kill him, break him in half. Or else Peevy and Hughes would have to seek altitude, depriving the giant of escape—and Cliff and Jenny as well. Peevy would have to sit helplessly and watch them disappear in a burst of flame. Trying to figure a way out, Cliff was at the end of his rope.

And then, miraculously, so was Lothar.

The tether was still anchored to the zeppelin and so, barely a few feet short of the rope ladder, Lothar was suddenly brought up short. He strained against it but it held firm, as it was designed to do. His thick fingers began frantically to work at the release clip on his belt, and then Jenny and Cliff surged past him toward the hanging ladder. Behind the trio their doom was literally hot on their heels.

Lothar turned in time to see a tidal wave of flame descending upon him. His hair and skin began to crispen and burn, and he screamed, not in pain, but in a burst of anger that superseded everything.

Peevy glanced at Hughes. They were at the point of no return—in a second the zep was going to go up, and if the autogyro didn't have the altitude, it was going to go with it. Yet Hughes, in the face of imminent demise, was not only calm but even had an amused smile on his face, as if he welcomed death to take its best shot, because he was ready for it. Which meant that Hughes was either incredibly cool or incredibly nuts.

Either way, it got Peevy to shout at the top of his lungs, "*Jump for it!*"

The rope ladder swung tantalizingly in front of them. Behind them the air was sizzling and exploding, and Jenny threw her arms around Cliff and breathed a prayer. Cliff timed the leap and then jumped for the rope ladder with outstretched hands, nothing keeping him airborne now except desperation and a fervent determination to survive so that he could kiss Jenny again.

He snagged the rope ladder as, just below them, Lothar burst into flames.

"Hang on!" bellowed Peevy, as much a signal to Hughes that they were clear as anything else. Hughes pushed the stick and the autogyro banked swiftly away, Cliff and Jenny in tow. And it was barely a safe distance before the fireball completed its consummation of the zeppelin's silver skin, ripping it to fragments.

As the airship disintegrated over the San Fernando

Valley, the autogyro descended toward the Hollywood Hills. On the rope ladder, Jenny clung tightly to Cliff as the dying glow played about them. He got to kiss her one more time, and had the funny feeling that it was far from the last time.

23 "Authorities speculate that the explosion was caused by a freak bolt of lightning, which resulted in the loss of the entire German crew."

In the Bulldog Café that morning, Cliff, Jenny, and Peevy sat at a table, the remains of breakfast before them. As the morning sun whitewashed the café, Peevy continued to read from the story headlined AIRSHIP DISASTER OVER HOLLYWOOD HILLS. Beneath it was an article about Doug Corrigan's flight and probably being let off by the authorities for all kinds of reasons except what Peevy knew to be the real one. He smiled inwardly and continued reading. "Film fans were saddened by news that actor Neville Sinclair also died in the tragedy when flaming debris fell on his touring car." He stopped and dunked a doughnut, shaking his head. "What a shame." When he saw Cliff's reaction, he simply shrugged and said, "Nice car."

Jenny looked across at Cliff, who stared out the window, lost in thought. "You're looking pretty sad for a guy who pretty much saved the world." At that remark, Peevy chuckled ruefully.

"I've got the cracked ribs to prove it," said Cliff, gingerly touching the taping beneath his jacket. And then he added softly, "And not much else."

Jenny edged over to him and rested her chin on his shoulder. "You've got me," she reminded him.

Suddenly a familiar droning filled the sky. Dishes rattled on the counter. Cliff jumped to his feet and rushed outside as the sound diminished in the distance, like a hunting dog leaping to the summons of a whistle. Jenny came up close beside him.

"What is it, Cliff?"

He was still searching out the sky. "Sounds like a racer. I missed her though . . . guess she's coming in over at the field."

She watched his face as he strained to hear the distant engine, and her heart broke for him. No GeeBee. No rocket pack. It was like watching the piteous flappings of a bird with two broken wings. She had no balm for it except time and patience and love. She took his hand, and together they started back toward the café.

Suddenly a shiny blue limo rounded the corner and slid to a stop before the Bulldog. Two men leapt out and cleared the street, signaling autos and pedestrians to make way.

And the roar of a GeeBee radial engine grew louder, not softer. Then, to Cliff's utter amazement, a brand-new GeeBee racer, black and white finish gleaming, taxied around the corner and eased to a stop before the diner. Leaves and branches were blown around, and Cliff, Jenny, and Peevy, who had just emerged, shielded their eyes in the prop wash.

Then the engine shut down, the canopy lifted, and Howard Hughes emerged, a canvas Windbreaker over his brown suit.

Now the rest of the Bulldog Café regulars emerged from the restaurant. His hand in Jenny's, Cliff approached the plane in wonderment as Hughes climbed from the cockpit.

"She's a beauty, Mr. Hughes!"

"Thanks," said Hughes, patting the plane fondly.

"Built her myself. By next month she'll be ready for the Nationals." He smiled graciously at Jenny. "Miss Blake, would you excuse us for just a moment?"

"Of course," she said with equal graciousness.

Hughes pulled Cliff a few steps to the side and leaned in close, speaking confidentially. "I've been meaning to ask you . . . what was it like, strapping that thing to your back, flying like a hawk?"

Cliff thought of everything his short and spectacular career as the Rocketeer had meant to him—the wind rush, the freedom, the spectacular grace and power the rocket pack had given him. The feeling that he could go soaring through the clouds and, perhaps, just for a second, brush fingertips with passing angels.

"Closest thing to heaven," he said.

And then Cliff looked past Hughes at Jenny, radiant in the morning sun, an angel on earth.

"Well . . . second closest," he admitted.

Hughes grinned broadly and nodded, as if approving something Cliff had learned. He shook Cliff's hand and said, "See you around . . . Rocketeer."

Hughes started back to his limousine and then, apparently remembering something, he turned and tossed something to Cliff. "Oh . . . and don't fly her without this."

Cliff caught it and stared at a pack of Beeman's chewing gum. Hughes continued to his car and Cliff looked around, confused. Fly what?

And then he stared incredulously as one of Hughes's assistants pulled a piece of masking tape away from the rim of the cockpit. Revealed in hand-lettered script were the words PILOT, CLIFF SECORD.

He was so stunned that he was only dimly aware of Hughes's limousine pulling away, and by the time the real world snapped into existence around him, and he felt the reality of Jenny's arm against him and the other fliers pounding him approvingly on the back, Hughes was gone. "I . . . I didn't get a chance to thank him," said Cliff in a daze.

Peevy grinned. "He saw it in your face, kid."

"Cliff?" said Jenny tentatively. "I have something for you, too. Actually, it belongs to Peevy. . . ."

She took a folded piece of paper from her purse and handed it to Peevy. He unfolded it and stared at it in disbelief.

"Oh, no!" he said.

It was Peevy's schematic of the rocket pack. Cliff and Peevy exchanged looks and Peevy held his head in consternation. Cliff, for his part, laughed, looking heavenward at the beckoning skies, and he swept Jenny up in a joyful embrace and held her aloft. She spread her arms wide, cutting a beautiful figure against the morning sky, the closest thing to heaven. . . .

And at that moment . . .

An ominous shadow fell across the plaster thigh of the Bulldog Café. A shadow wearing a fedora and leveling a pistol at Cliff, Jenny, and Peevy, trying to determine which target to shoot first.

Suddenly, wearing a tin pot on her head and a round oatmeal box tied to her back, Patsy swooped down from a tree on a tire swing. "Rocketeer to the rescue!" she bellowed, and tackled the would-be assassin, a little boy wearing his father's old, oversized hat, and brandishing a water pistol. Patsy and her playmate rolled across the lawn, kicking and laughing.

And in his mind and heart, Cliff Secord was already airborne. . . .

ABOUT THE AUTHOR

PETER DAVID, in addition to scripting such comic books as *The Incredible Hulk*, *The Amazing Spider-Man*, and *Dreadstar*, is the author of almost two dozen novels, among them *Knight Life*, *Howling Mad*, and *The Return of Swamp Thing*. He is also the author of four Star Trek: The Next Generation novels, including *Doomsday World* and *A Rock and a Hard Place*, both *New York Times* best-sellers. He currently lives in New York with his wife, Myra, and his children, Shana and Guinevere (and is soon expecting a third). He is at work on his next novel.

(Note: For the purpose of atmosphere, in the course of preparing this work we took some small liberties with the real-time occurrences of some events, such as the shooting dates of *Gone With the Wind*. We appreciate the good-natured tolerance of true period aficionados.)

The history of man in flight....

THE BANTAM AIR AND SPACE SERIES

The Bantam Air and Space Series is dedicated to the men and women who brought about this, the era of flight -- the century in which mankind not only learned to soar the skies, but has journeyed out into the blank void of space.

☐ 1: THE LAST OF THE BUSH PILOTS
   by Harmon Helmericks   28556-4 $4.95
☐ 2: FORK TAILED DEVIL: THE P-38
   by Martin Caidin   28557-2 $4.95
☐ 3: THE FASTEST MAN ALIVE
   by Frank Everest and John Guenther 28771-0 $4.95
☐ 4: DIARY OF A COSMONAUT: 211 DAYS IN
   SPACE by Valentin Lebedev   28778-8 $4.95
☐ 5: FLYING FORTS by Martin Caidin 28780-X $4.95
☐ 6: ISLAND IN THE SKY
   by Ernest K. Gann   28857-1 $4.95
☐ 7: PILOT
   by Tony Le Vier with John Guenther 28785-0 $4.95
☐ 8: BARNSTORMING
   by Martin Caidin   28818-0 $4.95
☐ 9: THE ELECTRA STORY: AVIATION'S
   GREATEST MYSTERY by Robert J. Serling
                                   28845-8 $4.95

Available now wherever Bantam Falcon Books are sold, or use this page for ordering:

DICK TRACY!

☐ DICK TRACY GOES TO WAR by Max Allan Collins 28890-3 $4.95

The morning headlines are blaring HITLER!!! and MUSSOLINI!!!, and true-blue detective Dick Tracy, now a Lieutenant Commander in Naval Intelligence, finds himself fighting for the War effort on the home front against Nazis, as well as the villains B-B Eyes, The Mole and Shaky.

☐ DICK TRACY A novel by Max Allan Collins based on the screenplay by Jim Cash and Jack Epps, Jr.   28528-9 $4.95
☐ *And* on audiocassette (read by James Keane)   45234-7 $14.95

The novelization of Touchstone's blockbuster film starring Warren Beatty, Al Pacino and Madonna. Big Boy Caprice is out to run The City, and all that stands in his way is Dick Tracy, and a mysterious person known only as The Blank. But is The Blank friend or foe....

☐ DICK TRACY: THE OFFICIAL BOOK OF THE MOVIE
   by Mike Bonifer   34900-7 $9.95

The official behind-the-scenes story of the Touchstone Pictures film, packed with photos and interviews with all the stars, makeup and special effects people, as well as actor/director Warren Beatty himself.

Read DICK TRACY GOES TO WAR, as well as the novelization of the Dick Tracy film and the DICK TRACY, THE MAKING OF THE MOVIE, available wherever Bantam Books are sold, or use this page for ordering:

The Man of Bronze is back....

ESCAPE FROM LOKI
A DOC SAVAGE ADVENTURE
by
Philip José Farmer

For close to sixty years people the world over have been
thrilled by the exploits of Doc Savage and his men.
Now, for the first time since 1949, a completely new Doc
Savage adventure has been written by acclaimed
science fiction author and Savage authority, Philip José
Farmer.

Every Savage fan knows that Doc met his men when
they were all POWs in WWI, but the story of that first
meeting has never been told in detail. ESCAPE FROM
LOKI is the story of how 16-year-old Clark Savage, Jr.
assembled the greatest team of adventurers and crime
fighters the world has ever known.

ESCAPE FROM LOKI marks the beginning of an all-new
series of DOC SAVAGE adventures. Available in June
wherever Bantam Falcon Books are sold.